10-25

MILADY'S REVENGE

MILADY'S REVENGE

Anne Herries

This first world edition published in Great Britain 2004 by
SEVERN HOUSE PUBLISHERS LTD of
9–15 High Street, Sutton, Surrey SM1 1DF.
This first world edition published in the USA 2004 by
SEVERN HOUSE PUBLISHERS INC of
595 Madison Avenue, New York, N.Y. 10022.

British Library Cataloguing in Publication Data

Herries, Anne
    Milady's revenge
    1.   Love stories
    I.   Title
    823.9'14 [F]

    ISBN 0-7278-6135-2

Typeset by Palimpsest Book Production Ltd.,
Polmont, Stirlingshire, Scotland.
Printed and bound in Great Britain by
MPG Books Ltd., Bodmin, Cornwall.

One

Damn it, but his head felt as if it were reverberating with a thousand crashing cymbals! And truth to tell it was no one's fault but his own. Fitz swore softly as his vision blurred for a moment. He paused, drew a deep breath and then walked on, vowing that he would never drink so heavily again, no matter what the cause.

Having spent the night at his club after an evening of careless drinking and gambling, both of which had left a bad taste in his mouth, Edmund Fitzroy, newly become Marquis of Lanchester, had chosen to walk home rather than send for his carriage. He needed some air to clear his head of the throbbing ache his excesses had inflicted on him. He was a fool to have let himself drink so much brandy, but he had taken the death of his father hard, particularly as they had quarrelled just before the carriage accident that had led to the late marquis's painful end.

Yet nothing of his inner feelings showed on his handsome face as he sauntered from the exclusive club in Brook Street towards his house in Grosvenor Square. A tall man, strong and athletic in appearance, his clothes fit him like a second skin, showing off the powerful shoulders and calves that needed no padding to set them to advantage. His neckcloth, so carefully tied before he left home the previous evening, might have come awry during the long night of indulgent pleasure, but his quality was not in doubt. To a casual observer he looked everything a wealthy and privileged gentleman in full possession of his health and youth ought to be.

Thus he appeared to Corinna Knolls as she was conveyed

in her father's carriage towards Hanover Square, which lay at the opposite end of Brook Street to that which the marquis was leisurely making his way.

She glanced out of the window, catching sight of his face as he paused for a moment, lost in thought. It was clear to her that his thoughts were far away, and that he had not noticed her. Lovely as she was, with eyes the colour of a summer sky and hair like moon-gold, Corinna was but a country lass, shy and unremarkable – unless one had the wit to look more closely and discover the woman who lay beneath. But even she was as yet unaware of the hidden depths she might call on, and being a natural, modest child did not imagine that so fine and handsome a gentleman would notice her.

Had he not been suffering under the dual burden of remorse and a thundering headache, Fitz would certainly have noticed. He had an eye for the ladies, and particularly those with a pretty ankle. Anyone who had been privileged to see them could have told him that he would not find prettier ankles than Mistress Knolls', nor yet a lovelier nature, but the only person who might have told him these things was now dead.

The marquis therefore continued on his way unheeding, unaware that he was heading for a course of action that would bring heartache to both himself and the sweet innocent he had passed without noticing.

'What do you think of my gel then?' Robert Knolls asked, half an hour or so later that morning, of the woman sitting opposite him in the elegant drawing room. 'Pretty little filly, ain't she? Find a good husband for her, don't you think?'

Sarah Mallory laughed wickedly up at him. She had been called similar names herself in the not too distant past, but a more accurate description of her present charms might have been a 'luscious piece'. Twice a widow and in her early thirties, Sarah knew that her beauty had become a little jaded of late. Her habit of indulging herself with rather too much wine and rich food had added flesh to a face that might once have rivalled Corinna's, but her two husbands had left her comfortably off and she did not spare her pleasures. She had a considerable appetite for the delights of both the table and the bedroom, and Robert Knolls was a fine-looking man, some years past his prime, but still vigorous.

'Oh, she's a lovely child,' Sarah said, giving him a flirtatious glance. She fluttered her long, dark lashes at him in the manner of a practised courtesan and was pleased by the dark flush that spread from his neck upwards. Why, the man was as innocent as a babe and would be putty in her hands! 'I am so glad you have come to me for advice, Robert. It shall give me great pleasure to introduce your Corinna into the best circles.'

'That's mighty good of you, ma'am. Mary always did speak highly of you.' He smiled at her, enjoying the flattering signals she was sending his way. A widower for the past eighteen months and not quite as naïve as the widow imagined, he had come to town for the dual purpose of marrying his daughter to a respectable gentleman and finding some amusement to enliven his own rather dull existence. It looked as if he might have solved both problems at one throw. 'Remembered you with fondness did Mary, Mrs Mallory.'

'Oh, but you must call me Sarah.' She ran the tip of her pink tongue over her full bottom lip, her manner clearly inviting. 'I feel that we shall be great friends, Robert. Perhaps more than friends should you wish it . . .'

'Well, that is a great relief to me, Sarah.' Robert was already imagining his head buried in the soft pink flesh of her generous breasts, his breeches uncomfortably tight. Damn, but she was an enticing piece and it was too long since he'd lain with a woman. 'Money isn't a problem. The gel shall have all she needs. I don't look for a lord or an earl, you understand, just a respectable match.'

'You need not concern yourself with the details,' Sarah assured him. 'Corinna is pretty enough to look much higher than you imagine, my dear. You will give her a dowry, I presume?'

'Five thousand guineas now and my fortune to her sons when I die,' he answered proudly.

'Then we shall have no trouble in pairing her off. You can safely leave everything to me – apart from the marriage contract, which is your part of course.' She stood up, offering him her hand, on which glittered several expensive rings, for she was an acquisitive magpie and her lovers were required to pay for her favours. 'And now I think there is something we should discuss more privately, my dear . . .'

Robert was on his feet with alacrity. Primed and ready to acquit himself with distinction, his daughter's future was relegated to the back of his mind.

Sarah smiled inwardly. She led him into her bedroom, where she proceeded to unfasten the pearl buttons on his fancy waistcoat. Half an hour in her bed and she would have him eating out of her hand – and paying handsomely for the privilege!

'Are you sure it is decent, ma'am?' Corinna looked doubtfully at her image in the elegant dressing mirror. Fashioned in the shape of a shield, with pale wood inserted into the dark mahogany, the looking-glass was like everything else in this house of plenty and a little too ostentatious for the girl's personal taste. Similarly, the gown Sarah had commissioned for her seemed rather too daring for a girl of her age. She was barely eighteen and had been sheltered by her loving mother, only beginning to attend evening gatherings in the last few weeks. Her darling mother's death had led to both Corinna and her father living very quietly for more than a year, but while she still grieved for her loss, the girl understood it was time to move on. 'I am not sure that Mama would have approved.'

'No one could disapprove,' Sarah told her. 'You look charming, my dear – but you may wear a gauze fichu over your shoulders if you choose. Of course, no fashionable lady does so in the evening, but . . .'

'I would not wish to appear dowdy, ma'am.'

'No, indeed, I thought you would not,' Sarah replied, smiling inwardly. The girl was naïve, a complete innocent. Not unintelligent, but young and shy. It should be no trouble to manage her. 'You will soon discover that most of the fashionable ladies wear their gowns cut much lower. You have pretty buds, Corinna, but they are slight. We must do what we may to give you a womanly promise, and this gown makes the most of your slender figure.'

In truth Corinna had a perfect form but Sarah, being plumper herself, liked to believe that gentlemen preferred a full figure. Besides, it would not do for the girl to be too confident. Better that she should retain her uncertainty and thus be easier to control. She was about to make her debut in front of Sarah's friends and with luck would be snapped up by a gentleman with both title and fortune within a very short time. It did not matter whether he be respectable or not, just that he could be persuaded to offer for the girl – and to pay Sarah a commission for arranging the match. And the sooner the better as far as she was concerned, for that would leave Robert looking for a wife to grace his home. Who better than the woman who had helped him get his daughter married to a nobleman? There were enough foolish old goats waiting for an innocent like Corinna and they would be salivating at the thought of bedding her once they'd seen her dressed like this.

Sarah inserted a long ivory wand beneath her wig, scratching at an irritating scab. The head she was wearing had not been changed for three weeks and was beginning to cause her discomfort. It was a nuisance, for the hairdresser she used was expensive, and his creations cost a fortune, but this one seemed to be infested and she could hardly bear it another minute.

Corinna was studying her reflection in the mirror. 'I suppose I look well enough, ma'am,' she said, still doubtful but willing to be guided by the lady her father had chosen to help present her.

'You look very pretty,' Sarah said and kissed her cheek. Corinna caught the odour of the heavy perfume Sarah wore with its underlying staleness. She recalled the fresh, light perfume her mother had always worn, but then her linens were always clean, unlike this fine lady's. 'Come, we must go downstairs. My guests will be arriving at any moment.'

Corinna gave her a fleeting smile. She was feeling extremely nervous at the thought of being introduced to the kind of people her hostess had described to her. She could have wished to make her debut in less exalted circles, for her ambition was to marry a respectable gentleman of moderate means and good manners and she looked no higher.

'It was kind of you to give a dance for my sake, ma'am. It must have been so much trouble and expense to you.'

'Nonsense!' Sarah took her by the hand. 'It is the greatest pleasure to me, Corinna.' Her father was paying – and in more ways than one. She smiled to herself at the memory of their pleasant encounter the previous evening. Robert Knolls was an enthusiastic if unskilled lover, and he learned what she had to teach easily. He would make a good husband one day. The girl would soon be out of the way, snapped up by one of the gentlemen Sarah had invited for the evening. Most were old enough to be Corinna's father, wealthy, bored and given to debauchery of all kinds – though in mixed company they displayed perfect manners, of course. Such a pretty, naïve child was tempting meat to a jaded palate. They would fight for the privilege of bedding her, and Sarah would find some profit for herself in the affair. If she had her way, Corinna would be sold to the highest bidder.

'Give me one good reason why I should attend Sarah Mallory's dance this evening,' Fitz Lanchester asked of his friend Marshall Rowlands. 'It is bound to be the same old faces. Besides, I do not care for the Mallory woman. She is grasping and I find her boring . . .'

The Honourable Marshall Rowlands grinned at him good-naturedly. 'Well, we all know that she is little more than a whore, Fitz, but she provides decent food and her morals are her own – no better nor worse than most these days.'

'Not all ladies sell themselves at Madame Elizabeth's bawdy house.'

'You can't be sure it was her,' Marshall said, quirking his eyebrow. 'No doubt it was merely a jest. Had you gone upstairs with her she would have laughed and unmasked.'

'Not her,' Fitz said and grimaced. 'When I refused her, she took Amersham and from what I heard he had his money's worth.'

'He might have had it at any time he chose if it *was* her,' Marshall replied. 'She has more appetite for the pleasures of the flesh than any woman I know.' He laughed and shook his head as his friend raised his brows. 'No, no, not from experience, I swear – but men will talk of their adventures, you know.'

Fitz smiled oddly. 'A wise head keeps a still tongue, Marshall. You would do well to remember that – though I daresay it is impossible in your case.' Marshall offered him a mock punch, which he neatly avoided. 'Well, I daresay it will not be more boring than any other entertainment on offer this evening. I sometimes wonder if I would do better in the country. At least a man can shoot and hunt when there is nothing better to do.'

'I've heard that dear Sarah has guests staying with her, which is why she is giving this dance – a country squire and his innocent daughter up to find the girl a husband, I daresay.'

'I pity the poor wench if Sarah Mallory has a hand in deciding her fate,' Fitz said, his interest momentarily stirred. 'That woman does nothing that will not benefit her in some way.'

'It will be interesting to watch them drooling over the girl,' Marshall said and laughed as his friend pulled a face. 'I've heard she is very lovely, though I've not seen her. She has been kept close to the house while her wardrobe is prepared, but Lord Phillips saw her go into the house one morning and he thought her beautiful.'

'I would not call him a bad judge,' Fitz said, quirking an eyebrow. 'Mayhap it may prove interesting after all.'

'I did not think you were in the market for a wife.'

'Nor am I,' Lanchester replied and pursed his mouth wryly. 'I have vowed that I shall not marry for at least five years – but sometimes the honey may be tasted without stealing the entire comb, my dear Marshall.'

'You wouldn't . . .' Marshall shook his head at him in disbelief. 'Besides, even Sarah wouldn't sink that low, Fitz. The girl is for sale – but only to someone prepared to marry her.'

'Who said anything about buying her?' Fitz smiled, mocking his friend who was always too eager to rise to the bait. 'I will take only what is freely given – now who could argue with that?'

Marshall looked at him doubtfully. He knew only too well that there was an imp of Satan that rode Fitz Lanchester at times, and there was no knowing what he might do if the devil was in him.

Corinna was horrified by what was going on around her. The way some of the men were looking at her made her squirm in embarrassment, and she had seen behaviour that her mother would definitely have frowned on had she been there. Surely this was not the cream of society she had been promised. Mary Knolls had told Corinna of her own debut some twenty-odd years earlier, and it had not been like this. Several of the men were already halfway to being intoxicated, and they made her feel as if she were a prime filly up for sale.

She glanced towards her father, hoping he would come to rescue her, but he seemed to have abandoned her to the hostess – who had introduced her to at least twenty gentlemen, none of whom she had found in the least appealing. Indeed, most of them sent shivers of disgust down her spine. Especially Lord Hugo Bent, a man old enough to be her grandfather, who leered at her constantly and smelled of an old, musty odour that was very unpleasant.

'Miss Knolls?' A voice from behind her made Corinna jump. She turned to look, and realized that she was being addressed by the first young man she had met that evening. Not only was he young, he was also handsome – and now that she had a moment to think, she knew that she had seen him once before. 'I know we should be properly introduced, but your hostess was busy. I am the Marquis of Lanchester, very respectable I assure you – and I wanted to ask if there is a chance that you have a dance free?'

'Yes, I think so,' Corinna said and handed him her dance card. She had reserved several spaces by the simple expedient of lying when asked by some of the disgusting men who had asked earlier. 'You may choose which you prefer, sir.'

'I see there are three left – and since that is the respected number allowed, I shall take all three. That is, if you will allow me the privilege . . .'

'Oh . . .' Corinna blushed, her heart beginning to race wildly. He was so handsome, so charming and so vital that her poor wits had scattered. Besides that, he smelled clean, like a wood of pine trees and the outdoors. 'I . . . Oh, thank you, sir. I should like to dance with you and I must confess that I do not care to with some of those gentlemen who have asked.'

'Then I am delighted to be of service to you, Mistress Knolls,' Fitz said and smiled, perfectly aware of what he was doing to the girl. She blushed beautifully; she was all that Marshall had described and more. He was extremely grateful to his friend for persuading him to attend an affair that he would otherwise have ignored. He raised her gloved hand to his lips, kissed the tips of her fingers and then bowed elegantly. 'I shall count the minutes until our first dance.'

Corinna watched him leave with regret. She had not been able to refuse all those who had asked and her next partner was already wending his way towards her. Sir Keith Miles

9

was perhaps one of the least offensive of Mrs Mallory's guests that evening and she was quite prepared to dance with him, though he was rather too stiff in his bearing to perform the steps well.

If the marquis was counting the minutes until their dance, then she was wishing them away. Yet she had good manners and she welcomed her partner with a shy smile. At least he did not have bad breath, nor did he leer at her in the disgusting way that some of the others did.

At the end of their dance she had nothing more to repine at than a sore toe, which her partner had inadvertently trodden on. She had dismissed his apologies with a charming smile, which left him more smitten than ever. Sir Keith was well aware that she was up for sale, and he was considering whether or not he was willing to pay Mrs Mallory's price. The girl was pretty, knew how to behave, and came of good stock. He, on the other hand, was rich and childless. His first wife had died giving birth to a daughter who had followed her mother to the grave within hours. His second wife had been barren. Until this evening he had thought to abandon all hope of an heir, but now . . . He decided to watch and wait. He would not be the only one interested.

Corinna was mercifully unaware of his thoughts. Her next partner was less well behaved than the first, and held her too close. She disliked the intimacy of his body pressed against hers, which made her feel hot and uneasy, but since he had been introduced as a particular friend of her hostess, she had been obliged to give him one dance. She would not make the same mistake again.

Her next partner was a gentleman in his middle years. Thin with receding hair and breath worse than a farm midden, he was better-mannered than the last and she was able to endure their dance with her dignity intact. And then it was time for her first dance with the marquis.

Corinna's heart raced as he came up to her. His smile made her knees go weak and she went into his arms willingly, eagerly, her eyes glowing with happiness. Even to a casual observer it was evident that she was falling head over heels in love.

The marquis was not only a wonderful dancer, holding her at the correct distance, his manner was also as respectful as it ought to be, and yet there was a hint of something that made her heart do a somersault of delight. The way he looked at her made Corinna feel special, his touch wiping away the sickness that had begun to lodge in her stomach.

'You dance like an angel,' Fitz told her. 'And your perfume is like wild flowers.'

'I am not wearing perfume – but the soap my mother taught me to make is scented by the essence of many wild flowers.'

'Other women use perfume to disguise the fact that they have not bathed,' he said. 'But you have the freshness of a perfect rosebud. Don't let yourself be despoiled by those old goats who lust after you, sweet innocent.'

'So you think as I do,' Corinna exclaimed artlessly with a little flutter of her fan. 'I must tell you frankly that this evening is not what I expected at all, sir.'

Fitz arched his brows, a wealth of meaning behind the polite words he uttered. 'Your hostess is a well-intentioned lady, I daresay – but this is not for you. I shall see that you are invited to a different kind of gathering, where you will not have to suffer the attentions of men like Bent.'

'Oh, I refused him when he asked for a dance,' Corinna said. 'I pretended my card was filled.' She looked at him shyly, hoping he did not think her forward because she had granted him the dances she had refused to others.

Fitz laughed, much amused. So she was not quite as naïve as he'd thought her. 'You did well, Mistress Knolls, but I fear you may have made an enemy. You must take care not to let him catch you alone, for he would punish you if he dared. And I know for a fact that he is a cruel, vindictive man.'

'Thank you for your advice, sir,' Corinna said, her heart missing a beat as she gazed into dark eyes that were serious now. 'Did you mean it when you said that you will arrange for me to be invited to a more select gathering?'

'It is already done,' Fitz said and the mockery was back once more. 'Besides, I want to make certain that we shall meet again after this evening – and I really do not care for our hostess or some of her friends.'

'But my father said she was quite respectable . . .'

'She is accepted into most circles,' he agreed with a twist of his lips that spoke volumes. 'Though there are some hostesses who would not receive her. However, I do not find her congenial. No matter, we shall contrive to make your visit to town a successful one and who knows what may happen by the time it ends?'

Corinna saw the expression in his eyes and her heart stood still before racing on wildly. Such a look – such words! Surely they must mean that he was thinking of . . . But no, she was letting her hopes lead her astray. The Marquis of Lanchester was one of the richest men in the country, of impeccable birth, though rumoured to be a direct descendant of one of King Charles II's mistresses. He could look so much higher for a wife, if indeed he was thinking to marry. He could not be much more than two-and-twenty, and might not marry for several years. And yet the way he looked at her seemed to promise so much.

At the end of their dance Corinna felt as if she were walking on air. It no longer mattered that some of her partners were old enough to be her grandfather. She hardly noticed them, replying in a vague way, her mind thinking ahead to the next dance with the marquis and then the next.

It was of the marquis she was thinking when she was left alone with her father and Mrs Mallory at the end of the evening, her mind caught up in dreams that cushioned her from her hostess's probing.

'So, I trust you enjoyed yourself this evening, Corinna.'

'Oh, yes, thank you, ma'am.'

'I know that your beauty was much remarked upon,' Sarah said giving her a false smile which hid her annoyance. The girl was getting above her station, and must be taught a few lessons. Things had not gone quite as she'd planned, and that had been due to the interference of a certain gentleman, with whom she already had a score to settle. 'I daresay we shall not have long to wait before at least two offers are made for your hand.'

'Oh, surely not so soon,' Robert said, saving his daughter from making a reply. 'I am not sure that I would see Corinna married to some of those lechers we met this evening, Sarah.' He smiled at the girl. 'She won't be rushed into a hasty marriage she might regret.'

'But you said your first priority was to see her wed.'

'Yes, but to someone she can respect and like,' he replied. 'Besides, I have been reliably informed that we are to receive several important invitations in the next few days. Lady Dorchester for one, and some others.'

'Lady Dorchester . . .' Sarah frowned at him. She was seething underneath, though she managed to look suitably interested. Lord Hugo Bent would not be invited to such a prestigious affair, for her ladyship neither liked nor approved of him. Sir Keith would probably be there, of course. He had hinted he might be interested, though the only one to offer her money to secure the marriage had been Lord Hugo. She had not taken his offer for the moment as she wished to push Corinna's price higher, but the girl might meet far more suitable gentlemen at the Dorchesters' affair. 'Who gave you this promise, Robert?'

'It was Lanchester,' he replied. 'Seemed a perfect gentleman, and interested in my gel himself I daresay.' He smiled at Corinna, who smiled back. 'And I imagine she is not indifferent herself, eh?'

'Oh, Papa,' Corinna said and blushed. She had fallen in love during their first dance and knew that she would marry the marquis instantly should he wish it, but she was sensible enough to know that gentlemen might say charming things without meaning them. 'I like the marquis very well, but . . .' She paused and looked helpless. 'I daresay there are many other young ladies more fitted to be his marchioness . . .'

'And where are they?' asked the proud father. 'No, no, my daughter, do not sell yourself short. You are lovely and good, a fitting wife for any man. Lanchester is interested, I am certain of it, my dear. Behave properly as a young girl should and I daresay he will come up to scratch.'

'And what if he does not?' Sarah asked, keeping the waspish tone out of her voice with difficulty. 'I do not myself think Lanchester in the market for a wife just yet. I would urge caution where that young man is concerned, Robert.'

'Well, we shall see,' he said and patted Corinna's cheek. 'If Lanchester fails to come up to the mark we'll put our thinking caps on – but there is time enough.'

Robert was enjoying himself. He had a lovely daughter who might bring him an entrée into the best circles, and he was aware that Sarah Mallory moved only on the fringes. He had found some of the company not to his taste that evening, but was willing to let it pass. Sarah was an obliging mistress and he had no wish to look elsewhere just yet.

For the moment he would let things run their course. At the moment they seemed promising, and not only as far as Corinna was concerned. He had been surprised to find that several ladies had smiled on him in an inviting manner, and he was feeling rather pleased with himself.

Alone in her bedchamber, Corinna sat dreaming before her dressing mirror. She had danced three times that evening with the most attractive man in the room. He reminded her of a romantic hero of old with his dark eyes, his air of confidence that some might call arrogance, and his mesmerizing eyes. Looking into them she had felt as if she were drowning, and now she felt as light as thistledown.

She had wished that they might go on dancing forever, and as she settled down into her bed, drifting into sleep, she pictured the marquis in her mind, remembering every word he had said to her, every look and gesture that had given her so much pleasure.

How delightful it was to be young and to have young men smile at her that way. If only she could spend the rest of her life with Fitz Lanchester . . . She blushed and dismissed the thought. She must not try to run before she could walk. They had only just met, but it seemed to Corinna in that moment that her dreams had all come true.

Two

'Stole a march on me,' Marshall complained to Lanchester the following afternoon when they met at the club they frequented. They had arranged to spend an hour or so fencing before moving on to the private lounge where they would indulge themselves in a glass or two of good wine. 'When I asked the beauty for a dance she said you had taken her last – all three of them!' He raised his brows. 'Are we getting serious here, Fitz? Three is pushing it a bit, isn't it?'

'Did you want to dance with her?' Fitz assumed an air of innocence. His features had the sculpted perfection of a Roman god, his dark hair waving softly back from a patrician forehead. Stripped of his coat in a white shirt and knee breeches, his lean, strong body was revealed to perfection. Yet it was his keen wits that were most admired. His expression rarely gave anything away, his thoughts a mystery to any that did not know him well. 'Only had to ask, Marshall. I would have thrown the dice for her.'

Marshall pulled a wry face. He was one of the few that knew enough of Lanchester to see beyond the mask. 'So you're up to something. I knew it! Just remember she's of good family, Fitz. Flirt with her by all means, but just remember to leave her her reputation. You destroy it at your peril, my friend.'

'I did not care to see her being molested by those rakes,' Fitz said. 'The way they were poring over her with their slimy hands made me sick to my stomach.'

'I can't say I appreciated it myself. Her father should be horsewhipped for allowing it.'

16

'I daresay he had no idea before the dance what kind of guests to expect. Seems a decent enough fellow – bit slow off the mark, perhaps, but straight. He was delighted when I told him I could get him and his daughter an invitation for Lady Dorchester's bash.'

'Not the Mallory woman?'

'Good grief, no,' Fitz said. 'Millicent would kill me on the spot. Even my beloved cousin wouldn't indulge me to that extent. But Mistress Knolls and her father, certainly – and I can arrange a suitable duenna if they wish for it, though her father is companion enough.'

'Watch out you don't find yourself hooked before you know it!'

Fitz smiled oddly. 'A mere flirtation, Marshall, to enliven things a little. I thought it might be amusing to see if I could make her the toast of the season. It has been damned dull of late.'

'You might break her heart.'

'Oh, I doubt it. She will find enough devoted suitors to make up for it at the Dorchesters', I daresay.'

'Well, just be careful your meddling doesn't go too far.'

'Neither Miss Knolls nor I will be hurt,' Fitz assured him with a casual shrug of his shoulders. 'I can make sure she has a happier time than might otherwise be the case – and I'm sure she will have enough proposals to choose from before she's done. You might even ask for her yourself, Marshall.'

'Fat chance I would have against you,' his friend replied, for he knew himself to lack the dashing good looks that the marquis took for granted. Shorter by a head, with sandy hair, he was plain by comparison and knew it. Fitz was the darling of the gods, a daring, sometimes dangerous man to know or love. 'Besides, I think you feel more than you admit, Fitz. It may be amusing to watch you become hoist by your own petard.'

'Hell will freeze over first,' Fitz said and laughed mockingly. 'If you hope to see me caught by Mistress Knolls' pretty smiles and simpers you will be sadly disappointed.'

'I'll make you a wager,' Marshall said. Mischief was in the air and he was caught by it. 'You'll end by asking her to be your wife. You'll get so entangled in this that you won't be able to cut clear.'

'I'll take your wager – what shall we say, a thousand guineas?'

'Paltry,' Marshall replied recklessly. 'Make it three and we'll shake on it.'

Fitz extended his hand with a mocking smile. 'Now the challenge becomes really interesting. How to have the beautiful innocent swooning in my arms and yet be able to walk away at the end.'

'And you call others lechers,' Marshall said and pulled a face. 'You'll not seduce the girl, Fitz?'

'A few kisses given freely, nothing more,' Fitz said and laughed. 'Nay, I'll not harm her. She may seem an innocent but I'll swear there's more to Mistress Knolls than any of us yet guesses . . .'

'Not invited?' Sarah screeched as she stared at the invitation, which had been delivered that morning, just two days after her own dance. 'But that is insulting. Millicent Dorchester knows that I am acting as the girl's chaperone.'

'Nay, you've as good as admitted that you do not count the lady amongst your special friends,' Robert said a trifle uneasily. He did not wish to upset Sarah further, but he was not prepared to refuse the invitation on such account. 'And Corinna needs no other escort than my own at this, the most prestigious affair of the season . . .'

Sarah ground her teeth silently. She was tempted to send him to the Devil and wash her hands of the whole business, and yet caution held her tongue. There was still the greater prize of becoming his wife when this was done. She lived well enough, but knowing herself to spend lavishly it was as well to provide for her future if she could. Her looks would not last forever and it would not be as easy to replenish her coffers once they had faded. She thought swiftly, not wanting to appear to give in too quickly yet knowing she must do so as gracefully as she could.

'Let me look at that again,' she said and then gave a little smile of regret as she glanced at the invitation. 'Well, I could not have attended on the nineteenth in any case. I am engaged to some friends for that weekend and shall be out of town.'

'Then there is no bother,' Robert said, clearly relieved by the excuse. 'And we already have invitations for many affairs that we may attend together.'

'Yes, of course,' Sarah said and gave him a small, hurt smile. 'I could always withdraw as Corinna's chaperone if you wish, Robert.'

'No, no, of course not, my dear,' he replied. 'There's not the least need. The Dorchesters may be a little high in the instep but we'll have plenty of invitations from other sources, I am very sure.'

In that he was to be proved right. It seemed that word had gone round concerning Miss Knolls and her father. The gel was generally thought a modest, sweet child, the father a country squire with few graces but a warm man, and Sarah Mallory was tolerated by all but a few of the elite hostesses. She was amusing, after all, and usually discreet. And there were few enough whose own reputation would bear intense scrutiny.

As it happened, all of the succeeding invitations included Sarah, which went some way to mollify her, though not to alleviate her dislike of the Marquis of Lanchester. Her reasons for disliking that young man were varied and of long standing, but she would have her revenge on him sooner rather than later.

The Dorchesters' dance was two weeks away. Corinna could not wait for it to arrive, to have an evening of freedom away from her chaperone. Sarah was very attentive to her, always appearing at her side whenever she seemed in danger of making friends with young people. An observant girl and more intelligent than Sarah imagined, she had noticed that her chaperone was less inclined to interfere when one of her own friends was with Corinna. She had met Sir Keith Miles at most of the functions she had attended, Lord Hugo Bent only once – for which she was heartily thankful.

Sir Keith was always polite and kind to her, the first to bring her drinks or ices at a supper party. She would have been foolish indeed had she not realized that he was paying her particular attention. Although she had done nothing to either encourage or discourage him, he remained constantly in attendance whenever they were in company together.

Fortunately for Corinna, the Marquis of Lanchester also seemed to be present at most of the dinners and card parties she attended during those two weeks. He proved skilful at dislodging her from both Sir Keith and her over-attentive chaperone, which made her laugh inside.

Indeed, they laughed together often, and Corinna found herself drawn more and more into his own circle. She had met his particular friend, the Honourable Marshall Rowlands, a gentleman she liked immediately. He had come to her rescue several times when Sir Keith had cornered her, and also once when she was unlucky enough to meet Lord Hugo at a dinner party.

'A most unpleasant fellow,' he told her with a smile as he claimed falsely that he had been sent to escort her into dinner. 'You were to have sat next to Lord Hugo, but I changed the cards. I hope you are pleased.' He winked as she whispered her thanks. 'That gentleman is not a fit companion for a girl like you. But I am sure you are up to snuff, Miss Knolls – it's wiser not to trust any of us too much, I daresay. Not even Fitz or myself if we're in our cups.'

'Oh, surely you do not mean that, sir.' Corinna laughed for she believed she was being teased. 'You cannot liken the marquis to Lord Hugo.'

'No, certainly not,' he said, half seriously, half in fun.

'That lecher is beyond redemption. I still have hope that we may save Fitz from himself.'

Corinna pealed with laughter, her eyes sparkling. Now she knew that he was jesting. It was a little contest between the marquis and Mr Rowlands to gain points from each other. She had come to expect a kind of mock rivalry between them and found it amusing.

She found it less amusing later that evening when Sarah warned her against both Mr Rowlands and the marquis.

'I imagine you find those young men congenial company, Corinna,' she said, managing to look concerned rather than spiteful. 'You will not take kindly to my warning you to be wary of their flattery – but I shall do so nonetheless. Neither of them would think twice of seducing you given the chance, and do not let yourself be duped by their compliments. I have it on good authority that neither of them is in a position to marry at the moment.' And she would lose a purse of golden guineas if things did not go her way. What with two new gowns of best silk and the second head in a month commissioned from that rogue of a hairdresser – and still she was not free of that irritating itch – she must needs repair her funds.

'Why, what can you mean?' Corinna stared at her in surprise. 'The marquis has recently inherited a fortune and Mr Rowlands is the only son of a moderately wealthy man.'

Sarah gave her a sour look. 'The marquis would indeed be suitable if he had thoughts of marriage, but I happen to know he is sporting an extremely expensive opera dancer as his mistress at the moment – and Marshall Rowlands has hopes of an heiress. Her father is a very wealthy merchant banker and the match has been secretly arranged for the past year. They will marry when the girl is eighteen, which will be next year.'

'Mr Rowlands' marriage plans are his own business,' Corinna said, hiding the hurt she felt at being given certain information in this manner. 'And I daresay a man in the marquis's position may have many mistresses before he marries.'

'And after,' Sarah sneered, her tone waspish for they were alone in the girl's bedroom and unlikely to be overheard. 'I know that kind of man, Corinna, and believe me they do not give up their pleasures after marriage. Oh, perhaps for a few months, but then the wife gets left at home in the country to breed while they enjoy themselves on the town. Lanchester is a rake. I know for a fact that he is a regular visitor at an exclusive bawdy house . . .' One that Sarah had visited herself more than once, though in disguise and for profit rather than amusement.

'I have no wish to hear that kind of talk, ma'am,' Corinna said, lifting her head proudly. 'My mother would not have approved.'

'Then Mary was a fool, as you will be if you continue to disregard my advice. Your father intends that you shall marry before the season is over, and I have seen no sign of any proposals as yet – though I know Sir Keith is interested. You cannot expect him to come up to scratch, however, if you continue to ignore him in favour of your other friends.'

'I do not wish to receive a proposal from Sir Keith – or any of the other gentlemen you seem to favour, ma'am,' Corinna said and then gasped as she saw the flash of anger in the older woman's eyes. Sarah's fingers worked at her sides and it was clear that she was on the point of striking her. 'As my father has told you, there is no hurry, ma'am. I believe he would prefer that I did not marry rather than force me to accept someone who was distasteful to me.'

'That was not my understanding of the situation,' Sarah said, though she was aware that she might have read too much into Robert's first indication that he wanted his daughter married. 'Very well, I shall say no more – but do not come crying to me when you find yourself in trouble.'

'I am not likely to be in that situation, ma'am.' Nor would she ask this particular lady for advice if she were!

Corinna turned away as the older woman went out, letting

the door close behind her with a bang. She did not like Sarah Mallory very much and wished that her father had not chosen to stay at her house, but she was not afraid of her. She had been painfully shy when they first arrived in town, but between them the marquis and his friends had done much to put her at ease with herself. No, she did not fear Sarah, for she would resist any attempt to marry her to a man she could not like, but Sarah's spite had hurt her more than she had let show.

Was it true that the marquis had a mistress? She supposed it must be, for there had been a hateful smile of triumph on the older woman's lips, as though she had known her information would hurt. And after all, it was not unusual. Corinna suspected that her father was having an affair with Mrs Mallory, and she knew that some of his friends at home had had mistresses.

She ought not to allow the spiteful words to hurt her, but it was difficult to ignore them. She had believed that Fitz, as she had begun to call him in her mind, was falling as much in love with her as she with him. Surely he would not continue to keep a mistress if that were true.

Wiping away her tears, which were foolish and would not help her, Corinna climbed into bed. She blew out her candle, closing her eyes and wondering where the marquis was now. Was he with Marshall, having a nightcap and thinking of her? Or was he with his mistress?

She tossed restlessly, her mind in turmoil. Oh, she was so foolish! She had given her heart to a man who could take his pick of any of the young ladies in the fashionable drawing rooms. Why should he be interested in her?

The sensible answer was that it was unlikely he meant more than flirtation, as Sarah had made clear. It was painful, but Corinna tried not to let it hurt. Perhaps he had truly fallen in love with her and all would be well.

'You do not come to see me now,' the lovely Dorita complained as Lanchester lounged in the upholstered, square-backed chair by the fireplace in her boudoir. 'I think it is that you have a new lover . . .'

Her liquid black eyes seemed to flash with ebony fire as she looked at him, her long hair falling to her waist in luxuriant waves. She was a beauty, passionate, tempestuous and possessed one of the most supple bodies that Fitz had ever seen. The combination was made for loving and she had kept him satisfied for the past six months, but suddenly he had begun to find her less amusing.

'If I had I should have told you,' he said with the lazy smile that had many another lady burning for his touch. 'I have other concerns, Dorita. You expect too much from me.'

'Once you came all the time,' she said, her beautiful face sulky, her mouth drooping at the corners. She was accustomed to being sought out for her favours, and most men would do anything to keep her – but this man had never been hers completely. There was something untouchable within him, and it fascinated while it frustrated her. 'I know there is someone else. I demand that you give her up or I shall leave you and find a new protector.'

She watched him from slit eyes, her lashes thick and curling on her olive-toned cheek, confident that her threat would bring him to heel, but he merely smiled.

'Have you someone in mind?' he enquired mildly. 'Please do tell me his name so that I can make it known to him that I have no objection. The poor fellow might otherwise fear a duel.'

Dorita lunged at him, her nails stretched like a cat's, ready to tear his skin. 'You insult me! I hate you. You are a pig!'

Fitz caught her wrists, holding her easily as she struggled against him. Now that she was near he could smell the heavy perfume she wore and it turned his stomach. He discovered that he no longer found it or her appealing.

'I am many things, my sweet,' he told her, his eyes alight with devilish laughter. 'But a fool I am not. I know that you entertained Devonish last week and that was the finish as far as I was concerned. I take no man's leavings, and besides, you bore me . . .' Her scream of rage as she fought wildly but uselessly against his superior strength made him laugh.

'I hate you! Pig! Beast!'

Fitz swept her off her feet, carried her to the bed and tossed her into the mess of silken covers and pillows. She gazed up at him, her rage suddenly over, her eyes melting with desire, hopeful, expectant, believing that he would take her now, wanting it, needing it. He stepped back, suddenly revolted and feeling the need for fresh air.

'You will excuse me, madam,' he said. 'Our arrangement is at an end. I shall send a small gift, for I am not ungrateful for your services these past months – but that is the end. I wish you well of Devonish and the others . . .'

He smiled as she screamed abuse after him. It was a pity her vocabulary was so limited, but then, he had never admired her for her wit, merely her body. It was time the liaison was ended, he thought with satisfaction. He would choose his mistress more carefully in future.

For some reason the sweet face of innocence came to his mind; a girl with eyes the colour of an azure sky and hair like moon-gold. He smiled wryly. It was true that Corinna Knolls had made him see that he was wasting his time with an Italian whore of uncertain temper and little intellect, but that did not mean he was in the market for a wife.

Outside in the fresh air, Fitz walked slowly, lost in thought. He was feeling restless and yet in no mind to go home or join his friends in a drinking bout at one of the many clubs of which he was a member.

Hearing a woman's scream, he looked for the source and recognized that it came from a dark alley nearby. He had wandered in a direction that he did not usually frequent, and he knew it was the haunt of thieves, prostitutes and foot-pads. His hand went to his coat pocket, where the gun he always kept ready reassured him as he crossed the road and went to investigate. When he saw a great brute of a man beating a girl who could be hardly more than twelve, he did not hesitate.

The fight was bloody, fierce and exhilarating, though shorter in duration than Fitz would have liked. He dispatched his victim with a few well-calculated blows that left the man lying unconscious in the filthy gutter.

'Yer've killed him,' the child said, looking up at him in awe. 'Bleedin' 'ell! I ain't seen no one wallop the life out of Blackie like that afore.'

Fitz wiped the blood from his mouth and grinned at her as his feeling of boredom vanished into thin air. 'Why was he hitting you like that?'

'He wanted me to go down the Dog and Pheasant wiv 'im,' she said. 'He says there's plenty of punters there as will pay to 'ave a bit of fun wiv me. I told 'im I weren't in the mood but he weren't havin' none of it.'

'Good grief,' Fitz said, genuinely shocked. 'You're only a child.'

'I've been at it fer a year now,' the child said and the look in her eyes was older than time. 'He made me – it were either that or go in the workhouse. Well, I ain't goin' in there, am I?'

'Aren't you?'

'Not on your nelly. The old master in there would have what he wanted fer free. I might as well make the flats pay for it.'

'Yes, I suppose you might,' Fitz agreed. 'Is there nowhere else you can go?'

'If I woz lucky I could get in one o' them there fancy houses,' the girl told him. 'The gents treat yer better there – at least most of them do, so our Sal says. She's been wiv Mrs George since she were twelve.'

'And how old are you – truthfully, girl?'

'Nearly twelve,' she said but it was clearly a lie. 'Another few months and I shall be.'

'How would you like to be a servant?' Fitz asked. 'You would have to work, but you would sleep in a bed and eat good food every day.'

'Nah, you won't catch me doin' that,' the child said. 'I

know what them fine ladies are – work yer ter death fer nothin' and chuck yer out if yer get into a bit of trouble. At least on the streets I can 'ave a tot of gin when I like.'

'And you would really like to work in a bawdy house?'

'Yeah . . .' The girl looked at him eagerly. 'Do yer know one what would take me in?'

'Yes, I happen to know a place not too far from here.' Fitz hesitated. He felt that he should find her a decent place – but where was there for a girl like this? He was shocked to discover that he could think of no viable alternative to the workhouse. 'Well, if you're serious, child, I'll take you there. She'll take you in if I ask her, and she's fair with her girls. Looks after them and has the doctor out when they need it.'

'It's better than workin' the streets fer Blackie,' she said. 'Want me ter give yer a quick one ter show yer what I can do?'

'No, thank you,' Fitz said and smiled at her. 'But with enthusiasm like that I imagine you will do very well.' The rogue in the gutter was beginning to stir. 'I think we had better go and see Mrs Rose before your friend wakes up . . .'

It was the evening of the Dorchesters' ball at last! Sarah Mallory had taken herself off to stay with friends earlier in the day, and Corinna was feeling wonderful as she looked at her reflection in the mirror. The gown she had chosen to wear that evening was a pale leaf-green in colour and had a swathe of white gauze in the very low *décolleté*, which revealed more than it hid of her lovely breasts. Corinna knew that it would still be modest by the standards of most ladies attending the ball and was no longer afraid of appearing fast.

Her expectations of the evening were high and she was not disappointed when their hostess seemed to single her out for particular attention. She was complimented on her charming appearance, introduced to several young people and told kindly that her hostess was there if she needed any help, and that Lady Dorchester would be keeping a discreet eye on her.

'Not that you need it, my dear,' that lady said. 'I have been reliably informed that you have perfect manners. But if any gentleman should behave less than honourably towards you, you may rely on me to point out to him the error of his ways.'

Corinna thanked her prettily and was left to mingle with the other guests. Before many minutes had passed, she was besieged by young men begging for dances, and she was hard put to save more than one for Fitz Lanchester. He was a little late in arriving, but when he did so he attached himself to her like a limpet. He danced with no one other than Corinna except for one duty-dance forced on him by his cousin. Although he did not actually compel other gentlemen to give up the dances they had reserved, he formed one of the circle about her for the entire evening, and it was he who took her into supper.

'I wish you were not so beautiful, Miss Knolls,' he told her afterwards when they saw a determined young man wending his way towards them in order to claim her.

'But why?' she asked, laughing as she saw his petulant expression. 'If I were ugly you would not mind giving me up and you would not want to dance with me yourself.'

'Such logic is unanswerable,' he told her and laughed deep in his throat. 'But perhaps a little less beautiful and I might have you to myself for a while.'

'I think you are a wicked flatterer,' Corinna told him. 'I shall dance with you later, sir.'

She smiled as her partner came to claim her. He was a charming young man, presentable, of moderate means and an excellent dancer, but his touch did not inflame her as another's did. The evening was as enjoyable as she had hoped, but still she could not wait for the last dance, which was to be with Fitz Lanchester, and at first she was a little disappointed when he asked if she would not prefer to sit it out with him. However, when he took her hand, leading her from the ballroom and out into the seclusion of the orangery, her heart began to race wildly.

There were lanterns strung from the roof of the orangery, but at one end it was almost completely in shadow and it was to this spot that Fitz led her. He stood looking down at her for a moment, gazing into her lovely innocent face before drawing her close. She trembled as his lips touched hers, gently at first and then with increasing heat. Her arms slipped up about his neck as she gave herself trustingly to his hungry lips, allowing the hot kisses as they reined on every exposed inch of her soft flesh. A flicker of doubt entered her mind as his tongue dipped below the scoop of her neckline, seeking out her breasts, his hand pushing the filmy gauze back so that he could circle the rose tips of her breasts.

'Oh . . .' Corinna breathed, her pulses racing between desire and fright. 'My lord . . . Sir . . .'

'Trust me, sweeting,' Fitz murmured against her white throat. 'You are so lovely, so adorable. I am burning for you, but I would not hurt you. Believe me, I shall never do anything that does not give you pleasure.'

All her instincts told her that this was wrong. She should not allow him such freedom, and yet she could not resist the sweet surging low in her abdomen, the need he had aroused in her, and she let him touch and kiss her as he would. It was he who drew back first, and she saw a strange blind look in his eyes as if he had been driven almost to the edge by his passion.

'Enough for now,' he said hoarsely. 'I want so much more, but to take it now would dishonour us both, my sweet. I must take you back to the ballroom.'

'Have I done something to displease you?' she asked, for she could see a pulse flicking at his temple and sensed some strange dark emotion in him.

'Nothing at all,' he said and smiled at her. 'I adore you, Corinna – but we shall speak more of this another day.'

Corinna's hand trembled on his arm as he led her back into the brilliant light of the crystal chandeliers that graced the huge ballroom. Their dance had not quite ended, and he held her close as they twirled to the other side of the room, and then Fitz presented her to her father with an elegant little bow.

'I return your daughter to you, sir – and I have been asked if you will both do my Aunt Rosalind the favour of staying with her in the country next weekend. It will be a small house party, just a few of her friends, Marshall and myself . . .'

'Delighted, sir.' Robert Knolls bowed and smiled. 'Delighted. And now, Corinna, my love, I believe it is time we were leaving.'

Corinna smiled and looked shyly at the marquis. Her cheeks were faintly pink for she was trying to come to terms with what had taken place in the orangery earlier. She was afraid that she had been a little too free with him and worried that he might think her fast. Yet how could she have resisted him when he was so persuasive?

But he kissed the tips of her fingers when she presented her hand and thanked him for his invitation. 'We are much indebted to you, sir, both for this evening and your aunt's generosity.'

'No, indeed, Miss Knolls,' he said, a strange, slightly mocking look in his eyes, 'it is I who must thank you for a delightful evening. I swear I have seldom known better. And I look forward to many equally as delightful in the future.'

What could he mean? Was he saying that he wanted to make love to her again?

She blushed and looked down, her heart behaving like a skittish lamb in spring. Her conscience told her that she had been foolish to allow this man so much licence, but when he looked at her – when he touched her – she was lost.

Three

'I trust you enjoyed the ball?' Sarah asked waspishly. She herself had spent a boring weekend with cousins in the country and was feeling put out to say the least. It seemed that her plans to enrich herself at the girl's expense were likely to fail. And she had returned to discover a pile of bills awaiting her in her dressing room. Besides the new fan made of chicken skin with a gold handle, she had purchased twelve pairs of white silk stockings, a silk ball gown, a velvet domino cloak and six heads in the last three months. Damn that hairdresser! She was sure he had infected the wigs with lice to spite her and she would take her custom elsewhere. He could whistle for his money, for she would not pay him a farthing. She glared at the lovely young girl, wondering why she did not suffer from the itching. 'Did Lanchester come up to scratch?'

Corinna blushed furiously. 'I do not understand you, ma'am.'

'Then you are either a scheming minx or more foolish than I imagined,' Sarah replied. 'If Lanchester was truly interested in proposing it was the perfect opportunity – but I warned you not to expect too much. If you pin all your hopes on him you will be sadly disappointed.'

'I–I do not expect anything,' Corinna said untruthfully. Oh but she did expect, she hoped desperately that the marquis's kisses had meant more than mere flirtation.

'If your father is disappointed in Lanchester he will probably accept the first who offers for you,' Sarah said. 'I should add another string to your bow if I were you, Corinna.'

Corinna did not answer her. Her hopes were centred on the weekend in the country with Lanchester's aunt, and she could only pray that he would ask her then to be his wife. Surely his attentions meant something. He would not have gone to so much trouble on her behalf if he did not care for her – would he?

Before the weekend that might change her life forever, Corinna had to endure a dinner party given by Sarah. Some of the people she most disliked had been invited, and her heart sank when she discovered that she had been placed between Sir Keith Miles and Lord Hugo Bent.

She did her best to be pleasant to each of the gentlemen, but it was perhaps the worst evening of her life. Especially when Lord Hugo put his hand on her knee. She moved her leg further from him, but that only put it closer to Sir Keith, who smiled at her as if he thought she had done so deliberately.

The meal seemed to drag on forever, and she was relieved when Sarah at last decided that the ladies would leave the gentlemen to their port. As she went to stand up, Corinna felt a man's hand grab at the top of her leg and for a moment clasp her between them in the most intimate way. She flushed, gasped and pulled sharply away from the table, almost knocking over her chair in her hurry. But she could not miss the evil leer in Lord Hugo's eyes and it sickened her. How could Sarah have subjected her to such an insult? Had she sat elsewhere it would not have happened, she was sure. No other gentleman would have behaved that badly!

Sir Keith came to her as soon as the gentlemen rejoined the ladies. She was seated on a chair by the window, looking out at the garden, her face pale, her senses still disordered from the shocking behaviour of a man who ought to have been a gentleman. He had made her feel like a common slut and the sickness was still in her stomach.

'I wanted to apologize to you, Miss Knolls,' Sir Keith said

at once. He looked at her in concern as she lifted a trembling hand to her lips. 'What that fellow did was disgusting. I can assure you that I have spoken to him severely and asked him to leave this house before he can offer you further insult.'

'Oh . . .' Corinna blushed. This was all so embarrassing! 'I . . . that was kind of you, sir.'

'It was the duty of a gentleman, my dear. You must know that I have the sincerest regard for you. I have not pushed my claim, for I know that I am not alone in my admiration – but if the time comes when you could look kindly on me I should be happy to oblige you.'

It was not quite a proposal of marriage but came very close. Corinna felt a little awkward but struggled to overcome her feelings. She would not hurt his pride for the world for he had been kind to her many times, and she preferred him to any of Sarah's other gentlemen friends. She did not wish to marry him, even if the marquis did not ask her, but she was content to number him amongst her intimate acquaintances.

'You are exceedingly obliging, sir,' she answered after a pause for thought. 'I shall not forget your kind words, but for the moment I can give you no further answer.'

'You have answered well enough,' he replied and looked rather pleased. Corinna fanned herself vigorously and hoped that she had not given him hope of something that she would never accept. It was so difficult, for he had done her a service and she had not wanted to offend.

She was relieved that Lord Hugo had taken himself off, though she sensed that Sarah was angry. The older woman came to her room when the guests had left and they were about to retire for the night.

'I do not know what you thought you were about at dinner, Corinna. Any young woman of sense knows better than to encourage a man like Hugo Bent. What happened was entirely your own fault.'

Corinna repressed the urge to abuse her, retaining her

dignity despite the extreme provocation. 'I did nothing to encourage him, ma'am.'

'He told me that you pressed your leg against his and urged him to touch you intimately.'

'You must know that is a lie,' Corinna said. 'I would rather die than have that man touch me like that again. If you persist in thrusting me into his company I shall complain to my father and ask that we take up residence elsewhere when we return from the country.'

'La! She gives herself airs,' Sarah said mockingly, her eyes glinting with sudden menace. 'Well, I know you for a sly minx, miss. I know more than you imagine. I have my spies even if I am not there to watch you – and I know what you did in the Dorchesters' orangery with Lanchester.'

'I have no idea what you mean,' Corinna lied, though her cheeks turned scarlet. Had someone else been there in the shadows? Had they seen or heard her with the marquis? Was she in danger of losing her reputation? If that happened she would have no chance of making a decent marriage.

Sarah's hand snaked out, grabbing her wrist, her fingers digging into the soft flesh. 'I'll let you run your course. If you can snare Lanchester, good luck to you, but I doubt he means to wed you. He'll have you if he can and then desert you, laugh at you behind your back if you're fool enough to give him what he wants – and then who will take you for a wife? You'll be lucky if even Bent will have you then, eager though he is to bed you.'

Corinna gasped and wrenched away from her. 'You have a viper's tongue, ma'am. Be careful you do not let my father feel it or you will find that he is not the fool you think him.'

'Take care you give me no power over you,' Sarah hissed at her, eyes bright with malice. She suddenly raised her hand and struck Corinna hard across the face. 'Run to your father with tales if you dare, but be warned, I shall not keep your secret then. If you slip from grace, miss, you will wish you had never lived.'

Corinna stared after her as she went out of the room. She

was shaking all over, a heaving sickness at the pit of her stomach. Sarah was a vicious, cruel woman and she feared for her father if he was fool enough to marry her.

She wished with all her heart that she could warn him, but she knew that he was well pleased with his mistress for the moment. Perhaps if things went well that weekend – if she received an offer of marriage . . .

Corinna remembered the ugly warning Sarah had flung at her and her stomach turned. Was she a fool to have fallen so much in love with the marquis? His smile and his manner made her feel that she could trust him, but supposing he seduced her and then deserted her as Sarah had warned . . .

No, of course he would not. Had he not promised he would never do anything that did not please her? What were a few kisses after all? She was so innocent, so naïve. She knew that most ladies would be flattered by his ardent love-making. She was letting Sarah get to her and that was foolish. The marquis truly cared for her, of course he did.

She bathed her face in water, its coolness taking away the sting of Sarah's slap. If only it were as easy to rid her mind of the cruel words. But she would not let Sarah win. Lifting her head proudly, she began to hum a lullaby that her mother had taught her. She had nothing to be ashamed of, and would hold her head high.

She smiled as she let down her soft hair. It hung in gentle waves about her face, framing her loveliness as she gazed unseeingly before her. If the marquis did not speak this weekend then she would give up hope of him and force herself to encourage someone else. She knew that more than one presentable young man might have been interested had she given them encouragement – but how could she? How could she think of marriage to anyone but Lanchester?

Corinna thought that she had never enjoyed a weekend more. Lanchester's aunt was a kind, gentle lady in her middle years, who had made both her and her father feel as if they were a part of the family. They had been riding together about the estate in Lady Rosalind's carriage, while the gentlemen rode beside or ahead of them, dined alfresco under the shade of spreading oak trees in the magnificent garden, and visited some charming ruins a short distance from the estate.

On this, the second from last evening of their visit, there was to be a small dance. 'Nothing grand or exciting,' Lady Rosalind had told them. 'Just some friends and neighbours who like to get up a few couples and dance. It is all very informal, I assure you.'

Corinna had spent the afternoon strolling in the gardens. It was a warm day and some of the guests were resting on their beds, but Corinna preferred to walk beneath the shade of some of the lovely old trees that graced the grounds, and Lanchester had joined her there.

'I saw you from the upper windows and came to find you,' he told her. 'You are not afraid for your complexion in this heat, Corinna?'

'It is delightful here in the trees. One is sheltered from the worst of the heat – do you not find it pleasant, sir?'

'Why yes, of course – but I should find it pleasant to be anywhere with you, Corinna.'

Her cheeks were a trifle pink as she looked up at him, though he would have been naïve to think it caused by the heat. 'And why is that, sir? I believe there are many places you would not wish to be, even if I were there.'

'Do you indeed?' His eyes quizzed her. 'I do not think I can imagine them.'

Corinna shook her head at him. 'You are a flatterer, sir.'

'I do not mean to be less than sincere,' he told her.

'I daresay it is a habit with you. I am not the first to receive your compliments, sir.'

Fitz looked at her thoughtfully. At the start she had appeared young and shy. Now he had begun to understand her rather more and to realize that perhaps Marshall had been right – if he were not careful he might find himself caught fast in her toils. There was rather more to Miss Corinna Knolls than most people realized. He was finding her enchanting, but she filled his mind more often than was wise, for he had no desire to marry just yet.

'No, perhaps not,' he said and smiled wryly. 'I think I shall go away and leave you to your pleasures, Miss Knolls.'

Now why had he called her that? Corinna asked herself as she watched him walk away. She had been Corinna to him for a while now. Had she done something to annoy him?

Had she been privy to his thoughts, she would have been even more confused, for they were in turmoil. He wanted her more than he had ever wanted a woman before; she possessed him waking and sleeping, and yet he was wary of being caught in the marriage trap. Why should he not have what he desired without the rest?

Fitz sipped his drink as he watched Corinna dancing with Mr Peterson for the third time in an hour. They had met only that evening and it was clear that the young man was smitten, and that she enjoyed his company. John Peterson was exactly the kind of young man she ought to think of marrying – an honest man of modest means who would make her a good husband.

If he were a gentleman he would leave the field clear for Peterson, Fitz thought as he finished his sixth glass of wine that evening. It was the honourable, the decent thing to do. He did not wish to marry her himself; the very idea of marriage appalled him – so why was he furious at the thought of Corinna enjoying herself with another man?

'Peterson has cut you out this evening,' Marshall said, coming to stand beside him. 'And a very good thing too, if you ask me. You've monopolized her for weeks and ruined any chance of her receiving a proposal elsewhere. Time to give it up, Fitz. Besides, it seems that she has found a new admirer she prefers.'

'Cut him out in an instant if I chose,' Fitz said with a sneer on his lips. He snatched a glass of wine from the tray of a footman passing amongst the guests. He wasn't exactly drunk but his thoughts were not as clear as usual and he was tormented by a feeling he dimly recognized as jealousy.

'I'm not so sure,' Marshall said. 'I think Miss Knolls has her wits about her. She must have realized you intend nothing but a flirtation and that if she is to stand a chance of a decent match she must look elsewhere.'

'Thousand guineas I'll have her before the night is out,' Fitz snarled and thrust his now empty wineglass at his friend as he saw Corinna leaving the room.

'Steady on,' Marshall warned, but the marquis was past heeding. He shrugged his shoulders. It was none of his affair, but it looked as if Fitz was heading for trouble.

Corinna found her way out on to the terrace. It was a sultry night and the gallery where they were dancing seemed stiflingly hot. She needed a little air, a chance to be alone with her thoughts. It had become clear to her that the marquis could not be serious in his intentions towards her, and she had decided that she must forget her hopes. She had liked Mr Peterson instantly, and though as yet she had no thought of marrying him, she believed their friendship might progress to something more – if she encouraged it.

She walked away from the house towards the little temple in the rose garden. If when she went back into the house she encouraged Mr Peterson, her flirtation with Fitz Lanchester would be at an end. She believed it might be for the best, but it was painful to make the decision. Yet perhaps it was already over, for he had not asked her to dance once that evening.

'Corinna!' Her heart caught as she heard his voice close behind her and realized he must have followed her. 'What are you doing out here? Have you promised to meet your new lover?'

She turned to look at him, her breathing difficult as she looked at him in the moonlight. Her heart caught with sudden pain. How handsome, proud and arrogant he looked standing there, his manner seeming to challenge her. His eyes were unnaturally bright and she sensed that he was angry – with her or for some other reason?

'I have no lover,' she replied, lifting her head proudly to meet the angry glitter of his gaze. 'I was perhaps a little free with you on one occasion but . . .'

Before she could finish, Fitz caught her to him, crushing her lips in a savage, hungry kiss that bruised her. 'You are a tease,' he muttered fiercely against her throat. 'You think to bring me to heel by smiling at him, but I do not play your game as you wish it, my sweet, only as I wish it.' He pushed the soft neckline of her gown down to reveal the curve of her lovely breasts, his mouth and tongue caressing the rosy nipples, and then his strong white teeth nipped at her, causing her to cry out. 'Yes, beg me,' he muttered thickly. 'Beg me to love you and I shall oblige you, for you have driven me mad with longing.'

'No . . . please, I beg you,' Corinna cried, trying in vain to push him away. But his strength was too much for her. 'Let me go, Fitz . . .'

They were inside the temple and she felt him bear her backwards to the little sofa placed there for the comfort of those who sought its solitude. The sofa's hardness was against the indent of her knees, and the pressure of his body made her fall back and he on top of her. His mouth and hands were everywhere as she made her protests. She tried to struggle against him, and against the feeling that was creeping over her, the desire and longing for him that she could not fight, the need to feel his body closer and closer to hers. She was trembling all over, on fire with a strange longing she only vaguely recognized as desire.

'My sweet Corinna,' he murmured against her breasts. 'My lovely, beautiful girl. How I want you. I swear I have never wanted another woman this way. I swear that I shall be good to you. I adore you . . . want you more than you know.'

'Oh, Fitz . . .' she whispered and then she was kissing him as fervently as he kissed her, her body eager for his touch, for the throbbing, urgent entry of his manhood that penetrated her virgin citadel. She cried out as he tore her in his urgency, but then he was kissing her again and the pain was forgotten in this wild feeling that had swept them both away on its surging tide. She gave herself to him unheeding, forgetful of all that she had been taught – of all that she knew to be wrong, to be foolish – for the glory that was now. And such glory, such wild sweet joy that for a few minutes she believed all well lost for it.

And then the madness was over and she felt him leave her. Her eyes were closed and she could not open them, could not look at him as the shame took over and she realized what she had done. She had allowed him to seduce her. She had begun by fighting, but then her love for him and her natural desire had led her astray. She could not cry rape for at the last she had given herself willingly.

'Forgive me,' he mumbled thickly, but she would not look at him, could not for the shame that was on her. 'Let me help you. You must go back to the house . . . your dress . . .' She felt him touch her shoulder with a gentle hand but she shrank away.

'Do not touch me!' she cried, her throat tight with tears that she would not let fall. She was already too ashamed. He should not see her broken and weeping. 'Go away. Let me alone. I do not wish to see or speak to you again.'

'Forgive me,' he said again and now the regret was plain to hear. 'I was drunk . . . jealous . . . I am sorry, Corinna. I should not have . . . I shall put this right somehow.'

'Go!' She screamed the word at him, her eyes suddenly open and blazing with anger. 'I do not want your pity. Leave me. I shall return to the house later alone.'

Lanchester stared at her helplessly. He was horrified by what he had done, shocked and shamed by his own behaviour. Never once before in his life had he forced a woman – and an innocent one at that! He had accused her of meeting her lover but he knew well enough why she had come out here alone. It was he who had hurt her and now he had ruined her. There was only one thing he could do and that was marry her.

'I shall make this right,' he promised. 'Do not be anxious, Corinna . . .'

'No! I want nothing more to do with you.'

Giving a cry of anguish, Corinna ran past him. She wanted only to escape from the shame and hurt of the situation, to be alone. She ran across the smooth lawns to the house, her heart feeling as if it had shattered into little pieces. She went in through the side door to avoid being seen, running up the stairs to her room and locking the door behind her. Then she threw herself down on the bed and gave way to her tears. The evening was over for her. She could not face anyone. At this moment she felt as if her life were in ruins.

'You disappeared suddenly last evening,' Robert said to his daughter when she came down the next morning. He looked at her pale face and the shadows under her eyes. 'Are you unwell? Lanchester approached me last evening, asked if he might call on me when we return to town – do you happen to know what that might be about?'

'No, Father,' Corinna lied. 'I cannot imagine why he should want to speak with you.'

'He has not spoken to you of his reasons?'

'No, Father.'

Corinna could not look at him. She had conquered her shame during a sleepless night and now she was angry. Lanchester might think he was doing the right thing but she could not forgive him for what had been close to rape. He had forced himself on her even though she had given way in the end – but she would not be the object of his pity. She would not be married out of duty because he had ruined her. Her feelings had turned to hatred and she would prefer to forget that she had ever known him.

'There is something wrong with you, isn't there?' Robert looked at her closely, noting the shadows about her eyes. 'Has someone upset you, my dear?'

For a moment Corinna was tempted to tell him, to beg

him to thrash Lanchester for her, to avenge her, but it would be her father who would suffer, not the marquis.

'I went to bed with a dreadful headache last night,' she said. 'It has left me feeling tired and listless this morning. Forgive me if I am a little strange in my manner.'

'You may be sickening for something,' her father said, looking at her with concern. 'I think we should leave as soon as possible, my dear. If you need a doctor you will be better in town, I daresay.'

'Could we not go home, Father?' Corinna asked. 'I have seen enough of London and wish for some peace and quiet.'

'Are you sure that is what you want?' Robert was puzzled. 'You seemed to be enjoying yourself before we left town – but the season is nearly done, so if it's what you want . . .'

'Oh, yes,' she said and smiled at him. 'Let us go home now. We may send for our things – and you may return to visit Sarah Mallory if you choose.'

'As to that . . .' Robert was silent. He had begun to see his mistress for the greedy, grasping woman she was, and to dislike what he saw. He had been misled, both by her and his own need of an obliging companion. It would suit him to end their arrangement, for he had other fish to fry. 'I've met a lady this weekend who I prefer, Corinna – a lady I might ask to be my wife one day.'

'Are you speaking of the young lady I saw you talking to last evening?' Corinna saw his blush and caught his hand, her pleasure for him banishing her own hurt for the moment. 'That is wonderful, Father! I am so pleased for you.'

He gave her an indulgent smile. 'Well, if all goes well, I think we may give you a little season in Bath next year. You are young enough, Corinna, and perhaps it was too soon for marriage. If Angela accepts me you will like a little trip to Bath in her company, I daresay?'

'Yes, very much, Father,' she said. As long as she was not forced to return to Sarah Mallory's house she could bear anything. She had decided that in future she would give no encouragement of any kind to any gentleman, and hope that she could be left in peace at home with her beloved dogs and horses. Marriage was now out of the question, for she was soiled goods and could not expect to find happiness.

'I shall write to Lanchester,' Robert said and frowned for he had expected something very different after the marquis's approach. 'He may put himself to the trouble of either replying or coming to visit us at home if he wishes. For it cannot be anything important if you do not know of it, Daughter.'

Corinna made him no answer. She was happy to have escaped the embarrassment of receiving an offer from a man she knew despised her only because she had allowed him to seduce her. Fitz Lanchester would forget her when he no longer saw her in company. If they met in Bath next year he would have put the incident from his mind, for no doubt she was one of many women to him – and perhaps she would have learned to forget.

In her heart Corinna knew that she could never forget. It was impossible for her to marry now. If her shame was known she would be ruined and she could not confess it, so she must remain unwed. Her father would be disappointed, but perhaps if she made herself useful to his new wife she would not be obliged to confess her sin. She was no longer fit to be a wife, for she had lost her innocence.

She could not love a man again for her heart was broken.

Four

C orinna and her father had returned to their home in the country. Fitz read the letter with a feeling of relief. He had been dreading the interview with her father, for it would be difficult if Corinna refused to see him. He would then have to confess his crime, which was still difficult for him to accept. He must have been mad! To do that to a girl of Corinna's background . . . An innocent, untouched young lady of quality . . . He could hardly believe that he had done such a wicked thing. He was sickened by himself, but there was no changing what had happened. He had only one course of action open to him. He must and would make her an offer of marriage.

This letter had given him a short respite. Perhaps by the time he settled various business affairs that would keep him busy for a month or so, she might have come to her senses and realized that a marriage between them was the only course open to them. He put the letter away in the coffer that held his private papers. He would think about this business of Corinna again in a few weeks. His mind turned to other matters.

One of his father's oldest friends had written asking him to visit. There was some business to discuss, a venture started many years ago that had turned out fortunately and would be to Fitz's advantage. His curiosity aroused, he decided to make the journey north. His conscience told him he ought to see Robert Knolls before anything else, but the letter had aroused his interest.

Surely a short delay could cause no harm . . .

*   *   *

Corinna wiped the spittle from her mouth, staring at herself in her dressing mirror in horror. Her face was pale with fright as she realized what this constant sickness, combined with the loss of her monthly courses must mean. She was carrying Lanchester's child!

No! No, it couldn't be so, she thought wildly. Perhaps she was ill or . . . But she knew that the sickness would pass and then she would feel perfectly well until the next morning. She was suffering from morning sickness. She had witnessed it in one of the servant wenches some months previously, and her father had dismissed the girl for wanton behaviour with one of the grooms. He had been so angry, and the thought of arousing such anger made her tremble inside.

Corinna looked at the singing bird in the cage, which her father had given her as a birthday gift, holding a piece of apple for it to peck. She had several birds, dogs and horses that she thought of as pets, and in her unhappiness of late they had become even more precious to her. Her dogs loved her blindly, without prejudice, and she could expect love from no one else once her shame was known.

What would her father say when he discovered that his own daughter was caught in the same trap as the servant girl he had dismissed? Corinna hardly dared to contemplate his anger, which she knew would be considerable.

Was there some way of escaping her fate? She realized now that she had been foolish to throw off Lanchester's offer so swiftly. At that moment she had hated him and wanted only to escape the scene of her shame, but she had not thought that this might happen. Some women were married for years before conceiving – and she had given into her foolishness only once. How unfair it was!

If there was some way of ridding herself of the child . . . the wise woman, perhaps? Corinna knew that there was an old woman in the village and it was whispered that she could sometimes cause a miscarriage. Dare she visit her? Dare she risk being exposed as a fallen woman? Yet what was her alternative? If she had the child . . .

45

A part of her wanted the child, but how could she face the shame it would cause both her and her father? Perhaps it might be better if she took her own life . . . She could drown herself in the river. That would end her unhappiness and give her father a chance to grieve without ever knowing of her shame.

Should she visit the wise woman or kill herself? The choice was stark indeed. Corinna's mind twisted and turned as she went downstairs. She could see no other way of escaping her fate.

'Ah, Daughter,' her father said, coming out of his study. 'I have this morning received a letter . . .'

'From the marquis?' Corinna asked, her heart leaping with sudden excitement. She was still angry, still shamed by what had taken place in that little summer house, but perhaps it might be better to accept an offer of marriage than face the shame that would otherwise be hers.

'No, not Lanchester,' Robert said and frowned, for he had seen the leap of excitement in her eyes. Was that what the girl had been hoping for all along? She had seemed strange that day at Lady Rosalind's, but perhaps that was disappointment. He was damned if he understood her! 'Sir Keith Miles has asked my permission to speak to you, Corinna. He will be here tomorrow and, if you agree, will propose marriage . . .'

She could not do it! Corinna felt the sharp sting of disappointment overwhelm her. For one wonderful moment she had hoped that her shame could be safely hidden from the world, but now she saw that there was no alternative. She must tell her father the truth. It would be very hard and she was afraid of his anger, but there was no other way.

'Please may I talk to you, Father?'

Robert looked at her strained face. Something was ailing the girl.

'You'd best come into the study, Corinna.'

She followed him silently, her heart beating rapidly. He stood by the fireplace, waiting for her to begin, an inkling of something unpleasant beginning to dawn in his mind. She had been behaving strangely for a while now. He hoped to God that it wasn't what he suspected.

'Well, speak out, girl.'

'I fear you will be angry, sir.'

'If I am there's no point in delay. Get it over with.'

'I – I am with child, sir.'

'And the father?' Robert barked. His fists balled at his sides, a vein bulging in his thick neck as he stared at her. 'Are you going to tell me the name of the rogue who dishonoured you – or can I guess?'

Corinna raised her head proudly. Inside she was quaking with fear but she would not allow it to show. 'I shall not tell you, Father. If I had not been foolish it would not have happened. I blame no one but myself.'

'Be damned to that!' Robert roared at her, beside himself with fury now that she was defiant. Had she wept and begged him to thrash the man who had despoiled her he might have found it in his heart to forgive her, but this pride – this shamelessness – made him want to strike her. 'You will tell me, girl. He shall be made to marry you.'

'I do not wish to marry him. I do not want to be an object of his pity or resentment.'

'You do not want . . .' Robert fumed, moving swiftly towards her. He struck her twice across the face as hard as he could, making her stagger backwards and almost fall. 'What of me? Tell me that, girl. What of my good name that you would drag through the mud? Will you shame your mother's memory and me? You will do as you are told or I shall thrash you so hard you will beg for mercy.'

'Send me away, Father. I can go somewhere that no one knows me – bear my child alone. Only give me a little money and I shall never ask you for more.'

'It is what you deserve,' Robert said, grinding his teeth as he stared at her angrily. 'I should thrash you to an inch of your life – kick the bastard out of your belly and send you to a nunnery or some house of correction.'

'It is what I deserve, Father.'

'And what would folk make of that then? I'll be a laughing stock when this gets out. No, you'll not make a fool of me, Corinna.' He glanced down at his desk, seizing the letter and waving it at her. 'You'll marry Sir Keith and keep your shame to yourself – either that or tell me who lay with you.'

'I cannot do that, Father.'

'You mean you will not – but you have no choice in the matter, Corinna. Either you tell Sir Keith that you will accept him or I'll kill you. The choice is yours – and if I discover the name of the man who put his seed in your belly, I'll kill him too. I daresay it was Lanchester. I've a mind to take a horsewhip to him!'

'No, Father. Please, I beg you . . . Let me simply go away. You need give me nothing. I shall never trouble you again.'

'You will obey me,' her father said. 'Disobey me and your dogs, your horses and your singing birds will be destroyed – and not kindly. If you have no fear for yourself, have a care for them.'

'You would not . . .' Corinna gasped and looked at him in horror. He could not mean that he would hurt innocent creatures unless she obeyed him. Yet as she gazed into his cold eyes she knew that he meant his threat. This was not the kindly man who had always indulged her, but a stranger who looked at her as if he hated her. It seemed that she had no choice. And in truth, what else could she do? 'But will Sir Keith want to marry me when he knows the truth?'

'You will say nothing to him of your shame,' her father instructed. 'You will act as if you are a virgin on your wedding night and he will be deceived. When the child is due you may claim to have a fall so that he believes it his own come early. You will not be the first nor the last to deceive a man in this way.'

'But, Father . . .' Corinna gasped as he raised his hand to her again, the blow sending her staggering back so that she almost fell. 'To deceive him so cruelly would be wicked . . .'

'Disobey me and you will see the pets you love put down.'

Corinna's eyes stung with tears. He had struck at her weakest point for he knew the softness of her heart too well. She could do nothing but obey this man she had once revered and looked up to with affection. For the sake of the pets she loved, she would take a man she disliked as her husband – and she would lie to him. But when they were married and her horses and dogs safe, she would tell Sir Keith the truth.

The day of Corinna's wedding was bright and warm, and she was met at the church by all her friends, who showered her with rice and dried flower petals when she came out on her husband's arm.

'You tremble, my dear,' Sir Keith said and looked fondly at her. 'You cannot be cold, so I fear that you are frightened of your duties. You must not be for I shall not hurt you. I care for you deeply and I shall always be kind to you.'

'You are very generous, sir,' she said, for he had given her many gifts since their betrothal, and his manner was always courteous and kind. 'I fear that I do not deserve your consideration.'

He looked at her oddly but there was no time to say more, for they were surrounded by well-wishers. Throughout the wedding breakfast, Corinna felt as if a shadow hung over her. She had asked that her dogs, horses and singing birds might be sent on ahead with most of her possessions to her new home. They were to spend a few weeks at Sir Keith's hunting lodge in Scotland before travelling south to his home in Hampshire.

Her husband was a wealthy man, something which pleased her father. He was relieved that she had obeyed him and that he had got her off without the scandal he had feared. Corinna cared nothing for her husband's wealth or her father's pleasure. She would have felt better if she had been allowed to tell her husband the truth, for she dreaded what he might think or do when she told him.

The coward in her whispered that he need never know. If

she cried out when he penetrated her he would think her a virgin, and she could perhaps contrive that some blood should be upon the sheets in the morning. Yet the honest core of her nature would not allow such deception. She must and would tell her husband the truth, but not until they were alone and away from this place she had once called home but that was now hateful to her.

'You must be tired, Corinna my dear,' Sir Keith said when they were shown to their rooms at the inn that night. They had travelled but a few leagues from her home to spend their first night at a fine hostelry where the food was good and the service excellent. 'Go to sleep, my dear. I shall not trouble you this evening. We have plenty of time to consummate our marriage.'

'You are so considerate, sir,' Corinna said and her eyes filled with tears. He was being so kind to her and she hardly knew how to tell him something that would make him angry. 'But I have a confession to make and I must make it now or I may not have the courage to do so later.'

He nodded, his eyes narrowing as he looked at her pale face. 'You want to tell me that you do not love me, that there was someone else – is that not the case?'

'Yes . . .' Corinna's courage almost deserted her, but her honesty would not let her continue to deceive him.

'I knew as much when I gave you time to discover for yourself that Lanchester was a wastrel. He led you a merry dance but never had the intention of wedding you. It was for that reason that you took me.'

'Not quite, sir,' Corinna said. Her throat felt tight and she was breathing so shallowly that she thought she might die of fright. 'I would have told you this before the wedding but my father forbade it. He threatened to destroy my dogs and horses if I refused you or told you of my shame.'

'Your shame?' Sir Keith's eyes narrowed, his expression hardening. 'Speak out then, for I would hear of it, though I suppose I may guess.'

'I am with child, sir.'

'And by Lanchester, I suppose.'

Corinna stood before him, hands clasped, head bowed, neither admitting nor denying his accusation.

'Answer me!' he demanded and when she did not, he struck her a blow that sent her reeling, stumbling over a stool so that she fell to the floor and lay looking up at him. She had thought him kind, but now she saw that his manner had concealed his true nature. She should have lied and deceived him as her father bid her. 'Answer me, bitch, or you will wish that you had never been born. Your father made a fool of me and you with him – well, I'm a harder man than Knolls ever knew how to be. Your horses and dogs are as good as meat for the hounds unless you tell me what I want to know.'

'Forgive me,' Corinna cried. 'I did not wish to deceive you. Merely let me go and I will not shame you. No one shall know of this – only spare my poor dogs. I beg you, punish me, not them.'

'Punish you?' He smiled unpleasantly at her as she made to rise and kicked her in the side so that she fell gasping to the floor once more. 'Oh yes, I shall punish you, my dear wife. But you will not run away. Oh no, you shall stay and bear your punishment, and your child shall be mine – and it shall know what it means to suffer too . . .'

'Please.' Corinna wept. 'Please, do not . . .'

But he lashed out at her with his foot again, catching her full in the face so that she screamed with the pain and fell back, covering her face with her hands as the blood gushed from a cut on her lip.

'You may sleep alone tonight for I might kill you in my present mood,' Sir Keith told her icily. 'But be prepared to welcome me another night, Corinna. If you wish to spare your child you will pay the price demanded – again and again . . .'

Corinna stayed on her knees as the door closed behind him. She had thought him kind and generous, believed that he would be prepared to let her leave him. She had expected that he would be hurt, even angry, but she had not guessed at the vindictive nature he kept so well hidden. He was no better than Lord Hugo!

But there was little she could do about it now. She was his wife, his possession, and he would do as he pleased with her. As she rose to her feet, her face was as cold as marble in the candle glow, carved out of stone like the heart that still beat within her.

'Married?' Fitz stared at Marshall over the wine bottle that they were sharing. 'When did you hear that?'

'Oh, a week or so ago,' Marshall said and yawned. 'You were out of town on business, I believe. Besides, I thought you must know. If you were interested, which I doubted.'

'It was business with my estate,' Fitz said and frowned as he reached for the wine, filling his glass to the brim. 'It has been a dashed nuisance – some legal stuff my father neglected before he died. It appears that I have estates in the West Indies that I never knew about, and but for the honesty of a decent man would have lost them. I've had a devil of a time sorting it out.'

Corinna Knolls married! Fitz was not sure how he felt about that. He had meant to take that trip into the country, for he believed himself honour bound to make the girl an offer – and there was a part of him that still thought she was the only woman he would ever truly love. Yet he had been reluctant to take that final step. Confound it, he hadn't been ready to take a wife yet. He wanted to be free for a few years, free to enjoy himself as he would with his friends.

Now, suddenly, he had the taste of ashes in his mouth and the evening in front of them seemed pointless. He remembered the way Corinna had surrendered to him so sweetly at the Dorchesters' ball – and that sudden surging desire that had swept them both away in the temple. God but she was lovely, everything a man could want – everything he wanted. And she was married to someone else.

'Who did the wench marry?' he asked casually, as if it meant nothing. 'Anyone we know?'

'Sir Keith Miles,' Marshall answered with a grimace. 'I wonder if she knew what she was doing. I swear he's worse than that old goat, Bent. Oh, not quite as much the lecher, but there are worse things. I know for a fact that he has a mean streak. One of his grooms did something once – damaged a horse he prized. He had the man stripped to the waist and whipped him in the yard, in front of all his other servants – did it himself, mind you. He beat the fellow until the blood ran and his bones showed through the flesh, then he dismissed him without so much as a shilling or a reference.'

Fitz felt sick. He gripped his wineglass so tightly that the fragile stem snapped in his fingers; he hardly noticed the sting or the trickle of blood. Corinna married to a man like that! It made him want to vomit.

'How do you know this?'

'The groom was the brother of my own head groom. He tended his brother, asked if I would take the man on in some capacity. I did, of course, but the poor fellow was done for, fit only for sweeping up. He died that winter, broken in spirit and body.'

'Miles should have been hung for it.' Lanchester reached for a fresh glass and poured more wine. He was aware of the bestiality of man, more than he had been some weeks earlier, but he had not thought to find such behaviour in a gentleman. 'Why would she marry a creature like that for God's sake?'

'Probably had no choice,' Marshall said and shrugged. 'But if you don't know then I can't say.'

Lanchester swallowed half the contents of his glass in one go. Was it possible . . . had Corinna married because she was carrying his child? He stood up, turning away as a wave of grief and shame washed over him.

'I think I shall seek my bed,' he muttered thickly. 'Tomorrow I have a long overdue trip to the country.'

He would see her father. Ask for the truth . . .

And then what? For a moment he considered going to Corinna, snatching her from her husband and running off with her, but then he realized that was folly. She would not allow him to shame her further. He must suppose that she was content with her life. There was nothing he could do. She was the wife of another man and nothing could change that. He had lost her, lost all right to think of her, and yet the thought of her scarcely left him day or night.

It was a fitting punishment.

Corinna trembled as she heard her husband's step on the stair. They had been married for one month and five days, and for each of those days and nights he had made her wish that she had never been born. She crossed her arms over her belly, which had begun to show signs of the child growing within her, knowing that her husband would have it out of her if he could. He hated her with a cold, deep hatred, his anger whipped to fury by her refusal to tell him the name of the man who had seduced her.

When the door was flung open, Corinna felt the vomit rise in her throat as she saw he was carrying a cruel, thin cane and guessed his intention. So far he had beaten her with his fists and his feet, but he clearly meant to take his brutality one step further.

'Down on your knees, bitch,' he commanded, his face twisting awfully as she raised her head, looking proudly into his eyes, refusing to give way before his bestiality. 'Do as I say or you will wish you had never been born.'

Still she defied him, and in a rage he took her by the arm, jerking it behind her and kneeing her in the lower back so that she fell to her knees at last. And then he began to beat her; cruel, heavy blows that went on and on long after Corinna had slipped into unconsciousness.

She thought it was morning when she heard the voices. A woman was sobbing softly somewhere near her, and a man was telling her not to weep. She did not recognize the man's voice for it was strange to her. It was this voice, which seemed kinder than she had heard of late, that made her open her eyes. For a moment it was difficult to focus, but then she saw the face of a stranger, a man in his later years; he was a plump man, well turned out with a powdered wig and dressed in the fashion of some years earlier, but, she thought, from choice, not necessity.

'Ah, so you have woken at last, m'dear,' he said and smiled at her. 'Well, what a silly girl we were to fall down the stairs like that – and with such sad consequences.'

'My baby . . .' Corinna whispered, her throat caught with tears. 'Has something happened to my baby?'

'I am afraid you have miscarried,' the kindly man said as he sat his awkward bulk on the edge of the bed, taking her hand in his. 'There then, my dear girl, it does no good to weep. My poor dear wife lost five babies before she died of a fever. But you are young and with fortitude and fortune you will have another child.'

'No . . .' Corinna shook her head. She could never have another child . . . not by the man she loved. 'No . . .'

'Now this will not do,' the stranger said. 'It was fortunate I arrived when I did, child. I am your husband's uncle, Lord Dorling – you may have heard him speak of his Uncle Henry – and I have decided that you shall come on a little visit with me as soon as you are up and about again. And I shall stay here with you and my nephew until that time. There, will that comfort you a little?'

Did he know the truth of her miscarriage, or did he truly believe she had had a fall? Corinna closed her eyes on a sigh. Is was probable that she owed her life to his timely arrival.

'Yes, that's it, my dear,' the kindly voice said as she drifted back to sleep. 'This will all soon seem like a bad dream and you shall be happy again . . .'

'If you tell my uncle what caused the miscarriage I shall kill you next time,' Sir Keith said. 'I am allowing you to visit with him since he has asked for you, but you will return to me – and then we shall see how well you have behaved yourself.'

'You need not worry that I shall betray you, though you deserve nothing better,' Corinna said, raising her head proudly to look him in the eyes. 'But do not think to beat me again as you did, for if you do there will be a letter with Uncle Henry – a letter that will reveal you for the beast you are.'

'You tempt me sorely, wife. I am minded to refuse my permission, to make you stay here and learn proper obedience to your husband.'

'If you do that, Uncle Henry will know what kind of a man you are,' she promised, her eyes as cold as ice. 'I think you know what would happen then, sir. I believe he would leave his fortune elsewhere.'

'Damn you!' He moved towards her as if he would strike but then held back. 'Go then – but remember you will always have to return to me. I own you, just as I own my dogs and horses.'

Corinna felt the sickness in her throat as she looked at the man she had been forced to marry. It seemed she had been granted a short respite from his cruelty, but she would never be free of him. She was tied to him whatever he did to her, for there was no chance of her being allowed to leave him in this life. She considered taking her own life, for it was the only way she could be free – and yet why should she let him win? He would then be at liberty to marry again, and ruin another girl's chance of happiness. Let him do his worst – he would not break her!

She saw the anger in his eyes, the way his hands balled at his side, and knew that, for the moment, she had won. He was afraid of the power his uncle held over him, and so for the moment she was safe. But she would not forget his treatment of her. He had pretended to care for her, but he had lied. All men were false. All men betrayed. She had loved once, but now she hated. And one day she would take her revenge . . .

* * *

In London, Fitz considered a trip to the West Indies. It would be interesting to inspect the estates he had been assured were worth a great deal of money – estates his father had apparently forgotten. Had it not been for the honesty of Rupert Baird, his father's great friend and partner in the venture they started when both were young men, Fitz would never have known of their existence. Besides, what was there to keep him here?

He would be gone a year, perhaps more, and then he would return. It would give him a taste of the adventure he craved, and still the restless spirit inside him, at least for a while. Perhaps it would help him forget the endless ache, the sense of loss that pervaded all he did.

As for his other work, that would go on while he was gone. Phelps was a good man; he could trust him. When he returned he might find other ways of achieving what he planned, but for now the West Indies held a sparkling promise for a young man with a shadow at his back.

Five

'You are now an extremely wealthy woman in your own right,' the lawyer said as he faced Corinna across the desk in the late Lord Dorling's study. 'As you know, your husband left much of his fortune in trust, which means you have the interest but not the capital – that passes to a distant cousin if you marry again. However, Lord Dorling had a great respect and affection for you, and the only proviso to his legacy is that you should take his name.'

'Yes, thank you,' Corinna said and smiled slightly. She had talked of this with her husband's uncle many times these past months, and had known the terms of his will long ago. 'It was dear Uncle Henry's wish that I take his name, which has already been set in motion, as you know. We had hoped that it would become legal before he died, but it was not to be.'

She stood up and walked over to the window, gazing out at the park of the beautiful house that had been her home for some months. She was a beautiful, graceful woman, if a little cold. Lawyer Berry admired and respected her, for he knew that his late client had thought very highly of this lady.

The lawyer nodded as she turned to face him, wondering at the sadness in her eyes. 'Since he has adopted you legally you are entitled to bear both his name and the title, which may pass through the female line as well as the male. You are therefore Lady Dorling and in possession of at least ten thousand pounds a year if you leave your fortune invested as it is. Of course, if you choose to spend the capital . . .'

'I doubt that I shall need more than the income Uncle

58

Henry left me,' Corinna replied, her voice husky with emotion. 'It was our intention to visit London this spring – since I am at last out of mourning for my husband.'

'Ah, yes.' Lawyer Berry looked at her oddly. 'An unhappy business, ma'am. It was fortunate that Lord Dorling had invited you to stay with him at that time.'

'My husband was given to sudden and violent rages in the last few months of his life,' Corinna replied, suppressing the shudder that threatened to crack her composure. The nightmares still came in the dark hours, reminding her of things best forgotten. 'His illness was some kind of dementia, so the doctors told us, and he had become a danger to himself and others. Uncle Henry decided that I would be better off living with him, and I was grateful to him.' Had she not been living in his home, Corinna knew it might have been her that was killed instead of the unfortunate nurse her husband had strangled in his mad fit. Fortunately, his fit had been fatal and he had not recovered to face the consequences of his actions.

'Something for which we must be grateful, my dear,' Uncle Henry had told her after it was over. 'Had he lived we must have had him put away in a suitable place. Indeed, it would have been better if I had done it years ago. Forgive me, Corinna. I should have done it that first time, but the dementia was not apparent then and I hoped . . .'

'You did as much as – and more than – I could have expected,' she told him. 'My life improved immeasurably from that time on.'

These past years she had had many reasons to be grateful for the kindness of a man who had been more generous to her than her own father. Once Lord Dorling had discovered that his nephew was treating his young wife so disgracefully, he had done what he could to alleviate her suffering. After the accident, which had led to her miscarriage, Lord Dorling had insisted that she stay with him for some weeks. Corinna had never told him that it was a brutal beating that had caused her to miscarry, but she thought he knew. And she believed he had threatened to cut Sir Keith out of his will, for the beatings had ceased after his visit, and she had been subjected only to verbal abuse from then on. Nonetheless, it had been a relief to her when Lord Dorling insisted that she go to live with him because Sir Keith was too ill to be trusted.

'We must have him watched night and day,' Lord Dorling had told her. 'He might do himself or others an injury, my dear – and I refuse to allow you to be subjected to more of his cruelty.'

'Perhaps he has cause to hate me, sir.'

'Your child was not his – cause for anger but not bestiality,' he replied. 'You were honest enough to tell him the truth; he should have respected that, and found it in his heart to forgive you.'

'I wish it might have been you I married, sir,' Corinna told him with a smile of affection. He might be many years her senior, but she believed she would have been content as his wife.

'Had I seen you first it might well have been,' he replied jovially, his plump body shaking with mirth. 'I should have greatly enjoyed presenting the world with an heir and cutting Keith out – never did like the fellow. Something bad about his mother's family. A touch of madness there, I have no doubt. They kept it hidden but it came out at the last.'

A shudder went through Corinna. 'I had wished that I might give Keith a child to make up for what I had done, but it was not to be, and now I can only be thankful.'

'Indeed yes,' Lord Dorling agreed wholeheartedly. 'We want no more of that line. But it means my title must die out and I regret that . . . unless of course . . .'

He hadn't told her immediately, but when it became clear that Sir Keith would eventually die of his illness, it was decided that Corinna should be adopted so that she could inherit his title and his wealth. The papers had been drawn up and signed a few weeks before Uncle Henry's death, taking effect just a few days after.

'So that is everything, ma'am,' Lawyer Berry said, shuffling his papers together. 'I shall set up the accounts you have instructed me to do on your behalf – and will write to you as soon as suitable accommodation can be found.'

'I shall not wear black for Uncle Henry,' Corinna said as she stood up to accompany the lawyer to the door. 'It was his express wish that I did not and I shall obey his wishes in this as in all else. Please stay to dine with me this evening, sir. I daresay we may give you a better dinner than the inn, and it was good of you to come all this way.'

'I could not do less, my lady,' he replied, giving her a smile of approval. 'I shall return this evening for dinner if I may – but there are one or two small matters concerning the estate. If you will excuse me until this evening . . .'

'Of course.'

Corinna left him as he went out into the hall. Lord Dorling's butler would take care of him now and she was exhausted by the morning spent discussing estate matters, of which she was now the mistress. The responsibility was a pleasure rather than a burden, giving some meaning to her life.

She had taken over much of the work these past weeks while her friend was slowly dying. It was during that time that their friendship had become so strong, so loving, and she was going to miss him terribly. She recalled the long winter evenings, when they had sat together by the fire, sometimes talking, sometimes quiet, content to be together.

They had talked often of the improvements made by Thomas Coke, Earl of Leicester, to his own estate, and had begun to implant many of his ideas at Dorling Park. The earl often held open days at his estate so that others could meet and talk of radical new methods of farming. Corinna and Lord Dorling had attended one of the open days the summer before his death.

Now that she was alone, she meant to continue the work they had started together. She had perfect trust in the various agents and servants who ran the estate and house, believing she could leave them to look after things as they had for

Lord Dorling, but she was not certain that she would wish to live there alone.

It was a vast house with many rooms; so many indeed that she had got lost the first time she had stayed here. Uncle Henry had advised her to find herself a pleasant house in Bath or London.

'You should marry again, my dear,' he had told her, as he lay propped against piles of feather pillows, his hand trembling as he touched hers. 'I know you were unfortunate the first time – but not all men are like my nephew.'

'No, indeed, sir.' Corinna had smiled and kissed him. Much of the bitterness had gone from her, warmed away by the kindness of her friend. 'Some are like you and I have been fortunate to know you.'

And now her dearest, her only true friend had gone and she was alone. She had grieved for him in her own way for these past six weeks, putting off the reading of the will until she felt able to cope. She had, after all, known exactly what her position was, and had made her plans accordingly.

It was more than five years since she had been forced to marry against her will. Five long, unhappy years . . . No, that was not entirely true, she corrected herself. She had been happy with Uncle Henry these past months. As happy as her memories would allow her to be. But the grief at the loss of her child, the humiliation she had endured for too long at her husband's hands, and the memory of betrayal, had never left her.

At the age of three-and-twenty Corinna had a beauty that surpassed that of her youth. Poise and charm had replaced the shyness, her quick wit honed to a razor's edge by her many debates with Uncle Henry. He was an intelligent and cultured man, and he had helped his protégée to improve her education and her knowledge of the world. Their happiest moments had been in reading the newspapers and discussing important events of the time.

Uncle Henry was a great admirer of William Pitt, who had the previous year become the First Lord of the Treasury.

Corinna knew that Uncle Henry had been very angry at the bungling and meddling on the part of His Majesty King George III, which he believed had played a large part in the loss of the American colonies in 1783. England had been forced to recognize the United States of America after several defeats on the battlefield. For as he had often remarked, 'Had they listened to Wilkes and applied more diplomacy at the beginning, some settlement might have been reached before it came to such a state that the Americans were driven to a declaration of independence.'

Their debates had been the source of much pleasure to Corinna. Uncle Henry had helped to restore the spirit that her husband had almost succeeded in crushing – almost, but not quite. Now they were over and the evenings seemed long and lonely.

What was she to do with her life now? She looked out of the long windows at the beautiful vista of the park. It was early spring and the dew was still upon the grass, the trees bursting with fresh green and pretty blossom, a pale sun glistening on the waters of a distant lake. She sighed as she turned away, unable to be lulled by the idyllic scene. She was still young. Thanks to Uncle Henry, she was wealthy and had a well formed, independent mind – but inside her was a festering sore that even his kindness had not been able to heal.

Over the years she had grown a protective shell around her heart. During her marriage she had learned not to love or care for anyone or anything: a pet might meet with a cruel accident if she was careless enough to fuss over it, a maid she liked might be summarily dismissed. It was safer to appear cool and detached. Even now, she seldom laughed freely, for her laughter had brought swift punishment.

She must learn to forget the past, put it to rest. Her husband could not hurt her now unless she allowed him into her thoughts. She was becoming stronger. Perhaps one day she would be able to forget.

She would go to London for the intended visit, set up her

own salon and perhaps then she might find peace of mind. Yet a part of her knew that she would never rest until she could find a way to punish the man who had brought her to abject misery. Had it not been for Lanchester's betrayal, she would never have been forced to marry Sir Keith, and might never have suffered the hurts that had been heaped on her by her vindictive husband. She had forgiven her father, for he had begged her to after receiving a letter from Uncle Henry, putting him in possession of certain facts. She could never love or trust him as she once had, but she had forgiven him. Perhaps if Lanchester showed a similar regret she might forgive him, too.

It would be pleasant to inflict some hurt on the man who had ruined her, Corinna thought. He ought to at least suffer some remorse for his careless behaviour, but how to teach him a lesson? That was the question. If she were a man she might be satisfied to take a horsewhip to him, but as a woman her only weapons were her wits.

'Did you receive an invitation from Lady Dorling?' Marshall Rowlands asked of his friend when they met at their exclusive gentlemen's club that morning. 'They say she is a beauty and hath a sparkling wit – besides being disgustingly rich. She is Lord Henry Dorling's heir, you know, and I believe she is in possession of more than ten thousand a year as well as substantial capital.'

Fitz Lanchester yawned and flicked a speck of dust from his immaculate blue cloth coat. Having returned from the West Indies eighteen months earlier, he was already beginning to find London life a bore. He understood Marshall's turn of thought, for after a run of shocking bad luck at the gaming tables, he had been forced to take stock of his life. He wasn't ruined, far from it, for besides vast properties in the West Indies, which had gained him a fortune, he had a thriving estate in Hampshire and had recently invested in a new tin mine at his smaller estate in Cornwall, which seemed to promise a healthy income. However, a sustained run of losses such as he'd been suffering would take its toll on even the richest man in time, and Lanchester had no intention of ending in Queer Street.

'Would you marry me off to her?' he asked with a wry smile. It was amusing that even his friends knew nothing of his secret lives. Fitz Lanchester was known by many names, and had many strings to his bow. 'Are you such an advocate of wedded bliss, my friend?'

'Damn you, Fitz,' Marshall exclaimed, for his own marriage had proved less than blissful these past four years or so. He had married his merchant's daughter and lived in relative comfort on the income allowed him by his father-in-law, but that was not as sweet as he had hoped, and he had not been faithful to his wife, who now resided in the country to care for their two sons. 'I would not see you wed to a crow, but this lady is far from it. Anyway, I intend to go to this card party of hers. They say she invites Pitt and his cronies as well as artists, poets and others of like minds.'

'A blue stocking then,' Fitz said and yawned again. 'Dash it, these late nights will be the death of me. I shall have to take a trip to the country to recover or I'll be done up.'

'So you won't come, then?'

'Haven't been invited,' Fitz replied. 'Can't say I know much about the lady, other than that the whole town seems besotted with her of late. We haven't met yet, though I heard that she might be at my cousin's bash next week.'

'She ain't invited you?' Marshall looked at him in surprise, for Lanchester was considered the most eligible of London's bachelors, despite his recent losses. He was lionized at most events, always sure to be surrounded by both ladies and gentlemen, and generally much admired. His years abroad had lent him an air of mystery, his lean, fit body the power of a man who was ready for whatever life might throw at him. 'Bit queer, ain't it?'

'I do not see why she should invite me to her house, nor do I think I should accept if she had. Don't much care for that type – I prefer my women to be pretty and amenable.'

'I believe she is perfectly amenable,' Marshall replied. 'Ain't like you to take against anyone without seeing them. Any particular reason, Fitz?'

'No, none,' he replied. Marshall was not the first to prate to him of Lady Dorling's wit and beauty, but for some reason all this excitement about the newcomer had irritated him. He could give no reason for his reaction, but it was some inner instinct that told him the lady spelled trouble – and especially for him. 'I daresay I shall like her well enough when we meet.'

'Oh, well.' Marshall shrugged. 'I was hoping you might be there. It might turn out to be a damned dull affair after all. Where are you bound for this evening?'

'I was invited to sup with Shepherd and his cousin,' Fitz replied. 'But I am in no mood for gaming at the moment. I may spend an evening at home.'

'Are you sickening for something?'

Marshall looked so horrified that Fitz laughed. 'Do you not think me capable of spending an evening in quiet pursuits? Do you never like to sit with a good book and a glass of wine, my dear fellow?' He had spent many evenings doing just that on the veranda, enjoying the lingering warmth of the sun, and there was a part of him that wondered if he would do better to return to his sugar plantations.

'Not for a whole evening,' Marshall replied and pulled a face. 'One must sometimes be content with such pursuits on a wet day in the country, but in town . . . You must be coming down with something, Fitz. Shall I call a doctor for you?'

'Good grief, no,' Lanchester said and quirked his brow mockingly. 'I wish you joy of Lady Dorling, Marshall. You may dine with me tomorrow at Brooks and tell me all about it if you will.'

'Delighted,' Marshall said, preparing to take his leave. 'But if I hear that you are ill I shall not be surprised.'

Left to himself, Fitz wondered if his friend was right. Perchance he was sickening for something, for he had no desire to spend the evening at the gaming tables. Indeed, if the truth were known, he was bored with his life. He had resided at his Hampshire estate for most of the winter, paying a short visit to Bath – the town that Beau Nash had made fashionable and that the Methodists had deemed Satan's headquarters. Far from being wicked, Lanchester found the delights of Bath society rather innocuous. He longed for something to engage his wits, arouse his interest, for otherwise he was in danger of losing his edge, of becoming nothing more substantial than the empty-headed dandies he so despised. He was about to summon a servant and have his horse brought round, when an unexpected guest was announced. He stood up as his nephew came rather sheepishly into the room.

'To what do I owe the pleasure of this visit, Tobias?' he asked. 'I do hope you haven't found yourself in dun territory again so soon, for I meant what I said the last time, you know. Pray make it short for I have an appointment in an hour's time . . .'

Corinna welcomed her guests, smiling at Mr Pitt who had brought several gentlemen of superior intellect in his party. She greeted him graciously, directing him to people whose company she knew he would enjoy, turning next to a young man whose poetry she admired almost as much as Mr Cowper's.

'I am delighted that you could come this evening, sir,' she told him. 'Have you brought anything for us, Mr Blythe?'

John Blythe blushed as she smiled at him. He was already in love with her. Both because she made him feel that he might one day achieve greatness with his poems, which he privately often thought terrible, and because she had spent some guineas in subscribing for a small book of his poems and had distributed them to her friends.

'I have a little something, but for your eyes only,' he told her shyly. 'It needs more work and I shall appreciate your keen eye before I dare offer it to others.'

'Then you shall read it to me later,' she promised and sent him in the direction of a lady who had enjoyed his published poems. Fanny Burney, herself a novelist and author of the acclaimed *Evelina*, thought Mr Blythe showed talent, though he was inclined to be slightly undisciplined about his work

Although the great man himself had sadly died recently, his keen mind much missed, several members of Doctor Johnson's literary club, which continued to flourish in spirit in drawing rooms such as this, had accepted invitations that evening. Corinna wished that she might have known him, for she had heard much of him, his looks and reputation. His face and limbs disfigured by a form of St. Vitus's Dance, from which he had suffered, he was often known as the Great Oddity. Yet his reputation and that of the men who had belonged to the Club would live on long after his departure.

Corinna feared that her own affair could not compare with the distinguished company who had met regularly with Johnson. However, she had done her best to gather men and women of serious minds as well as leaders of fashion. Besides cards for those gentlemen who wished to play, there were to be readings and discussions that all were invited to join in. Marshall Rowlands was a late arrival, having come with his cousin, who had wanted to call in at a soirée given by Lady Manchester, and they were just in time to hear a reading from Mr Cowper's latest work, 'The Task', which Corinna had subscribed to at its publication.

A discussion of the poem followed and, yawning behind his hand, Marshall was about to repair to the card room when his hostess saw him and came swiftly to greet him.

'Forgive me, I had not seen you, Mr Rowlands,' she said and smiled at him. 'You are just in time for supper, sir – and

I believe there is a spare table if you and your friend wish to play cards.'

'We were late,' Marshall apologized. Damn it! She was a beauty, though rather severe in her dress and manner – but those eyes! Magnificent! Fire beneath the ice, if he were any judge. 'I crave your pardon. I came with Jolly Peters and he had another engagement earlier.'

'I am happy to see you here, sir. It was good of you to spare us a little of your time.'

Marshall felt a tingling at the base of his spine. He would swear he had met her before, though the name did not ring a bell with him. He could not remember her face and thought he would be sure to had they met, and yet there was something about her eyes . . .

'It was generous of you to invite me, ma'am. I think we have not met before.'

'Oh yes, many times,' she said and laughed, amused by his puzzled look. 'No, no, I shall not tell you since you have forgotten me – but I will tell you that it was more than five years ago. I was very young and silly then, so I daresay I did not make much impression on you.'

'Five years is a long time, Lady Dorling,' Marshall replied, puzzled more than ever now. 'I think you shall have to tell me, for my wits have gone awandering.'

'Shame on you, sir,' she teased. 'I know that five years can be an eternity in certain circumstances . . .' For a moment her eyes were bleak, shadowed by memories. 'But I would not have thought your life so terrible . . .'

'No, indeed.' Did that mean hers had been? Marshall suddenly wished desperately that he could recall what had happened five years earlier, but nothing of any magnitude came to mind. 'I shall remember, ma'am. You have foxed me for the moment, but I shall recover.'

'I am glad to hear it,' Corinna said, a wicked smile about her mouth. 'For I should not want to be the cause of your decline. Now, who would you wish to meet, sir – or perhaps you know everyone here?'

Marshall knew most by sight if not intimately, but to his surprise he found himself confessing a desire to join the circle about Mr Pitt, a group of worthy gentlemen who were bent on discussing the affairs of the country.

Corinna walked him over, told her friends that he was an earnest gentleman with an inquiring mind and left him in favour of Mr Blythe, who wanted to read her his poem.

So she had captured one of the gentlemen who had been involved in that part of her past that she wished to erase from her mind. If she remembered him correctly, Marshall would take his curiosity to his friend Lanchester – and then they would see what they would see.

Corinna felt a tingling at the base of her spine. The moment of her revenge was very close, and it filled her with a strange excitement mixed with apprehension. What would it be like to see him again after all this time?

Alone in her room that night, Corinna considered her position. Now that she was on the verge of seeing Fitz Lanchester again, she felt nervous, apprehensive. For a long time she had thought of the pleasure she would derive from punishing the man who had brought her to the lowest point of her life, but now she was not so certain.

What exactly did she mean by punishment? Was she prepared to ruin him at the card tables? If it could be done, of course. Gossip had it that he had struck a run of ill luck. She herself was an excellent player, and there were others who might help her contribute to his downfall if she asked. Of course, they might ask for payment . . .

She could not be unaware that more than one man found her attractive, despite her cool manner. Several were married and perhaps hoped for a clandestine relationship; others might offer marriage if prompted to it.

She was willing to surrender her freedom to none of them – even for the pleasure of punishing Fitz for his careless behaviour all those years ago. Perhaps it might be possible to make him fall in love with her and then give him the brush-off just when he thought he had won her.

Yes, that was a tempting thought. She smiled at her reflection in the mirror. For some reason the idea of Fitz being disappointed in love was very pleasing, however unlikely.

Corinna laughed at her own thoughts. She was being ridiculous. It was unlikely that Fitz would be attracted to her sufficiently to cause him grief – and if he was . . . Ah, what then?

'The hell of it is that I know I've met her before, but I'm damned if I can recall when.' Marshall frowned. He had called on Fitz at the earliest opportunity, finding him in his library seated in a chair by the window, a book in hand. 'She claims we met several times and that it was more than five years ago – but who can remember that long back?'

Fitz's eyes narrowed. He had no difficulty in remembering the events of five years earlier, nor the remorse he had felt after his trip into the country. The discovery that Corinna Knolls had been married off to a man who was not fit to kiss her boots simply because she was carrying his child had played on his mind for many months. Robert Knolls had been near to having an apoplectic fit when Fitz confessed to being the seducer of his daughter. He had demanded reparation, which Fitz had paid without demur, despite the size of the sum demanded. The angry father had told him the money would be placed in trust for his daughter should she need it, but as Knolls had afterwards married a pretty girl who had proved expensive, it was doubtful if Corinna had seen a penny of the money.

Marshall's chattering droned over his head as he let his thoughts drift back to that time. He had been young and foolish when he'd seduced Corinna in a fit of drunken jealousy, and for a time he had sincerely regretted his mistake. However, the distressing incident had been gradually forgotten, for there was nothing that he could do for Corinna once she was married. Nor did he flatter himself that she would be grateful for any help he tried to give her. She had made her feelings clear enough that night in the temple. Had she been prepared to listen to him then it might all have been settled between them.

'What is Lady Dorling like?' he asked now, trying to picture Corinna in his mind, but her image was faint and would not come no matter how hard he tried. There had been women in his life these last years, none of them important, but they had helped to ease the hollow aching inside him for a time. 'What colour are her eyes and hair, for instance?'

'Her hair is blonde, golden rather than pale yellow,' Marshall replied, trying hard to put into words the glorious beauty of the woman with whom he had already fallen half in love. 'Her eyes . . . her eyes are like the cloudless blue of a summer sky!' he finished in triumph, elated with his efforts, which were remarkable for a man not given to poetry.

'I see.' Lanchester smiled oddly. 'You have fallen in love with the lady, Marshall. I shall hope that she attends my cousin's ball, for I must admit that I am curious.'

'You will find her charming, I am sure,' Marshall said, colouring, for he knew his friend's mockery was deserved. 'Everyone remarks on her wit and understanding as well as her beauty. I believe she has been married, though she is known only as Lady Dorling.'

'I didn't know her husband,' Lanchester replied with a frown. 'Dorling kept much to the country, I believe.'

'For the past few years, yes – but he wasn't her husband. He adopted her apparently, made her his heir so that she could carry on his name.'

'He had no other heir then?'

'I believe she might have been married to the nephew,' Marshall replied with a frown. 'No one seems to know much about her – bit of a mystery.'

'You make me almost eager to meet the lady,' Fitz said, laying aside a tooled leather copy of Oliver Goldsmith's novel *The Vicar of Wakefield* that he had recently commissioned to make up a set of the author's works. 'Though, unlike Mr Goldsmith, I doubt she will live up to expectations . . .'

Six

'Are you looking forward to this evening?' Anne Crabtree asked. A widow left in difficult circumstances, she had accepted with pleasure Corinna's invitation to be her companion in London. They had known each other only a few months – since, in fact, Corinna first took up residence in Lord Dorling's establishment – but she thoroughly approved of her benefactress. Some people thought Corinna cold because she did not gush or exclaim as so many ladies did, reserving judgement and speaking thoughtfully, but they did not know her. They did not know of her generosity to others or the way she concerned herself in charitable affairs. 'Your new gown is most becoming.'

'Green suits me,' Corinna replied and did a little twirl in front of the mirror. 'It is one of the most becoming colours for me – though I have not worn it for some time.' She had been wearing green the night Fitz Lanchester seduced her and it had unpleasant associations for her. However, it had been a deliberate choice for this evening.

'Most colours suit you,' Anne told her with a smile. 'You are so beautiful that you might wear anything and look lovely.'

'You are prejudiced in my favour,' Corinna replied and laughed softly. 'It is very good for me to have you with me, dearest Anne. I have made many friends since I came to town, but you are the kindest of any.'

'Oh no,' Anne replied, looking serious. 'I could never repay your kindness to me, Corinna. My life was very dull until you took me up.'

'As was my own until Uncle Henry carried me off to live with him,' Corinna said with a sigh. The ache inside her had not yet been eased, even though she had been made much of since her arrival in London. People had been flattering and she was much sought after, by both the gentlemen and the ladies, but there was still an emptiness, a wariness inside her that would not let her believe in the compliments showered upon her. She had found only empty promises during her last visit, and until that memory could be exorcised there was little hope of her being truly happy, though she was no longer as lonely as she had been. 'But we shall be sure of a good evening tonight. Lady Dorchester is a generous hostess.'

'You have met her before?' Anne looked at her curiously for she knew very little of Corinna's past, save only that her marriage had ended tragically.

'Oh yes, when I was here five years ago – before my marriage.'

Anne saw the shadows in her eyes and wondered, but she did not ask questions. Life had taught her that there were some things of which others did not wish to speak, and she would not intrude into her friend's privacy without invitation.

'So, we are ready to leave,' she said and smoothed her long white evening gloves on her plump arms. 'I daresay the carriage awaits. We should not keep the horses standing.'

Fitz saw her at once and knew her. At first he felt a tingling at the nape of his neck that warned him, and then his gaze travelled upwards to the lovely face and glorious hair, which she wore high on her head with one long ringlet allowed to fall on her white shoulder. He had struggled to recall her features earlier and failed, but his instincts had not failed him. Somehow he had sensed that the newcomer would cause disruption in his life and now he knew why.

'There she is,' Marshall said from just behind him. 'Standing with Lady Bickling. Beauty, ain't she?'

'She always was,' Fitz replied. 'The years have lavished their bounty upon her. As a girl she was pretty, but now she is a moon goddess.'

'Moon . . . my God!' Marshall's jaw dropped as he suddenly realized why she had looked familiar. 'Corinna Knolls! But she . . .'

'Married Sir Keith Miles, and I imagine Lord Dorling was in some way related to her husband.'

'Now you mention it, I believe he was Dorling's nephew,' Marshall said and struck his forehead with the palm of his hand. 'What a dunce I am not to realize it before this. It never crossed my mind.'

'Why should it?' Fitz asked with a lift of his broad shoulders. He was dressed that evening in a coat of blue, an embroidered waistcoat and pale grey breeches. His figure was well proportioned, muscled, without an ounce of fat, his legs and shoulders needing none of the padding that so many gentlemen sported, his thick dark hair worn au naturel and tied back with a ribbon. Several heads turned as he walked towards where Lady Dorling stood, a dozen pairs of eyes watching him intently, for there was such an odd look on his face.

Fitz knew that he must make himself known to Corinna at once. It would not do if she were to see him and feel discomforted by his presence. He had waited for this opportunity for years, and meant to apologize to her at the earliest opportunity.

'Ah, Lanchester.' Lady Bickling smiled at him ingratiatingly. 'It is pleasant to see you here this evening. Your cousin was telling me that you seldom grace her affairs these days and she must be gratified that you have come tonight.'

'I doubt Lady Dorchester feels the need of my presence amongst so many,' he replied, his teeth bared in what passed for a smile. There was something of the wolf about him then, preparing to leap on its prey. 'Lady Dorling, you have been pointed out to me. I hope we need no introduction, for I believe we have met before.'

'Have we?' Corinna's heart was pounding but there was no sign of agitation on her face as she gave him a cool stare. This was the moment she had dreamed of, longed for and yet feared. Every line of his face was remembered, every nuance of his voice as well known to her as her own, but she gave no sign as she continued. 'You must forgive me, sir, for if we have met I have forgotten it.'

This lie was delivered with such a cutting edge to her voice that Fitz's worst fears were realized. He knew without a shadow of a doubt that she meant to make him pay for his past treatment of her. So be it. She was entitled to her anger, entitled to take what payment she would of him, for he doubted that she had received a penny of the compensation he had paid her father.

'Indeed, you must know that this gentleman is the Marquis of Lanchester,' Lady Bickling said simperingly. 'His company is always much sought after and any hostess wishing to be thought a success does her best to encourage him.'

'Indeed?' Corinna's brows rose as if she doubted this. 'Then I shall claim a prior friendship with you, sir, and invite you to my next soirée.'

'You may be certain that I shall call upon you at your earliest convenience, ma'am,' Fitz said. 'Would it be too much to hope that you have a dance left on your card for me this evening?'

'I fear that it would, sir,' Corinna said with a challenging lift of her head. How dare he act as if nothing had ever happened between them? She wanted to strike out in anger but retained her dignity. 'I am so sorry – but you came a little late.'

She made it sound as if he had committed some dreadful crime. Her eyes seemed to scorn him, her every word seemed a barb meant to penetrate his flesh. Fitz had never met a woman who could cause him such discomfort with just a word or a look – but perhaps it was his conscience that pricked him.

'It is not my habit to come early to these affairs, ma'am.'

'Then I fear you need to learn the error of your ways, sir. And now you must excuse me, for Mr Hanson was not late in arriving and I am promised to him for this dance.'

Fitz watched as she welcomed her partner with a warm smile. Why was it he felt that he had spent two rounds in the ring with a bare-knuckle fighter and come off worst? A wry smile lingered on his mouth, a mouth that had a sensuous appeal, which, had he known it, had sent waves of shock winging through Corinna's entire body.

He spent the rest of the evening watching as Corinna danced and flirted discreetly with her partners. She was like a brilliant candle, attracting moths to her flame, yet remaining cold at the heart. There was something distant about her, something untouchable. Her smile when it came was dazzling, but it was rare enough.

He had thought she was lying when she refused him a dance, but he soon discovered that she was one of the most popular ladies present that evening. When supper came he tried to reach her in the hope of taking her in, but found that there were ten other gentlemen with the same idea in mind. Any other woman would have known he was interested and extricated herself from her other admirers to favour him with her company, but she seemed to deliberately encourage them in order to keep him at a distance.

His frustration turned to amusement as the evening wore on. She was certainly a fascinating creature, and he supposed her ten thousand a year did her cause no harm. It looked as if she was batting fair to become the sensation of the season, which meant that the triumph was all hers. To become one of her admirers would mean standing in line, something he was unused to doing. He was unlikely to get her alone even for a few minutes at an affair like this, and clearly she would not make it easy for him to present his apology. She had not looked nervous when they met and he believed she was an extremely confident woman, wealthy, and of good social standing – a very different proposition to the young girl who he had seduced five years earlier.

Clearly she had not suffered from the experience. Over the years he had sometimes wondered about her life. He had heard that Sir Keith could be violent and cruel at times, but perhaps he had been so besotted with his young wife that he could not do enough for her. Fitz would make it his business to find out as much as he could before he paid the promised call.

Leaving his cousin's house an hour or so before the ball was over, Fitz decided to walk home. It was a fine evening, still a little warm after the sultry heat of the past few days, and he thought the air would clear his head. His thoughts were still with Corinna, his mind rejecting the suspicion that had begun to haunt him. No, it was foolish to imagine that there was something between them – it was merely a matter of unfinished business. He must take the earliest opportunity to apologize to her.

Fitz was not sure when he became aware that someone was following him. His senses were alerted just in time for him to round on the rogue who was about to strike him.

'No, you don't, sir,' Fitz said and drew the little pistol he carried in his coat pocket. His finger rested on the trigger, the safety catch off as he aimed it straight for the villain's heart. 'Be off with you or you'll be crows' bait before morning.'

For a moment the man stared at him, eyes glinting with malice, then he backed away, keeping his eyes fixed on Fitz until he suddenly turned and bolted down a side street, disappearing into the blackness from whence he had come.

It was not unusual for unwary revellers to be attacked at night. No doubt the man was a footpad bent on robbing Fitz's pockets of any gold he carried. Well, he had gone empty-handed this night for he had mistaken his man. Fitz had kept a clear head for he had not been interested in wine that night.

He smiled oddly to himself as he continued on his way. It was not the first time he had been stalked by such rogues, and thus far he had come off best. He was a skilled swordsman and reputed to be the best shot in London. At one time he had been forced to fight several duels, and on one occasion had killed his man, something that had led to him being forbidden the court for some months. Since then most gentlemen had stayed clear of quarrelling with him, and he had learned not to be careless with the wives of hot-tempered gentlemen.

He was more than a match for the thieves and footpads who haunted the dark streets of London. He had other activities, which few of his acquaintances knew about, and was unafraid of the dark, secret world that swirled beneath the veneer of respectability masking so many so-called gentlemen. The lights and gaiety of his cousin's ballroom were far removed from that other world.

His work was not that of the pimp, thug or murderous cut-throats he sometimes met in his secret visits to the underworld, but he mixed with them, knew them – even understood them.

Corinna looked at her reflection in the dressing mirror. She had let her hair down and was in the process of brushing it, which she did every night, with at least one hundred strokes of the brush. It was a habit she had learned during the first months of her marriage when she had needed to calm her nerves. She had never known when her husband might enter her bedroom, nor what kind of mood he would be in. There had been nights when he had simply wanted to possess her body, and that had been the easiest to bear, for the act was never long in duration. On those nights he left her once he had relieved his need, allowing her to rest in peace, but then there were the other nights . . .

But she would not let herself think of those terrible times. They were over now. Her husband could never torment her in that way again – or at least only in her dreams. These days she seldom had one of her nightmares, but there were memories that she could not entirely eradicate from her mind.

And none of it need have happened if that man had not

seduced her so carelessly! Corinna's fingers tightened round the handle of her elegant silver brush. She was angry – angry that he had dared to approach her so confidently, apparently without a shred of remorse. All that pain and suffering, all the humiliation she had been forced to endure – and it was all because of him, his selfishness!

Her honesty forced her to remember that she had responded to his love-making, but she had been a young girl, naïve and in love. He should never have treated her so badly, never have abandoned her.

Until this evening she had almost convinced herself that she could forgive, could put the past behind her once she had seen him again. Now she discovered that the bitterness burned inside her like a physical thing. She had wanted to strike out, to lash the self-confident expression from his handsome face. He was so sure of himself and his position. Supposing she could bring him down in some way – punish him for what he had done to her . . .

She did not know what she could do to a man like Lanchester. He would be impervious to her barbs, for how could she hurt a man who cared so little for the opinion of others? No, it was not enough to taunt him, perhaps make a fool of him in public. She wanted a more tangible revenge – but how to achieve it?

Corinna sought her bed. Until this moment she had not really thought beyond her first meeting with Lanchester, believing that she would realize her anger was unworthy, as perhaps it was. He was not truly worth expending time and energy upon – and yet there was a need in her to see him suffer in some way.

But it was ridiculous to let her thoughts run wild. She might prick him occasionally with her thorns, perhaps humiliate him if the chance came, or win a sum of money from him at the card table, but there was little else she could do. If she were a man she would take a horsewhip to him, but had that been the case there would be no score to settle.

*   *   *

'My God!' Fitz stared in dismay at the agent he had employed. His report was more terrible, more revealing than he could ever have guessed. 'Sir Keith Miles died after a fit of insane rage – are you certain of this, sir?'

'Indeed, milord,' the agent replied. He was generally employed by the Bow Street Runners and known to be efficient at his work. 'I checked most carefully. It was all hushed up, of course, but he killed a nurse employed to care for him by means of strangulation. The man who gave me the information had been employed by the gentleman as a footman, and often helped to restrain him when he was violent. He said that the madness had been coming on for years and that Sir Keith had treated his wife very badly. On one occasion he had had three of her dogs and her horse destroyed because she had done something to displease him. Any maid who showed her kindness was dismissed without a reference, and they say he beat her.'

'That is vile,' Fitz said, his face white. His stomach turned and he felt the rage boil inside him. To think of Corinna being treated in such a way – beaten, humiliated and tortured! It angered him to see whores treated roughly by their pimps, but that a gentleman should behave so to his wife! How could any man do that? It was beyond imagination. 'I wonder that she stayed with him so long.'

'He would not allow her to leave,' the agent said. 'The only time she was allowed away from her home was when Lord Dorling insisted that she stay with him. Apparently Sir Keith was a little afraid of his uncle, for as head of the family he could have had him put away if he chose.'

'I see . . .'

Fitz began to see a great many things. It was clear now why Lord Dorling had decided to adopt his nephew's widow and to leave her his fortune. Such a scandal must be hushed up, and perhaps the old man had had a fondness for her. A marriage between them would have been distasteful to a man of conscience, because of the close relationship. It was also crystal clear to Fitz why Corinna had treated him so coldly at the Dorchesters' ball. She must blame him for her suffering. And indeed he was in some part to blame for what had happened to her . . .

He was pricked with remorse. One careless action on his part had led to unimaginable suffering and humiliation for her. It was true that he had sought her father out, had paid compensation – but had he acted sooner, as he ought to have, Corinna might have been his wife instead of that monster's. Oh God, what she had endured! His senses reeled. It was enough to send a man mad just thinking of it.

For some reason he was swamped by a sense of bitter loss. He had been such a fool, such a careless, unthinking fool! And what now? He had been determined to apologize, but was she likely to forgive him? It was doubtful after all that she had endured. However, he must make the effort, he decided. He must do what he could to make amends for the harm that had been done her.

The pain twisted and turned inside him as he imagined her feelings, the hurt she must have felt for so long. And it was because of him, because of his selfish, careless behaviour that she had suffered so much. She must hate him. Any woman would hate the man who had caused her to fall so low.

Corinna glanced at the pile of cards waiting for her when she arrived home after a pleasurable morning spent shopping and at the lending library. For a moment her heart caught as she saw the rather plain but elegant card on top. The Marquis of Lanchester had called again. He had called three times now and had been told that she was out; twice she had truly been out, but on the first occasion she had been upstairs and had instructed her maid to tell him that she was busy and could not see him.

She tore the card up and threw the pieces on to the silver salver. If he persisted in calling she might be forced to admit him in the end, though she was loath to do so. She glanced through the pile of invitations that had arrived that morning. It was impossible to attend every invitation that came for her, but she picked out three and sat down to reply to them in the affirmative.

She then opened her leather writing slope and began to compose letters to her friends. Writing letters was one of the most pleasurable pastimes of the age, and most ladies indulged themselves in this way. Corinna found the art of constructing a letter that was both beautiful to look at and a delight to read very rewarding. Her writing was an art form and a joy to look upon, so beautifully did she form each letter.

Her correspondence done, she was about to go upstairs to change for the afternoon when the door knocker sounded. For some reason her heart raced and she was not surprised to hear a gentleman's voice in the hallway. He was here again! Clearly he did not mean to take no for an answer.

'The Marquis of Lanchester begs to see you, milady.'

Corinna hesitated, tempted to instruct her maid to send him away, but she realized that was a waste of time when the door of her sitting room was thrust open and a very angry man walked in.

'I was not aware that I had admitted you, sir.' Her eyes met his defiantly. He glared at her but she merely raised her head a little higher as if challenging him.

'I am tired of being dismissed, Corinna. I was certain you were here and I am not prepared to be refused again.'

The maid gasped and looked to her mistress for instruction, but Corinna dismissed her. 'Since you are here, sir, we may as well get this over with. You may go, Sally.'

'Did you imagine I would simply go away?' Fitz asked as the door closed behind the shocked maid.

'I had hoped you might have learned some manners since we last met, sir. A gentleman would have waited to be admitted to a lady's private parlour.'

A wry smile touched his mouth. 'Then we must agree that

I am not a gentleman, Corinna. Enough of this nonsense. I have come here to apologize.'

'Indeed?' Her look would have frozen water in the glass. 'Am I supposed to be grateful that you have condescended to apologize for your disgusting behaviour after all these years?'

'I spoke to your father soon after your marriage and made reparation to him.'

'Did you so?' Corinna glared at him. 'And that cleared your conscience, did it? A debt paid so easily.'

'I am aware that you received nothing . . .' He was cut off by a look so acid that it would have buckled the knees of any other man. 'And I daresay you would not have considered money a fitting recompense.'

'You are correct in that respect, sir. You pay whores for their services, I believe? I am not flattered to be considered on a par with such unfortunates.'

'No, of course not,' he said, keeping his temper on a tight rein. 'I meant no such insult. What else could I offer? You were already married to a wealthy man.'

'Against my will.'

'Yes, I know that now – but I was truly not aware of it then. Nor did I understand . . .' He broke off as her eyes narrowed, sensing that she would reject any show of sympathy on his part. 'I am truly sorry for what happened that night, Corinna. I had been drinking heavily and—'

'Do you imagine that serves as an excuse?' She would not allow him to finish. 'Does that wash away your guilt?'

'I was also jealous. You had been flirting with that other fellow . . .'

'And that gave you the right to treat me as you did?'

'No, of course not. I had no right. It was a cruel, thoughtless act and I have regretted it.'

'For a moment, perhaps,' she said. 'I doubt it has weighed upon you much these past years. I do not see that you have changed greatly, sir. You are as arrogant and presumptuous as ever. A gentleman would have waited to be asked, not come striding in here as if he had the right. Believe me, sir, there have been times when I wished you dead, and others when I longed for the strength to take a horsewhip to you myself.'

'I knew that you would not see me,' Fitz said. He was angry now, pricked by some devil, just as he had been all those years earlier. He wanted to lay hands on her, to shake her, to . . . As he realized where his thoughts were leading, he checked himself and frowned. 'Very well, ma'am. I see that it is useless to appeal to your better nature. I had hoped we might be friends, that I might be of service to you in some way – but clearly it is useless to hope that your nature might allow you to forgive. I shall not make the same mistake again.' He turned and walked away, slamming the door behind him as he went out.

Corinna was trembling when he left. The vomit rose in her throat and she had to breathe hard to keep herself from giving way to tears. How dare he? How dare he . . .

Her eyes were stinging as she blinked away the angry tears. She was standing with her back to the room, looking out at the garden which was bathed in sunlight and quite beautiful, when the door opened again. Someone coughed and she turned angrily thinking that the marquis had returned, but she checked her furious retort as she saw the gentleman standing there.

'You asked me to call, Lady Dorling, and Mrs Crabtree thought you might be in here,' he said. Then, seeing her face, 'But you are upset . . . is something the matter?'

'Sir Maxwell . . .' Corinna tried to gather her scattered wits. She had asked him to call but she could not for the life of her recall why. 'No, nothing . . . Yes, I shall tell you, sir. The Marquis of Lanchester was here. I do not like him . . .'

'Nor I,' Maxwell Everard said and looked angry. 'Damned arrogant, and a rogue to boot if you ask me. Shall I go after him – call him out? It's time someone taught him a lesson.'

Corinna had begun to recover her composure. She saw the

book in his hand and smiled. 'You have brought me Pope's masterpiece, *The Rape of the Lock*, which you told me about. It is so kind of you, sir. I had quite forgotten.'

'I have many earlier works of equal merit in my library,' he told her with a smile. 'One day perhaps you may take more advantage of it. I should be happy to read with you throughout my life, Corinna.'

It was the closest he had come to declaring himself, though she had been aware for some days that he was courting her. He was a pleasant companion, some ten years her senior, but courteous and generous. There were moments when she wondered if it might not be comfortable to marry a gentleman of his temperament, for she missed the evenings spent in lively conversation with Uncle Henry, but then she remembered her late husband and realized that she could never marry again. She could never submit herself to the domination of a man, risk the humiliation and pain of being used that way.

'You are very kind, sir,' she said, recovering herself. 'Would you care for some refreshment before you leave?'

'No, I thank you. I merely thought to leave this on my way to an appointment – but I believe we may meet at Burton's card party.'

'Yes, I believe we may.'

Corinna had offered hospitality, for she could do no less, but she was relieved when the door closed behind him. She rang for her maid, told her that she was not at home to any visitors for the rest of the day and went upstairs. For the moment she needed to be quite alone.

Corinna would have been happier not to be forced to meet the Marquis of Lanchester in company, but there was simply no avoiding it. Wherever she went, he seemed to make an appearance sooner or later. She did her best to avoid him whenever possible, but for his part he seemed to go out of his way to speak with her. It was deliberate, of course – done to annoy her – and they had several rather sharp exchanges, which were exciting because they stimulated her mind, despite her dislike of him.

It was at the Burtons' card party that they next met. Corinna was asked to join a party of four at whisk. She had accepted readily since a gentleman she admired for his philanthropy was one of the four, and it was not until she came to the table that she realized the second gentleman was Fitz Lanchester.

'I am so glad that you are to be one of our set,' Lady Rush told her, making it impossible for her to withdraw. 'For you play well and I hate poor play. Cannot abide careless discards. One must always study one's partner and follow his lead, do you not agree?'

'Yes, in the matter of cards, of course.'

She was relieved that her own partner was not Lanchester but the gentleman she admired and she smiled at him as he drew out a chair for her.

'I am delighted to have this opportunity of furthering your acquaintance, Mr Selby. I have heard of your work with the Foundling Hospital and must tell you that I am most interested in learning more.'

'You are so kind,' he replied eagerly. 'Might you be interested in becoming one of our patrons, Lady Dorling?'

'No talk of business,' Lady Rush said crossly. 'Lanchester, I believe you should lead this first hand.'

'Willingly, ma'am,' he replied, an odd smile on his lips. 'I agree that cards must be the business of the evening.'

'Do you not consider that sensible discussion of a social problem, which ought to be the business of us all, allowable at any time?' Corinna challenged with a glare. 'Or do you find all such conversation dull?'

Fitz gave her a bland look that irritated her beyond bearing. He looked powerful, arrogant, and far too attractive for his own good – or Corinna's peace of mind. 'Idle gossip may be allowable at the card table, ma'am, but I think you owe it to your partner to concentrate on the game in hand.' He scooped up the trick Corinna realized belatedly might have been hers. She had thrown away a small card when she might have played a Jack and won the trick. 'I believe Selby's project is a worthy one that we may all admire – at the appropriate moment.'

A sigh of exasperation from Lady Rush closed the topic. Corinna's eyes flashed blue fire at the marquis but she made no further reply, bending her mind to the battle on the card table, for she was determined to beat Lanchester if she could.

In the end it proved an enjoyable evening, for she acquitted herself well and the honours were equal. Indeed, she was in good humour when they all repaired to the supper room, and she was at last able to have a few words in private with Mr Selby. An arrangement was made for her to visit the hospital the next day, for she wished to see for herself the work that was done there before committing herself to becoming a patron.

'We are looking for larger premises,' Mr Selby told her with a hint of pride in his voice. 'I am delighted to tell you that since I took over from Mr Phelps as chairman of the board of our hospital, I have collected enough monies to consider taking in the children of those in need as well as orphans.'

'Is that not the duty of the parish?'

'Have you ever been inside a workhouse run by the parish, Lady Dorling?' Mr Selby shook his head at her sorrowfully. 'It is a sobering experience, I can tell you. That is why Thomas Coram resolved to build a Foundling Hospital in 1703, for it was not then an unusual occurrence to see the body of a child by the roadside. Many notables of the day, including Hogarth and the great Handel, helped Coram, but the project was barely begun in his day and opened in the year of 1743. We have greatly improved upon his ideas since then.'

'Indeed, I have never been inside a workhouse,' Corinna replied. 'But I have given it some thought, sir. It is surely for us, who have so much in life, to help those that have so little.'

'A worthy thought, Lady Dorling,' said Lanchester from behind her. She had not been aware that he was at her shoulder and she jumped slightly as she turned to look at him. 'But beware of seeming too earnest, or you may find that you are labelled a crushing bore.'

His eyes held a distinct challenge, which made Corinna wish to attack him physically, but she sensibly held her temper.

'I would prefer to be thought dull than an empty-headed nitwit who thinks only of his own pleasure, sir.'

Mr Selby looked shocked, for her remark was clearly intended for the marquis. 'My lady . . .' he began, but was silenced by Lanchester with a lift of his brow.

'I do not believe anyone could think of you as such a person, Lady Dorling.' Fitz smiled at her in that irritating way of his. 'One must admire your courage if nothing else.'

Corinna ground her teeth. 'I thank you for that, sir – if nothing more.'

Fitz's head went back as he laughed out loud, drawing several pairs of curious eyes their way. 'Touché, ma'am. I give you best in this instance, though I reserve the right to re-engage another day.'

Corinna resisted the urge to smile. He undoubtedly had charm and a ready tongue, which in another she might have found amusing. This time she refused to be drawn, merely inclining her head before moving on to speak with other friends. After supper she abandoned the card room in favour of idle gossip with some of the other ladies. Fresh tables had been made up in the card room and she declined to be included in the company, saying that she intended to take her leave quite soon.

Fitz, too, left after supper, for he had an appointment to keep elsewhere, an arranged meeting in a place that would have made his hostess of the evening raise her brows had she known. Fitz thought that Corinna might have approved had she been privy to his thoughts, but of course she was not, and probably never would be.

Fitz shared his secrets with very few, and only those he trusted beyond doubt. Lady Corinna Dorling was not one of the few.

Seven

C orinna slept well that night and rose feeling refreshed and much lighter of spirit than she had for some time. Her companion was to accompany her on the visit to the hospital, where she had arranged to meet Mr Selby at eleven o'clock.

He was there when she arrived promptly, and a tour of the common rooms and wards left her with feelings of pity for the afflicted and kindness for the gentleman who had devoted so much of his time to helping the poor.

'I think the children are lucky to have someone like you, sir,' she told him as she left at the end of her tour. 'I shall send you a draft on my bank to help with your funds and you may add my name to your list of patrons. If I can be of further help, you may call on me when you wish.'

'You are very generous, ma'am,' he said as he escorted Corinna and Anne to the door. 'Thank you for visiting us, ladies. And depend upon it that I shall not be behind in asking for your help.'

They were standing outside in the street, which was rather rundown, the hospital being, for the moment, in a building that had seen better days. The gutters were filthy, running with water that carried all kinds of unimaginable debris. Across the road was an inn, which judging from its appearance was not the kind of establishment that Corinna cared to frequent. She noticed that the people in the street looked thin, their faces pale with deprivation, their clothes filthy and rotting. She knew that many of the poor suffered from terrible diseases and were close to starvation. It was no wonder that the children of people like this ended up as orphans, most of them thrust into the workhouse due to the lack of establishments such as she had just seen.

'I too would like to do whatever I can,' Anne Crabtree said to Mr Selby. 'And . . .' What she meant to say was lost as a young lad of perhaps twelve came rushing by them and snatched Corinna's purse from her hand. 'That rogue stole Lady Dorling's purse! Thief! Stop thief!' She set off after the lad, calling out to him to stop at the top of her voice.

'Come back, Anne,' Corinna cried. 'It doesn't matter. There were only a few guineas in it . . .'

Anne was deaf to her pleas, her indignation aroused to the point where she was unable to stop herself charging after the lad. People in the street had begun to yell and shout, some agreeing with Anne, but, Corinna feared, many more encouraging the lad to make off with the money. She heard cries about rich gentry deserving what they got and sensed that the mood of the crowd was against them. Something awful might have happened had a man not come out of a building at the far end of the street. Seeing what was happening, he stepped forward, caught the lad, boxed his ears, rescued the purse and returned it to Anne with a little bow.

Corinna was surprised to see that it was Sir Maxwell Everard who had dealt with the situation so swiftly, for she wondered what his business might be in such a place as this. He brought Anne back to her immediately.

'Lady Dorling,' he said and presented her with the purse with a little flourish. 'What brings you to such a place as this?'

Corinna thought she might have asked the same of him, but smiled and told him the reason for her visit.

'I own some property in this area,' Sir Maxwell said, answering her unspoken question. 'I have been offered a generous sum to sell it and have been making a last inspection before agreeing to the offer.'

'Ah, I see,' Corinna said. 'It was fortunate for us that you were here, sir, for I was afraid things might turn ugly – there were certain elements of the crowd who appeared ready to make trouble.'

'This is not the kind of area in which I would expect to see a lady of your quality,' Sir Maxwell said. 'These people spend most of their lives with their wits befuddled by cheap gin, though it is not so cheap and readily available as it once was, of course. May I escort you back to the river, Lady Dorling? For if you are not careful you may be accosted again, and the watermen may cheat you.'

'The one that brought us here was a surly devil,' Anne told him. She was red-cheeked from her exertions and feeling a little foolish now. 'I hardly understood a word he spoke.'

'It is their cant,' Sir Maxwell replied with a little smile. 'These boatmen are a law unto themselves. Their rag sauce would test the patience of a saint. By that I mean their chatter, of course.' He gave her a knowing smile, which Corinna thought a little condescending.

'He was talking about a scampsman, whatever that might be,' Corinna said, accepting Sir Maxwell's arm gladly as they walked down to the river's edge. 'Said something about him being sure to scrag, and that his slummery would not save him this time.'

Sir Maxwell laughed, amused by her puzzled look. 'He was talking of a highwayman the Runners took yesterday, I daresay. Scrag means that he will hang and slummery is another word for gammon – to bamboozle someone with words, I believe.'

'Yes, of course,' Corinna said. She smiled, entertained as he intended. 'It is all clear to me now, sir. You are well versed in this cant.'

'I have had reason to visit the area from time to time,' he replied. 'And I made it my business to understand what was being said. But enough of this nonsense – did you enjoy your evening at Burton's? I had hoped to make up a four at whisk with you, but I was cut out by Lanchester.'

'I enjoyed the evening apart from being forced to play at

the marquis's table,' Corinna said with a slight frown. 'He is a man of remarkable skill, but I cannot like him.'

'That has been noticed,' Maxwell told her with a slight smirk. Again there was something in his manner that she did not quite like. 'Some find it amusing that he continues to pursue you so particularly despite your feelings. I have heard it said that he has met with too many reverses at the card tables and must marry an heiress.'

Corinna was shocked. 'You cannot think that he . . .'

'I have not given it much thought,' Maxwell replied. He glanced over his shoulder at Anne, who was walking just behind them. 'I was sure after what you said to me the other day that you would not entertain the idea.'

'Nor should I,' Corinna replied. She was annoyed at the speculation being created, for she knew that it must be the source of much gossip and laughter in the coffee houses and drawing rooms of London. 'Indeed, I do not care for the man at all.'

'He is an arrogant rogue, ma'am,' Sir Maxwell said and there was a note of petulance, even anger in his voice. 'I sometimes think that he needs to be punished as much as the scampsman of whom your waterman spoke.'

'I have wished to punish him,' Corinna agreed on a spurt of temper. Annoyed by his report of the gossip concerning Lanchester's attentions, she spoke without careful thought. 'There have been times when I would have liked to wipe that infuriating smile from his face. But what can one do against a man like that? He cares naught for the opinion of others. I have made my dislike plain enough, but it seems only to amuse him. I can do nothing but prick him with my little thorns and they mean nothing to him.'

'There might be a way to teach Lanchester a lesson . . .' Sir Maxwell mused thoughtfully.

'Would that there were!' Corinna said with feeling, and then almost instantly regretted it. 'No, no, I should not have said that. It is better to ignore him, I believe.'

'Perhaps,' Sir Maxwell replied, but still looked thoughtful.

'You know that I would do anything to make you happy, Lady Dorling – may I presume to call you Corinna, perhaps? I think our friendship has progressed enough for me to do so in private?'

'Yes, of course,' she replied, for she was indebted to him for his kindness in rescuing her companion and for lending her books from his library. 'In private it would be perfectly acceptable.' To use her first name in public would seem too particular; it might cause more gossip and speculation.

'I make no presumptions,' he told her. 'But I am your devoted friend and would be more, Corinna. I would win your good opinion and perhaps in time my reward.'

'If you are asking me to consider . . .' She paused for a second. 'I have no thoughts of remarrying, sir.'

'No, no,' he said quickly, his manner servile and humble, but somehow unconvincing. 'Not just yet, for I know that we have not progressed that far. I ask only to serve you and to hope for the future.'

What could Corinna do but smile and incline her head? She had no idea what he was hinting at in the matter of wishing to serve her and could not refuse an offer of marriage unless it was made.

All further conversation was ended between them as they reached the steps leading down to where the boatmen waited to row passengers across to the other side of the river. Corinna listened as Sir Maxwell bargained with the surly man who had brought them across, understanding only a few words of what was said. But an agreement was arrived at, two shillings paid for their fare, and the ladies settled comfortably in the boat.

'I shall take my leave of you, dear ladies,' Sir Maxwell said. 'But I hope to call on you at home soon. Perhaps then I may have news for you, Corinna.'

'Do you like Sir Maxwell?' Anne asked of Corinna as they waved goodbye to him. 'It was good of him to come to my rescue that way – but there is something that I do not quite trust about him. I think he might lie to create an impression to suit himself.'

'He's a fly one, that flash gent,' the boatman said and winked at Anne, touching the side of his nose. 'Ain't no flat, carries a barking iron in his tog, and knows how to use it. You be careful, missus, or he'll chizzle you like as not.'

Anne turned red and gave him a stony look. 'You mind your work, sir. I was not addressing you.'

'Your mistress knows what I mean, mumps face.'

Corinna made no comment for she was able to understand a little of his slang. He was warning them that Sir Maxwell was a man to be wary of and that he carried a gun in his coat pocket, something she had noticed for herself.

'What did you make out of that?' Anne asked when they had left the river behind and were seated in the comfortable cab they had hired to take them back to their lodgings. 'What a rude fellow he was, to be sure!'

'Oh, it was all nonsense,' Corinna said, but she was aware of some unease. She had thought Sir Maxwell was merely talking for effect when he spoke of punishing the Marquis of Lanchester, but now she was not so certain. She would have been even more concerned had she been a fly on the wall that very afternoon, when the two men met to discuss a matter that concerned them both.

'I must warn you not to meddle in my business, Lanchester,' Sir Maxwell said, a tide of hot colour rising up his neck. 'That property was sold until you interfered.'

'It could not be bought without my consent, and I do not give it,' Fitz replied coldly, giving him a look that had been known to intimidate many a rogue. 'The walls are unsound in places and the roof leaks. You expect too much, sir. We shall offer you no more than half the sum you ask, and that is being generous.'

'I was not aware that you had the casting vote, Lanchester.'

'I am but one on the board,' the marquis replied with a

slight smile. 'But I believe you will discover that the others will abide by my advice.'

'I take it amiss that you have chosen to deny what is rightfully mine.' Sir Maxwell glared at him. He was well aware that the board would not move a muscle if Lanchester was against it. 'Perhaps if I offered . . .' He quailed at the expression in the marquis's eye. 'Be damned to you, sir. I shall refuse to sell for such a paltry sum.'

'You may find there is an order served on you to make the building sound or pull it down.'

'You have no power to do that!'

'Have I not?' Lanchester smiled and flicked a speck of dust from the immaculate sleeve of his coat. 'I have friends in high places. You may discover that pressure is brought to bear in one way or another.'

'That is blackmail!' Sir Maxwell fumed. Lanchester was a formidable adversary and he could see his hopes of a quick profit disappearing before his eyes.

'I do not deny it – but you have no use for the building. It has become the haunt of thieves and highwaymen. Was not that highwayman they took recently hiding there? One could wonder how he came to be there and who it was that betrayed him. It is a sad thing when thieves fall out, is it not?'

Sir Maxwell's face turned deadly white. 'What are you implying, sir?'

'Implying?' Lanchester's mouth thinned. 'Why, nothing – except that the rogue must have been betrayed by someone he trusted. Perhaps he went there to meet a fence, what think you? They might have argued earlier over some trifle or other.' Fitz yawned behind his hand. 'Neither you nor I know what was in the mind of those rogues, but it must be a worry to you to have your property so misused, sir. You would do better to dispose of it and be saved any further bother.'

'You'll be sorry for this,' Sir Maxwell muttered. 'One day I shall wipe the smile from your face . . . Very well, I accept your offer. My lawyer will see to the business.'

'Selby and the others will be grateful to you,' Lanchester said. 'And you may think of it as your contribution to a worthy cause.'

Sir Maxwell swore beneath his breath, turned on his heel and left without another word. Fitz stared moodily after him. He was not sure what devil had prompted him to provoke the man, except that he had seen Corinna walking with him towards the river. She had been smiling up at him, clearly amused at what he was saying. Knowing Sir Maxwell for the knave he was, Fitz had felt a surge of rage. If he could prove what he knew to be true, he might have called the Runners to arrest the cheat then and there – but knowing was one thing, proving it was another.

Besides, it was no crime to own property, even if that property was used for evil purposes. Sir Maxwell had a finger in some of the worst brothels and gaming hells in London, but was discreet enough to keep his name clean. The beatings, thievery and extortion that went on in some of those houses were inexcusable. Girls were forced into a kind of slavery, made to lie with any man willing to pay, and then, when diseased and of no further use, they might be thrown out on the streets to die, or into the river. Young fools cheated of their fortunes met with no better treatment at the hands of those who fleeced them, some dying in the filthy alleys that surrounded the gaming houses, their throats cut. The government was either powerless or uninterested in making laws to control those who ran these places, and their existence was a blot on the reputation of the city.

Fitz was one of a small group of gentlemen pledged to clean out some of the worst offenders. Working in secret, they often took the law into their own hands, and were known to each other as the Lords of Reform. It was a dangerous business, rode very close to breaking the law, and gave Fitz the excitement his life would otherwise lack. As a part of that work he often rubbed shoulders with cut-throats and prostitutes, who gave him information about the men he sought to root out and expose for their evil-doing.

This, however, was merely a part of his work, for he was on the board of several charities pledged to alleviate the plight of London's poor, and it was in this capacity that Everard had first come to his notice. Several properties that the board were interested in purchasing had changed hands suddenly and been offered at a higher price by the new owner – Maxwell Everard. Clearly he had thought to pull the wool over their eyes, believing that the men whose names appeared on the charity's board were simple fools. However, he had not reckoned with the man who oversaw many of the trusts, though as a secret partner, and unknown to all but the privileged few.

Fitz Lanchester was a powerful man, himself immensely rich – although again this was known only to a few. He chose to use his power to help those that could not help themselves, and did so ruthlessly, with little regard for the law. Those who really knew him understood that he was a law unto himself. His respect for the government of the day was scant, and with others of like minds he rode out like the knights of old to right wrong where he perceived it. Those who called him arrogant were right in so far as it went, for he was accustomed to wielding power without asking, and to having his own way in most things. That he stood for justice in a society that offered little to the poor was to his credit, but in doing so he had made enemies.

It angered him that Corinna should give her trust to such a man as Maxwell Everard, while reserving her poisoned barbs for him. Had she guessed that most of them went home, causing him some anguish, she would no doubt have laughed heartily. He laughed at himself as he realized he was the world's worst fool for allowing her to get beneath his skin.

He should find an obliging whore and lose himself in the pleasures of the flesh, or simply take himself off to the club and get drunk in the company of friends. But neither solution appealed. Of late his life had seemed empty and meaningless, despite his many activities. He had discovered that he wanted only one thing and that was way beyond his reach.

Corinna would not have him if he were the last man alive!

'Is something upsetting you?' Anne Crabtree looked at Corinna anxiously as they sat comfortably together a day or so later, Anne busy with her embroidery, while Corinna read some of her correspondence. 'You seem to be out of sorts, my dear.'

'I have been a little offhand,' Corinna admitted with a rueful smile. 'Forgive me if I have offended you in any way, Anne dearest. My mind has been elsewhere, I fear.'

'No, you have not offended me. I thought that you seemed . . . unhappy is not quite the word, but not your usual self.'

'I have been down in the dumps,' Corinna said and laughed. 'Yes, I know it is true, but the devil of it is that I do not know why. Perhaps I am missing Uncle Henry. And then . . . This came earlier.' She handed Anne the letter she had been reading. 'It is from my father and a little sad. He married a girl of about my own age and she has led him a merry dance. He believes she has cuckolded him and he thinks the child she carries is not his own.'

Anne frowned as she read the letter. 'He asks to see you, to be reconciled.'

'Yes, that is what has been pricking at me,' Corinna said. 'I swore I would never see him again, and yet . . .'

'Now you think you ought to?' Anne looked quite annoyed for such a gentle soul. 'I know the conventional answer would be to tell you to forgive and forget, but I do not subscribe to that line of thought. If your father stepped beyond the line of what was forgivable, you should not give him the chance to hurt you again.'

'My father cannot hurt me,' Corinna replied with a sigh. 'He has no power over me, for Uncle Henry did everything necessary to protect me. I do not particularly wish to see my father – but I think I may write and tell him to call if he will.'

'Well, that is your choice,' Anne said. 'But are you sure it is wise?'

'I am not sure it is wise to go on hating,' Corinna said. 'Hate is a corruptive thing, Anne, and I do not wish to become bitter or twisted. Perhaps if I could forgive my father . . .' She sighed as the real problem nagged at her once more. She had believed that she could never forgive Lanchester, that she desired revenge, to see him humbled at her feet, but her feelings toward him had begun to change of late.

She did not know why, for he constantly irritated her whenever they met, but now she was more inclined to laugh inwardly at his attempts to challenge her. There was something about him that commanded respect. She had seen it in other men, known that his words were listened to and accepted. Despite herself, she had begun to look for him at the affairs they both attended and to feel disappointed if he were not there.

She glanced through the pile of invitations on her desk, frowning as she saw one to a card party. It was for that very evening and must have been overlooked. She had not seen it previously and would be unable to attend since she had a prior engagement.

'I must answer this at once,' she said to Anne. 'It would seem careless not to, and I should not care for that.'

'I have an errand,' Anne told her. 'I shall leave you in peace – is there anything I may bring you?'

'You may return that book to the library for me,' Corinna said and handed her the book of poems she had been reading. She laughed wryly. 'Thank you for putting up with me, Anne. I daresay I should be a sad creature without you.'

Anne smiled, shook her head, and went out. Corinna penned her note of regret, rang for a footman and sent it off immediately. She wished that she had seen it when it arrived, for she imagined that Lanchester would be at his friend's house that evening. And, if she admitted the truth, she would prefer the card party to the invitation she had already accepted.

Had she been less well mannered, Corinna might have considered crying off and suiting her own preference. Indeed, had she done so, she might have saved herself and others a great deal of distress.

'I see Maxwell Everard is here,' Fitz said with a wry twist of his mouth as he glanced about the room that evening. 'I should warn you not to encourage him too often, Marshall. He is heading for . . .' He broke off as if recalling himself. Marshall was the best of fellows but inclined to gossip. 'No matter. Just as long as he does not ask me to make up a table with him.'

'Well, he will not, for I have already reserved that right to myself and two others with whom I know you have no quarrel, Fitz. Rochester said you took five thousand guineas from him last week, and he wants a chance of revenge.'

Fitz laughed softly. 'He is welcome to try, as are you all, my friend. I believe the streak of ill fortune I had a while back has left me. I have been winning of late.'

His luck at the tables had seemed to change since the night he played a game of whisk with Corinna for shillings. Usually he played for much higher stakes, but that night he had rediscovered pleasure in the game for its own sake, and since then he had been unable to lose.

There was a sprinkling of ladies present that evening, but most of the company consisted of gentlemen Lanchester had known and played cards with all his adult life – but Sir Maxwell had come upon the scene only a few months earlier. There was some question about the source of his wealth, for he had only an insignificant estate in the south of England, and was rumoured to have spent some years abroad. Some kind of scandal had caused him to leave when he was a young man of merely eighteen, but it had been forgotten by most.

Fitz was having the man investigated to see what more could be discovered other than his property deals, for although he knew him to have a finger in some of the less reputable hells in London's murky back streets, as yet no significant details had been revealed. At the moment it was all speculation and proof was needed if he were to be brought to justice. If none could be found it was possible that one day the gentleman might wake up to find himself on a ship heading for some far-flung destination. Rough justice, but effective!

However, he could tolerate the man in company if forced, and nodded politely, if distantly, to Maxwell as the company talked and laughed for a few moments before moving to the card tables. His luck was in once more and he won hand after hand, causing the Earl of Rochester to bemoan his bad luck when they paused for supper.

'I'm damned if I know how you do it, Lanchester,' he said. 'I've never seen a man with such luck.'

'Luck – or is there more to it?'

Silence greeted Sir Maxwell's words. He had spoken in a loud voice and everyone stared at him in silence. From his manner and the flush in his cheeks, it was obvious that he had been drinking far too much of his host's good brandy.

'I say, hang on,' the earl said, embarrassed. 'I meant no such thing. We all know Lanchester wouldn't . . .'

'He is a rogue and a liar,' Maxwell said belligerently, his eyes bulging. 'None of you know what he might be capable of. I say he's a cheat.'

'You'd better take that back, sir,' Marshall said. 'I will thank you to apologize and leave. If you insult my friend, you insult me.'

'I shall not apologize,' Maxwell said defiantly, though his face had gone white now.

'Then get out of my house this instant!'

'Nay, my friend,' Fitz said, laying his hand upon the arm of his indignant host. 'A charge has been made and must be answered.'

'We all know it is rubbish . . .'

'It seems that Sir Maxwell does not,' Fitz said, a wolfish smile on his lips. 'Will you name your friends, sir – and your choice of weapons?'

'Johnson and Baxter,' Maxwell said instantly, naming two

of the gentlemen with whom he had played cards earlier. 'And pistols. I know you for an expert swordsman and I cannot match you, but I can fire a pistol as well as any man.'

'You're a fool,' said the Earl of Rochester. 'With a sword you might have hoped to escape with a prick; with the pistols you're dead. Lanchester never misses.'

Maxwell looked sick, but his head went up, eyes defiant.

'You will stand with me – Rochester, Marshall?' The two men inclined their heads in agreement to Fitz's request. 'Very well, my seconds will call on you in the morning, sir. I think it best to give you a day to clear your head, for I do not take unfair advantage of a drunken man. If you decide to make a written apology it will be accepted.' He smiled at the earl. 'And now, Rochester, if you care to try your hand, we shall see if I cannot win some more of your guineas.'

'Try if you will,' the earl replied and grinned at him. 'I'll have my revenge, you'll see. No man's luck lasts for ever.'

The rest of the company laughed, turning their backs on Maxwell, who, after hurried speech with his reluctant seconds, left the house. Whatever happened, he would not be welcomed in that house again, nor yet in many others.

'It was good of you to see me, Corinna.' Robert Knolls looked at his daughter awkwardly. They were alone in her private sitting room, Anne having retired discreetly when he was announced. 'I thought you might refuse me.'

'I considered it,' Corinna replied and raised her head, meeting his eyes fearlessly. She thought he looked older and tired, and felt a pang of regret. 'We did not part on the best of terms, Father.'

His face creased with distress, regret writ plain. 'I was wrong to do what I did. Wrong and cruel. I realized that very soon after your wedding, Corinna.'

'Unfortunately, that was too late,' she replied. 'It was not a happy time for me.'

'I know something of what you suffered,' he told her.

'Lord Dorling wrote to me when Sir Keith became ill. I am very sorry. Had I known . . .'

'You did not stop to consider, sir. You must have known I could not want to marry him.'

'But there was the scandal to be thought of. I did not know then that Lanchester meant to marry you . . .'

'Meant to marry me?' Corinna stared at him, her face suddenly pale, her knees going weak. She clutched at the back of a chair to steady herself. 'What do you mean? I know he paid you compensation, but . . .'

'The money was meant for you, but I fear it has been spent.' Robert sighed. 'He came to see me, told me that he had been delayed or he would have been there sooner. He was going to ask for permission to approach you formally – and I would have given it, Corinna. I had always hoped for it.'

Corinna turned away, going to stand at the window and look out at the garden. Why had she not been told this long ago? Yet since she had sent back any letters from her father unanswered, perhaps she had only herself to blame . . .

She squared her shoulders and turned back to look at her father, her face void of emotion, though she was finding it hard to control. The ice inside her had begun to crack – it had begun when she first saw Fitz again – and now it was melting, letting the feelings flow freely once more. And they hurt; they hurt terribly. 'It was his duty to offer me marriage. I should not have accepted him.'

'No, he did not come for that, Corinna. He accepted the blame for what had happened – but he said that he was jealous, in love with you.'

'I cannot believe that!' It made everything so much harder to bear. She might have been Fitz's wife!

'I believed him,' Robert said. 'He tried to explain his behaviour, his hesitation. He was young, restless, and unsure what he wanted of life. He knew that he loved you, but was not truly ready for marriage. After that night he delayed when he should have come to me immediately, but that was partly our fault, Corinna. If we had returned to town I am certain that he would have kept his appointment.'

'Perhaps . . .' What would her reaction have been if Lanchester had come after she knew that she was carrying his child? She could not be certain. Her anger might have cooled by then, especially if she had believed that he was truly in love with her. Her emotions were stirred, her mind in sudden turmoil. Her father's revelation put a different complexion on matters – both past and present. She sighed. 'But that is in the past. We cannot change what has been done, sir. We can only move on.'

'I know there is no going back,' Robert said and echoed her sigh. 'God knows I would reverse many things if I could, but there is no use in repining for what cannot be changed. All I ask is that you will be generous enough to forgive me, Corinna. I have wronged you and I shall make what reparation I can in my will . . .'

'I have no need of money,' she replied. 'Uncle Henry saw to it that I would always be financially secure. However, I find that I may be able to forgive you. I cannot forget . . .' She shuddered. 'I do not think that I shall ever be free of the shadow that my husband cast over me – but I shall try to forgive.'

'Thank you, Corinna.' He moved towards her as if he would embrace her, but she stepped back and he hesitated. She seemed to ward him off, though her manner was not hostile.

'No kisses or tears,' she said, but softened the words with a smile. 'I am no longer the girl you once knew, Father, but a very different woman. Do not expect me to melt overnight.'

'No, of course not.' He hesitated awkwardly. 'My wife – Angela – has begged me to bring you to stay with her.'

'Not for the moment,' Corinna said. 'Perhaps in a few months. I make no promises, but I shall give the matter some thought.'

'That is all I ask. I shall leave you now.' Robert walked towards the door, then stopped and turned to look at her. 'I don't know if this interests you at all, but Lanchester fought a duel this morning with a man called Sir Maxwell Everard. I understand that Everard fired too soon but missed his target, hitting Lanchester in the shoulder and wounding him – he himself was killed . . .'

'No!' Corinna gasped and staggered, sitting down abruptly. It was shocking news. Fitz wounded, Sir Maxwell dead! She felt sick and shaken, her hands trembling as she clasped them in her lap. 'Pray tell me, why did they quarrel?'

'I understand it was over the cards, though I am not sure of the details,' her father replied. He studied her pale face in concern. 'Forgive me, I did not know he still meant something to you or I should not have told you so carelessly.'

She shook her head, lying instinctively to protect herself. 'No, he does not. It was just the shock. Was Lanchester badly hurt?'

'Not fatally, but severe enough for him to be laid upon his bed, I understand.'

'And Sir Maxwell was killed?'

'Instantly. He gave Lanchester little choice, for he was trying to reload his pistol . . .'

'But that is against the rules of duelling, is it not?'

'Exactly. He was no gentleman, Corinna. Had Lanchester not aimed true the man could have been arrested for attempted murder – but he might have got in another shot and killed either the marquis or one of the other gentlemen present.'

'Will . . . will Lanchester be arrested for killing him?'

'There may be some sort of inquiry before the beak,' her father replied. 'But there were several witnesses to testify that the marquis was blameless. The most that will happen is that His Majesty may demand that he retire to the country for a few months, though I believe he has powerful friends and may escape with no more than a mild reprimand.'

'I see . . .' Corinna swallowed hard. 'I am glad you told me, Father, even though it was a shock. I knew Sir Maxwell and . . .' But she could not speak of what was in her mind. It was too shocking, too disturbing.

'I do not think you should grieve for him,' her father said. 'By all accounts he may have been a rogue.'

'Yes . . .' Corinna lapsed into silence once more. It did not behove her to speak ill of the dead, especially when she suspected that this was what Sir Maxwell had meant by being of service to her. He had declared that Lanchester deserved to be punished and she had agreed. She had agreed! How many times she had wished the words unspoken.

'May I call your companion to you, or your maid?'

Corinna raised her head, composing herself. 'No, thank you. I was shocked, but I am much better now. I would prefer to be alone for a while.'

'Yes, of course. Forgive me.'

Corinna made no reply as he went out. Her head was in a whirl, her emotions in turmoil; a mixture of guilt, regret – and thankfulness that the man she had once loved was not dead. Yet he was injured, and such wounds as his often proved fatal. If he should die, then she would never forgive herself.

Eight

There was little more news to be gained that evening or the next day, but on the third day, Anne came back from a trip to the lending library to tell her that the Marquis of Lanchester was gravely ill.

'Lady Rush told me that she had heard he might die of his injury.'

Corinna got up at once and went over to the window, trying to hide her anguish. If Fitz Lanchester died, believing that she hated him, it would break her heart for a second time.

'She also told me that it is all coming out about Sir Maxwell now,' went on Anne behind her. 'Apparently he was involved in all kind of nefarious business, and might have been taken up by the Runners quite soon.'

Corinna turned to look at her. 'Do you know exactly what he was accused of? I had suspected something, but . . .'

'You know Lady Rush,' Anne said. 'She is all hot air and knows nothing . . . But it was strange how he understood all that stuff about highwaymen and hanging, did you not think so?'

'Yes, I did think there was something odd about him that day.' How she wished she could take back the hasty words she had spoken! Had they contributed to Sir Maxwell's intent, or had he been bent on destroying a man he disliked?

Corinna was in a state of anxiety all day. How could she obtain news of the marquis? They had no engagements that evening for she had decided to refuse the invitations they

110

had received in favour of a quiet night at home, but there was no possibility of her resting now.

It was not until quite late in the evening that she made up her mind.

'I am going to Lanchester's house,' she told her companion, causing Anne to stare at her in dismay.

'But you cannot! It would be most improper,' Anne said, her gentle soul shocked by the very suggestion. 'You must not think of it, Corinna.'

'I have thought of nothing else all day,' she replied. 'I shall not rest until I have news of him.' She stood up determinedly. 'Please call for my carriage while I go and get ready.'

'If you are to go then I shall come with you.'

'No, I do not wish it.' But Corinna relented as she saw Anne's stubborn look. 'Very well, you may accompany me, but you must abide by what I do and say nothing. I must have your word now.'

Anne opened her mouth to object and shut it again, merely inclining her head.

'Thank you,' Corinna said. 'I know you do not approve, but it is something I must do.'

'I should advise you to wear a hood,' Anne said. 'I myself shall go masked, for we must try to hide your identity to avoid scandal.'

'Yes, certainly, I shall heed your advice in this matter. I had thought of pretending to be the marquis's cousin if need be.'

'Well, I shall say no more.'

Anne compressed her lips. She thought it a foolish idea but knew that Corinna would go alone if she persisted in warning her against it.

A stately butler answered Anne's demanding knock at the door of the marquis's imposing house. He looked at them suspiciously.

'Yes, what do you want at this hour? There is a sick man in the house.'

'That is why we are here,' Anne replied curtly. 'My mistress has come to see her cousin. She has travelled a long way and must be admitted at once.'

'Mistress Lawson?' The butler stared at Anne. 'Why didn't you say so at once?' He glanced at Corinna, whose face was shadowed by the velvet hood she wore and the gauze scarf draped across her mouth. 'Forgive me, miss, I did not know it was you.'

'I must see him,' Corinna said in a choking voice. 'Is he very ill, sir?'

'The doctor was here earlier,' the man said, shaking his head. 'It looks bad, Mistress Lawson.'

'May I see him now?'

'I'll take you up.' The butler looked down his long nose at Anne. 'Your companion may wait in the salon to the right. Someone will see to her in a moment.'

Corinna followed him up the stairs. Candles burned at intervals along the gallery above, but she had no time or inclination to stare at the magnificence of her surroundings, though she could not be unaware of them. It was a truly impressive house.

The butler paused at last before the door at the far end of the passage. 'This is the marquis's bedchamber, miss. I do not know if it is proper for me to allow you to enter . . .'

'My cousin is like to die,' Corinna said. 'This is no time to think of the conventions. I must and shall see him.'

In the face of her determination, the butler could do nothing but bow his head and indicate the door. He hesitated as she knocked softly, then walked away as she opened the door and went in. His master's valet was in attendance and would no doubt see to the young woman now. He had never met Mistress Lawson before that night, but from all accounts she was a fiery young lady, much given to impetuosity.

Corinna went hesitantly inside, for despite her stout words to Anne, she knew that she was breaking all the laws of society. If it was generally known that she had visited the marquis late at night her reputation would be gone forever.

A man was standing by the bed looking down at the marquis, who was tossing restlessly upon his pillows. He turned as she entered, a finger to his lips.

'He is in a fever,' the valet said softly when she came up to him. 'The doctor was here earlier and told me to keep him as cool as I could – are you his assistant? He said he might send someone to help me care for the marquis.'

'No, I am Fitz's cousin,' Corinna replied, deciding to stick to her story. 'I was anxious when I heard he was so ill and came to see what I could do for him.'

'We have never met,' the valet replied. 'I am Reed, ma'am, the marquis's man. He has spoken of you to me but I thought you were in the country.'

'I have recently come to town,' Corinna lied. 'But I may help you if you will allow it, sir. You must be tired if you have nursed him alone since he was hurt.'

'I have been with him constantly. At first he laughed it off, said that it was but a flesh wound, but then he took a fever . . .'

She heard the concern in his voice, and bent over the marquis to lay her hand on his brow. 'He is burning up,' she said. 'If the doctor's advice was to keep him cool I think we should strip all but a sheet from the bed – and it might be a good idea to bathe him all over.'

'I shall do that, ma'am,' Reed said, 'if you will strip away the bedclothes, and make up his medicine. You will find the bottle and instructions on the dressing chest.'

Corinna smiled inwardly for she knew he was trying to protect her. She was supposed to be an unmarried girl. Reed could not know that nothing about a man's body would surprise or shock her. But to save his feelings, she obeyed him, returning to the bed only when the sheet was once more in place.

'Lift him up a little,' she said, 'and I shall pour the medicine down his throat.'

'He will fight you. My master is not a good patient.'

'We shall overcome him together.'

Her smile was one of such sweetness that Reed could do nothing but obey her. She held the glass to Lanchester's lips, but he had stirred somewhat and set his mouth against it as if reluctant to swallow.

'Now, do not be stubborn, Fitz,' Corinna said in a coaxing tone. 'You are worrying poor Reed and I refuse to stand for such foolishness, my dear.'

'Corinna . . .' Lanchester said, opening his mouth and his eyes for a second. 'Corinna? How come you—' He was cut off as she poured the brown liquid into his mouth; he choked slightly and spluttered as though he found it distasteful. 'Damn you, Reed!' Lanchester's eyes closed almost as soon as his head touched the pillow.

'You did well, miss,' Reed said. He looked slightly puzzled, for he knew that his master's cousin was Miss Mary Lawson. 'He usually refuses to open his mouth for me.'

'We . . . we were fond of each other some years ago,' Corinna said. 'He was surprised, that's all.'

'Yes, miss. Thank you for your help. Perhaps you ought to leave now. I could arrange for a room to be made ready . . .'

'Nonsense,' Corinna replied. 'You are tired and I shall not be able to be here all the time. You must rest for a few hours and I shall keep vigil. You may trust me, I promise you. Should the marquis need you, I shall ring for you.'

'Perhaps . . .' He saw the determined gleam in her eyes and smiled. 'Yes, of course, Mistress Lawson. I do need to rest and you seem very capable.'

'I shall do whatever is necessary. Go and rest now, Reed. Your master is safe with me.'

He smiled at her and left the room. Corinna went to the bed, laying her hand on the marquis's forehead again. Was it her imagination or did he seem a little cooler?

'You must rest, dearest,' she told him softly. 'I am sorry for all the hurts between us – and if my careless words contributed towards what happened between you and Sir Maxwell . . .' A little sob rose to her lips but she held it back. 'So sorry . . .'

She sat down in a chair near the fireplace, preparing to watch over him throughout the night if necessary. How foolish she had been all this time, telling herself that she hated him when plainly she did not. Several times she got up to check on his progress and to her relief the fever did not seem to get worse. But it had not gone, for he moaned and spoke a name indistinctly in his sleep, throwing his arms out as if he had bad dreams – or memories. Once she thought she heard her own name, but then he was crying out for someone else.

'Forgive me . . . Father . . .'

Had he quarrelled with his father at some point? It must have been years ago, Corinna thought, and yet she could see it troubled him still. She felt something tug at her heart strings and knew suddenly what she had strived to hide from herself these many weeks. She was in love with him. Perhaps she had never stopped loving him. The bitterness and anger she had felt against him had been stripped away, leaving only remorse and fear – fear that he might die and never know that she loved him.

'You will be better soon,' she promised, stroking his forehead. 'And then we shall be friends again. We shall forget the past and—' She broke off as the door opened behind her and his valet entered the room.

'You should not have come so soon.'

'I have rested,' Reed told her. 'Besides, you ought to return home before you are missed. Your companion is most anxious for you.'

'Oh, poor Anne!' Corinna cried. 'I had quite forgot her. Yes, we must go – but I shall return tomorrow evening. You may expect me at the same time.'

'Yes, ma'am.'

Corinna went quickly downstairs, where she was met by Anne, to be told she had been given blankets and a sofa to lie on, and that their carriage had been sent away.

'The marquis's butler said we could not keep the horses standing all night, and that he would arrange for us to be taken home.'

'Yes, I see,' Corinna said. 'We shall allow ourselves to be taken a part of the way, Anne, and then we must get out and send the carriage away.'

'Yes, I had thought of that myself,' Anne replied. 'And now we must hurry away, for it will be light in another hour or so and the servants will be wondering where you have been all night.'

Corinna said nothing, merely smiling at her companion's concern for her reputation. At this moment nothing seemed to matter other than the fact that Fitz was still alive.

'My goodness, you are cheerful this morning,' Anne said as Corinna greeted her with a smile that lit up her face. 'I made sure you would be still asleep.'

'Oh, no, I was awake at my usual time,' Corinna replied. 'Quite often I sleep no more than three or four hours.' It was a habit she had developed during her marriage and now could not break. However, she was feeling remarkably well, and happier than she had for a long time.

'Well, we must hope that last night's episode will not cause you trouble,' Anne said. 'I do not think anyone saw us returning to the house this morning.'

'If they did it would not be so unusual. A casual observer would think only that we had been to a late-night revel.'

'Perhaps – but not if they saw us leaving Lanchester's house. You took a terrible risk, Corinna.'

'And I shocked you,' Corinna said with a smile of apology. 'Well I am sorry for it.' She made up her mind that she would slip away that evening without alerting either her companion or her servants. It should be easy enough to retire early with a headache and then slip out of the house and hire a cab herself . . .

'I am glad to see you so much recovered, sir,' Reed said when he found his master sitting up against the pillows later that morning. 'You really gave us quite a shock, my lord.'

'You should not lose faith so easily, Reed,' Fitz mocked.

'Do you not know that I have an iron constitution?'

Reed shook his head, knowing his master's disregard for personal safety of old. 'You were very ill, sir. Enough to bring your cousin hurrying to your side.'

'My cousin?' Lanchester raised his brows. 'To whom are you referring?'

'Mistress Mary Lawson,' Reed replied. 'She came to the house late last night and helped to nurse you, sir. I did try to tell her it wasn't proper, but she would not listen.'

'That sounds like Mary,' the marquis replied with a frown. 'But I imagined she was still in Italy with her mother. Are you sure you did not imagine it, Reed? I thought I was the one with the fever . . .' He looked thoughtful. 'I seem to recall something . . . soft hands and a voice . . . *her voice*.' His gaze narrowed sharply. 'What did this lady look like?'

'She wore a hood over her head but it slipped back as she bent over you. Her hair was a pale gold, sir, and her eyes were blue.'

'Mary has red hair and green eyes,' Fitz said. His mouth thinned as his suspicion hardened. 'Tell me exactly what she said to you, Reed. Think carefully now; this may be important.'

'She said she was your cousin, that she had recently come to town – and that she must see you. She was most concerned, sir.'

'Concerned that I might live and denounce her, perhaps,' Fitz said with a snarl. 'If it was the lady I believe it may have been, I have it on good authority that she wants me dead . . .'

Reed gasped. 'No, surely not, sir. She was like an angel – beautiful, caring and—'

'False,' Fitz said curtly. 'Before he died, Maxwell told me that she had begged him to kill me for her sake. His reward was that she would become his mistress.'

Reed was shocked, unbelieving. 'You must be mistaken, sir. Surely she could not have done or promised such a wicked

117

thing?' It was impossible to believe. His master must still be in a fever.

'Why should a man lie when he is dying? Answer me that if you can. There were witnesses to hear his words.'

'I cannot say, sir – but I do not believe the lady who came here capable of such wickedness as to plot a man's death.'

'You are bewitched by her beauty as others have been,' Fitz replied, refusing to be swayed. 'I daresay she thought nature might take its course – that is why she did not take her chance while she had it – but she made a mistake. I am on my way to recovery.'

'She said that she would come back tonight at the same time . . .'

'Did she indeed?' Fitz's mouth curled into a sneer of mockery. 'Then she will be caught in her own trap, for there will be a surprise awaiting her . . .'

Her plan had worked well, Corinna thought as she success-fully escaped from the house without detection and walked swiftly to a place where she knew carriages were always to be found for hire at the kerbside. She had no trouble in finding a driver willing to take her to her destination and settled back against the squabs, ignoring the slightly sour smell of the interior and trying to ignore her guilt.

Anne had been concerned when Corinna complained of a headache earlier, and though she hated to deceive her friend, she felt it was best in the circumstances. Anne disap-proved of her visiting the house of an unmarried man at night, but Corinna could not rest without news of Fitz. If she were told that he was much recovered she would leave at once, but if he was worse . . . The thought sent such shivers running through her that she could not bear it. Her nails dug into the palms of her hands as she remembered her careless words to Sir Maxwell and wished once again that she could recall them. If only she had not spoken so carelessly . . . but she had not dreamed of such terrible consequences.

Corinna's thoughts were tangled and far from happy as she was set down before the marquis's house. Perhaps it was foolish of her to come here, she thought, almost turning away before the door was answered. Fitz would not thank her for her concern – and yet she was driven by a need inside her. The need to see him, to know that he was still living was paramount. Before she could lose her courage entirely the door was opened to admit her, and this time the butler seemed to be waiting for her.

'We hoped you would come, miss,' he told her in a voice muffled by emotion. 'My master is gravely ill . . .'

Corinna did not wait to be told more. Gathering up the hem of her skirt, she ran past him and up the stairs as swiftly as she could, arriving at Lanchester's bedchamber breathing hard. She paused for a moment to compose herself and then went in, her heart racing wildly. Only one small candle was burning in the room, and she could see the dark shape of the man lying under the bedcovers. No one was there! How could Reed have left him alone when he was so ill? Perhaps it was already too late. The thought that he might already be dead brought a rush of emotion and tears to Corinna's eyes.

She went swiftly to the bed. She would see for herself how ill he was and then demand that the doctor be sent for immediately. She bent over him, her hand reaching towards the covers. Too many covers! Why had they not been keeping him cool?

'My lord,' she said softly and then gave a startled cry as someone grabbed her from behind. She struggled violently but whoever held her was very strong. She was lifted bodily and tossed upon the bed, where she lay gasping for breath for a moment before looking into the face of the man bending over her. 'You! But I was told you were very ill . . .'

'My man did as I bid him,' Fitz said, his face set and angry in the dim light of the candle. She noticed that he held one arm stiffly and his skin was white, as though he felt some pain from the struggle between them. 'Had you been told I had recovered you might have gone away and I should have lost my opportunity.'

Corinna was more angry than frightened. She pushed herself up against the pillows, the bolster having been cunningly used to deceive her. 'What on earth do you imagine you are about, sir?' she demanded. 'Why have you attacked me like this? I came here to help you and this is my reward?'

'To help me or to make certain that I did not recover?' Corinna was too shocked to answer immediately so he went on, 'Did you imagine that no one would know? Everard told me before he died that you had persuaded him to call me out for the purpose of murdering me – and that his reward was to have you for his mistress.'

'That is a lie!' Corinna cried. 'I was part of no such pact, sir. I may have expressed my dislike and said I felt you deserved to be punished . . .' She broke off as his eyes flashed with fury and she shrank back against the pillows. He looked as if he were angry enough to do anything. She was suddenly aware of how vulnerable she was there alone with him. 'You cannot believe so ill of me?'

'Why not?' Fitz asked. A small pulse was throbbing at his temple and his hands balled at his sides as though he could barely keep from striking her. His anger had grown steadily all day, the thought of her plotting with his enemy forming a red mist in his brain. 'You have made it plain enough that you hate me, ma'am. Why should I not believe that you want me dead?'

'Because I do not,' she said. 'I will not deny that there was a time when I might have wished it, when I felt a certain bitterness towards you, but I would never have agreed to such wickedness.'

'You may cry your innocence now that you have been caught,' Fitz said. 'But why else would you come here if not to make certain I was not like to recover?'

Corinna opened her mouth and then shut it again. If she told him the truth he would laugh at her, despise her, as she was beginning to despise herself. She had been a fool to let herself care for him! Clearly he was not worth her concern or her tears.

'So you have no answer for once? Well, that makes a pleasant change. I have suffered enough of your poison barbs of late, ma'am. You have done your best to make a fool of me. Everard tried his damnedest to murder me, but as you see I survived.'

Corinna refused to answer. The evidence against her was damning, for she had no way of proving her innocence. If she told him she had been unable to rest because of her anxiety for him he would not believe her. He was determined to think the worst of her and she could not explain without making herself seem a fool. She would not give him the satisfaction of knowing how vulnerable she was!

'Obviously I wasted my time in coming here,' Corinna said and attempted to swing her legs over the edge of the bed. He seized her ankle, refusing to let her get up. The touch of his hand against her silk-clad flesh made her jump with shock. 'Unhand me, sir! I wish to leave this house at once.'

'I daresay you may,' he said grimly. The warmth of his hand gripping her ankle was sending tingles running through her. 'But I have no intention of letting you plot against me again, ma'am. I imagine there are other gentlemen who might be willing to oblige you by sending me to an early grave, and the next one might succeed. No, I have other plans for you.'

'You have no right to keep me here!'

'None at all,' Fitz agreed with a smile. 'But I do not imagine you will be here long.'

Corinna shivered as a cold chill started at the base of her spine. There was something ruthless about him, something that made her think he might be capable of anything. 'What do you plan to do with me? Am I to be murdered?'

His smile was icy, his eyes hard as flint. 'Murder? It is one option, of course, but I feel it would be a waste to destroy such beauty as yours, ma'am. It should be allowed to flourish for others to enjoy. Since you were willing to sell yourself to Everard so cheaply, why should you not put your talents as a whore to good use? I daresay we could find a place for you in some bawdy house – or perhaps a sea voyage to the harem of an Eastern potentate.'

'You would not!' Corinna could not believe what she was hearing. 'I have never heard anything so monstrous!'

'Have you not?' He raised one eyebrow mockingly. She was so beautiful with that glorious hair and those eyes – and yet she was a consummate liar. 'Then your education must have been sadly lacking. You would not be the first troublesome girl to be sold to the highest bidder – and with hair like yours you should fetch a good price in the eastern world.'

'Do not be ridiculous! You cannot hope to get away with such a thing! My absence will be noticed by morning. People will come here looking. My companion will raise a search for me. I have friends . . .' There was a note of almost farcical desperation in her voice. This was so ridiculous – it could not be happening.

'None of whom will have the least idea what has happened to you,' Fitz replied. 'It seems you came alone this evening and in a hired carriage. It would have been more difficult to silence your companion, but you made things easy for me, Corinna.'

'Anne will know where I went,' Corinna said. 'Besides, I do not believe that you mean a word of this, Fitz. You are merely saying it to frighten me. Do you imagine I shall go quietly?'

'No, I fear you will not,' he said, his mouth set hard. 'That is why I shall have to oblige you to swallow a sleeping draught.' He reached for a glass of wine that had stood unnoticed on the table beside the bed. 'It was prescribed for me by my doctor and is quite harmless. I assure you that it will not make you ill, only sleepy.'

'I shall not drink it!'

'Oh, but I think you will,' he said and his eyes glittered

dangerously. His tone was that of a man who meant to be obeyed – cool, calm and authoritative as though he knew she could not resist. 'Do not make me hurt you, Corinna. I should not like to do that, my sweet. But make no mistake, I shall if forced to it.'

Corinna did not know what wild spirit possessed her, but for one strange, courageous moment she was willing to die if he had set his mind to it. Taking the glass in her own hand, she swallowed the contents defiantly, looking up at him directly and calmly, making him frown.

'There, I have taken your wine, whether it be poisoned or merely drugged. Indeed, I would prefer poison to the life you have described to me. I have suffered at the hands of men too much to be surprised at anything they may do. Why should I believe you are any different? Know that if you carry out your threat, sir, you are sending me to my death, for I would rather die than submit to the lechery of men who disgust me.'

Fitz's expression was unreadable as she lay back against the pillows. The sleeping draught took its effect and she felt a peculiar lassitude creeping over her. Her eyelids were growing heavy, closing, the drugged sleep claiming her. But just before she drifted into a thick, heavy blackness, she was conscious of a hand stroking her brow softly.

'Hate me if you will,' a voice murmured close to her ear. 'For there are moments when I have come close to hating you . . .'

Corinna awoke to a shaded room that was not her own. She was aware of feeling fear, a sense of terror creeping over her as she sat up and looked about her. The room was beautifully furnished in shades of rose and cream and were it not for the heavy drapes at the windows she might have felt the warmth of the sun. Her head was aching and she felt a little sick as she pushed herself up against the pillows.

Where was she? Her mind was oddly fuzzy, but as her thoughts began to clear she remembered well enough what had taken place the previous night. She had gone to Lanchester's room alone and he had tricked her into thinking he was ill in order to make her his prisoner. This was not the room she had been in when she was drugged, she was certain of that much as she pushed back the bedcovers and tried to get up. Her head began to spin and she fell back against the pillows with a groan, closing her eyes again. She felt weak and somewhat unsteady, as though she had been ill.

Could Fitz Lanchester really have meant to do with her as he had threatened? She recalled whispered tales of such places and shuddered at the thought that she might already be imprisoned in a house of ill repute. The madam would no doubt try to force Corinna to lie with her patrons, but she would resist. Indeed, she would take her own life rather than let herself be used like that!

But somehow she could not believe that the man she had loved, perhaps still loved, could be so ruthless. He had been angry and he'd wanted to punish her. He had a right to his anger, she admitted, though he could and ought to have found other ways to punish her. She knew that a few words dropped in the right ear would have finished her in society. If people believed the lies Sir Maxwell had told Lanchester as he lay dying . . . But why would he have lied so basely? Corinna found it difficult to understand the malice behind such an act. Clearly they had been meant to hurt, but still she did not understand why.

Gradually her head cleared and after a few moments she tried to get up again. This time she was able to put her feet to the floor before her head swam, but she clutched at the bedpost and remained standing until the dizziness passed. She walked very slowly to the window, drew the curtains aside and looked out. To her surprise she saw that she was in the countryside and that she must be in one of the bedrooms at the back of an important house. She could see one wing of the building set at an angle to the main block, and it looked rather beautiful, its warm yellow stone mellowed and softened by time. She could also see a cobbled courtyard and beyond it a park with ancient trees, their branches so heavy and sweeping that they touched the earth in some places. In the distance there was a temple that was most likely a summer house, and beyond that she caught a glimpse of sunlight on water. So there must be a lake within pleasant walking distance.

Had Lanchester brought her to his country seat? Instinct told her that this was indeed his home. Why? Had he some reason why he had not carried out his threat immediately? Perhaps she was to be punished further for her sins . . .

Her thoughts were suspended as the bedroom door opened to admit a young maid accompanied by a footman carrying a tray.

'Are you feeling better, ma'am?' the maid asked and signalled to the footman to set down the tray. 'Wait outside, Fred.' The footman went out and the girl looked at her. 'Are you well enough to be up, ma'am? His lordship said as you've been proper bad.'

'My head aches but that is to be expected,' Corinna said, hesitating. 'Where am I?'

'At Amberly, ma'am – the Marquis of Lanchester's family home, of course. Where else would you be?'

'You forget that I have been ill,' Corinna said, playing along with her. 'When did I come here?'

'Yesterday afternoon. You've been sleeping all that time. The doctor has been to visit you twice and Mrs Martin, the housekeeper that is, has been looking after you herself.'

'I see . . . Thank you.' Corinna hesitated, then, realizing that she was beginning to feel hungry, said, 'What have you brought me?'

'Just some pastries and preserves, ma'am,' the girl answered. 'And a pot of chocolate. I could bring coffee or tea if you prefer.'

'No, that will be perfect, thank you. What do I call you?'

'Rose, ma'am.'

'Did you prepare this yourself, Rose?'

'No, ma'am, it was prepared by the chef and I was asked to bring it to you.' Rose looked puzzled.

Corinna wondered if the food or drink was drugged, but she saw no point in worrying too much. Lanchester would do with her as he pleased. She had an odd, fatalistic mood upon her, feeling caught up in something over which she had no control. Besides, her mouth tasted awful and her stomach was grumbling. She had to eat unless she wanted to starve herself. Now that she knew she was at Lanchester's house the feeling of fear she had experienced on waking had disappeared.

She ate three of the pastries, which were light and melted on her tongue, and drank two cups of the strong, dark chocolate. It was slightly bitter but chocolate was meant to be drunk that way and Corinna found nothing unpleasant or unusual in the taste.

Rose had left her to enjoy her breakfast alone, but returned some minutes later carrying a pretty morning gown of blue silk, which she laid out carefully on the bed.

'I shall bring you some hot water in a moment, ma'am. Will you wish for help with your dressing?'

'That is not my gown,' Corinna said. 'I have never seen it before.'

'His lordship said as your things had been sent for, my lady. I believe this belongs to his cousin. I think it will fit you.'

'What am I to do when I am dressed?' Was she a prisoner or not? Corinna was confused.

'The doctor said you could get up when you chose, but that you were to take things slowly for a few days.'

'I see, thank you.'

So she was being treated as a guest at the moment. Corinna went behind the screen to wash herself once the water had been brought, then stood patiently as the maid fastened the hooks at the back of her bodice and arranged her skirts. The gown fitted well enough, though it was a little tight over her breasts.

'Shall I dress your hair, ma'am?'

'I think I shall wear it loose this morning,' Corinna said. Her head still ached and she did not feel like having pins fastened to keep up the knot she often wore at her nape during the day.

When Rose left, Corinna got up and wandered over to the window to look out once more. She stiffened as she saw a man walking towards the house, two dogs following closely at his heels. He was carrying a sporting gun and a brace of wood pigeon and she knew him instantly. Lanchester was here!

Her heart raced as she drew away from the window. She did not know how she was to face him. A part of her wanted to run away so that she would not have to, but common sense told her that she would need to walk miles before she came to an inn where she might or might not find a means of transport back to London. That was clearly his purpose in bringing her here, and the reason why he was not bothering to keep her drugged or locked in her room. He knew quite well that she would find it hard to escape from this house, for she had no idea of her bearings or where to find help.

Yet her courage did not fail her, for she could not think that he meant to carry out the threats he had made. Had he intended to go ahead with one or the other she would surely have woken to find herself on board a ship or in some house of ill repute.

Well, she thought, there was no point in waiting here to be told her fate. She might as well go and face it. Raising her head, she left her bedchamber and began to walk along the landing to the head of the staircase. The runners were thick Persian rugs that cushioned the sound of her shoes as she walked, and to either side of her pier tables and mirrors adorned the walls. Gilded candelabras stood upon each table and would be lit at night to illuminate the sumptuous luxury of the beautiful house.

Sir Maxwell had told her that Lanchester was looking for

a rich wife, but it seemed unlikely to Corinna that the owner of a house like this would be in difficulty – unless, of course, he was deeply in debt and afraid of losing everything. She would hate to lose such a house if it belonged to her, she admitted, charmed by what she saw. The collections had been added over the years, and she could see evidence of tours to Rome and Greece in the artefacts that graced the hall. Huge Chinese porcelain vases stood at the head of the stairs, and she could see bronze statues below her in the hall.

When Corinna was halfway down the stairs Lanchester came in from a room to the side and rear of the lower hall. He stood gazing up at her, and for a moment her heart caught with fear as she thought he might be about to order her back to her room.

She stood like one of the beautiful statues that graced his home, waiting for him to speak . . .

Nine

'I fear you have been a little unwell, Corinna,' he said to break the silence at last. 'I must apologize for it. I believe the draught you were given was too strong and I regret that it was necessary to put you to such distress.'

Corinna's heart began to beat once more, though more rapidly than usual. She progressed steadily towards him, halting on a stair that allowed her to meet him on his own level, her eyes looking into his.

'I fail to see that your disgraceful behaviour can be excused, sir,' she said icily. 'If there is a quarrel between us, you have stepped beyond the limits of decency by kidnapping me and bringing me here.'

'But you drank the wine yourself,' he said with an odd smile. 'And I believe you have suffered no other harm. As you see, you are not a prisoner.'

'Do not mock me, sir! I know full well that it is almost impossible for me to leave this house without your permission. Your servants could restrain me at any time, and if by chance I succeeded in leaving the house, I might never find help before my escape was discovered.'

'Your sound reasoning does you credit, Corinna,' he said and smiled. 'It pleases me that you do not intend to do anything foolish. Some ladies I know would be screaming at this very moment, but you are remarkable. I believe that is why I find you so interesting.'

'I have no wish to be of interest to you!'

'No, perhaps not,' he replied. 'But we find ourselves in a coil, do we not? I was angry the other night and I may have

129

acted rashly, but we must both live with the consequences.'

She lifted her head proudly, giving him a hard stare. 'I see no reason why you should not immediately put your carriage at my convenience and have me conveyed back to my house in London.'

'Ah, but I see several,' he replied in a tone so mild that it drove her beyond bearing. 'I have brought you here while I make up my mind what your punishment ought to be . . .'

'That is ridiculous,' Corinna snapped. 'I have already told you that I did not plot to have you killed, sir. I must admit I might have taken a horsewhip to you had I the power – indeed, were there one to hand it would give me the greatest pleasure at this very moment.'

Fitz laughed, amused by her vehemence. 'You have such spirit. I have always admired it. It is a pity that we are enemies, Corinna. I think we might have dealt well together under other circumstances.'

'You may thank yourself for that, sir!'

'Yes, I do not deny it,' he replied in a calm, reassuring tone that she found truly irritating. 'It is the reason you are here and not on board a vessel bound for Constantinople. Believe me, it would have been easy enough – and is still possible.'

'Empty threats,' Corinna said dismissively, though her heart thumped wildly as she saw the gleam in his eyes. 'Civilized gentlemen simply do not behave in such a way.'

'And what makes you imagine I am a gentleman, civilized or otherwise?'

'I am certain you are not, sir!' Her eyes flashed with sudden temper. 'If you intend to keep me here to torture me with your taunts, I can tell you that you are wasting your time. I have experienced such grief at the hands of a master and you are no match for him.'

The gleam died from his eyes. 'I believe you suffered greatly at the hands of that monster, Corinna. I wish there were something I might do to wipe the pain from your mind, but I know that to be impossible. I would beg you to forgive my part in it if I thought you might find that achievable.'

She felt a twist of pain about her heart, blinking to keep back the sudden sting of tears. 'I do not blame you for my husband's cruelty, merely for abandoning me to my fate and thus leaving me to his mercy.'

'I should have come to speak to your father immediately,' Fitz replied and the note of regret was clearly sincere. 'I, too, was in confusion, and I hesitated too long. I assure you that I have regretted it.'

'Do you expect me to believe in your remorse, sir? I have seen no sign of it.'

'Have you not?' He lifted his brows. 'Should I prostrate myself before you with tears and beg for your forgiveness? You mistake the man, Corinna. It is not my way to beg.'

'No, indeed, I know that well enough. Instead you drug me, kidnap me and hold me against my will,' she snapped. 'A fine remorse, sir!'

'Sadly, you speak the truth,' he agreed, a flicker of humour in his eyes. 'As I said earlier, it is a coil. I acted on impulse, out of anger and jealousy. You may recall that I did so once before. It is a regrettable trait that I must learn to conquer – but it is done. The question is, what do I do with you now?'

'I have no idea,' Corinna replied. 'I do not know why you chose to bring me here, sir. Perhaps you think to repair your fortunes by forcing me into marriage.'

Fitz laughed. 'Have you been listening to the gossips, Corinna? Shame on you. Look around you, my sweet. Does it appear that I am in need of a fortune?'

'Then if you do not need a rich wife, why have you brought me here? Why not carry out your wicked threat or simply allow me to leave?'

'I have been asking myself the same question for the past day or so,' he told her with a wry smile. 'But you are here, and it would cause too much of a scandal to allow you to leave. In your present mood there is no telling what you might do or say . . .'

'Have you no concern for my companion's feelings? She will be out of her mind with worry.'

'No, I do not think so . . .' He shook his head as she glared at him. She was in a fine passion, though doing her best to control it. Her cool composure, for which she had been much admired in town, had sadly deserted her. 'Rest easy in your mind; the lady is not in the least worried about you. She believes she knows exactly where you are.'

'Fiend!' Corinna stamped her foot. Her hands worked at her sides and she longed to strike him, to wipe that arrogant, self-congratulatory look from his face. If he found this amusing, she did not! 'Oh, if I but had a weapon of some kind . . .'

'Would you shoot me with my own pistol – or stab me to the heart?' He seemed intrigued by the idea, which served only to increase her fury. 'No, I do not think you have the stomach for it, Corinna. Indeed, I wonder that I believed Everard's lies so easily. I thought a man would not lie on his deathbed, but I have had time to consider and I believe I see what he was about.'

'I wish that I did!'

'We were enemies for reasons I shall not disclose,' Fitz told her. 'He had his own reasons for wanting me dead – and for wanting me to believe that you had persuaded him to kill me if he could.'

'I should never have done such a thing!'

'Such passion,' Fitz murmured, laughter lighting up his eyes with devil fire. 'Now, I wonder why . . .'

'Any woman of sensible feeling would be outraged at the very idea of plotting the death of a man she . . .'

'A man she what? Pray, go on, Corinna.'

'I have said more than enough. You deserve that I should never speak to you again.'

'That is quite possible,' he said, the glint of humour back in his eyes. 'But somehow I cannot believe that you are capable of such restraint.'

'Devil!' Corinna raged and then laughed, because he

clearly knew her. One thing she could not bear was to be silent. She had had enough of silences, of long, lonely hours when there was no one to talk to and no one to help ease the hurt inside her. It was better to let emotion spill over, to rage, lose one's temper – laugh. 'Impossible! You are the most infuriating man I know. I do not know why I no longer hate you, sir. I have reason enough.'

'That is undeniable, but we do no good by repeating ourselves. I suggest that we should begin to ponder on the future.'

'So it *is* your plan to marry my fortune!'

'I was thinking along other lines. You amuse me and you owe me something, Corinna. I might take payment of another kind – I have a fancy that I could teach you to like me better.'

'No! I have no wish to marry ever again.'

'That would be a sad waste,' he said and looked into her eyes. Grief and sadness still lingered, despite the pride and courage with which she had chosen to face the world. 'But something tells me the lady doth protest too much.'

'Do not come near me or . . .'

'I have no intention of forcing myself on you at this moment,' Fitz said with a lift of his brows. 'You will not have it so, Corinna, but I am a reasonably civilized man. There is a time and a place for everything. I am determined that you shall pay for your unkindness and we shall have a reckoning. But for the moment you are my guest. Feel free to use my home as you will – but do not wander too far from the house. Someone might feel bound to protect you.'

'From what?'

'Oh, the dogs or an itinerant rogue who might attack you.'

'The only rogue I see is you, sir!'

'We shall deal very well together, Corinna,' he said, laughing softly. 'And now I beg that you will excuse me, for I must change before I am fit to be good company.'

Corinna turned to watch as he went past her up the stairs. He was whistling, clearly much amused by the situation. Well, she certainly was not amused! If he imagined she was about to fall into his arms . . . Her thoughts suspended themselves as she suddenly realized that that might be very enjoyable . . .

A cold collation was set for lunch and, thinking she was living in some kind of mad dream, Corinna sat down to partake of it for all the world as if she were the marquis's honoured guest. When summoned to the meal she had thought the food would stick in her throat, for she had spent the morning walking in the gardens thinking wildly about escape. To her surprise, she discovered that her appetite did justice to the excellent fare, and was smiled on with approval by her host.

'I am happy to see that you eat well, Corinna. I should not care for a . . . mistress who picked at her food. I like a woman who is flesh and blood and not all bone.'

'Are you implying that I am fat?' She glared at him. He seemed determined to taunt her, to punish her.

His eyes assessed her knowingly. 'I would say you have a perfectly balanced figure. You are neither so slim that a puff of wind might blow you away, nor are you given to excess flesh.'

'So I'm plump,' Corinna said crossly, refusing to be mollified. 'Perhaps you would be kind enough to tell me of any other faults you have noticed about my person, sir.'

'I have not yet had sufficient leisure to observe you and therefore cannot give an opinion, but your tongue may be your least favourable asset, ma'am, since it seems to have been dipped in lemon.'

'And you, sir, deserve to be whipped at the cart's tail!'

'But you provoked me, Corinna. I was merely trying to promote pleasant conversation between us.'

'Indeed?' She smiled at him with acid-tinged sweetness. 'Then perhaps I should respond in kind. While you are undoubtedly a fine figure of a man and reasonably attractive, I find you excessively irritating. You are entirely too sure of yourself and your place in society. I fear you were spoiled in your nursery.'

'Is that how I appear?' Fitz nodded, looking thoughtful. 'I fear I have been spoiled, ma'am, though not in the nursery. I was caned often enough as a boy. However, since I came to town, I have been looked upon by doting mothers, searching for a husband for their daughters, as an object worthy of interest. I have also been much pursued by ladies wishing to replace a clumsy husband with a considerate lover in their bed. I suppose I have come to take such things for granted, though I do not think of my own consequence, I assure you.'

'You surprise me,' Corinna replied. 'I had imagined you enjoyed the adulation you receive.'

'I assure you I do not even notice it.'

'Such modesty,' Corinna said, but found that her anger was abating. 'Do not tell me that you did not notice Lady Fellows when she tried to interest you in her daughter the other night. I cannot believe that lady could go unnoticed by anyone.'

'You mean the battleship with the timid child in tow?' Fitz's eyes gleamed with laughter. 'I did my very best not to, but I must admit even I was not able to ignore that lady completely.'

'I daresay such encroaching mothers are something of a trial to you, sir.' She was finding it hard not to smile for his description was so apt.

'Will you not call me Fitz, Corinna? I believe we shall be friends before too long and I think we should start out as we mean to continue. After all, if we are to be much in each other's company formality will not do.'

'The remedy is in your own hands, sir.'

'Alas, I fear you are not yet ready to kiss and make friends.'

'You mock me, sir.'

'But you look so beautiful when you are angry. Forgive me and say you will use my name.'

'If it pleases you,' she agreed and sipped her wine. 'Since we are to be friends, why do you not let me go home? I shall not speak of this unfortunate incident and—'

'Oh, but I could not be sure of that,' he said quickly. 'Besides, I have discovered it is very pleasant to have you here with me, Corinna. My life has been rather boring of late and this encounter between us has given me something I find vastly stimulating.'

'I daresay you may be enjoying this, but you are not being held to ransom, sir.' Her eyes flashed at him, her fingers drumming on the table.

'There, you have broken your promise to call me Fitz already,' he said, his eyes bright with mischief. 'How can I let you go, Corinna? You would likely have me arrested as soon as look at me.'

'You deserve that I should!'

'I know it – so now you see my dilemma, my love. I must keep you here until I can be sure of you.' His wicked eyes challenged and mocked her. 'I feel that with some gentle persuasion you may be brought to see my point of view – perhaps to enjoy your visit. It could be pleasant for us both, Corinna.'

'And how long do you intend that I shall stay?'

He shrugged his shoulders carelessly. 'Who knows . . .' His smile dimmed as she stood up, pushing back her chair to leave the table. 'But you have not yet had your pudding and it was made especially for you, Corinna. Do please return and I shall promise not to plague you . . .'

Corinna did not deign to glance back. She was angry with him for teasing her, and even more angry with herself for beginning to enjoy it.

The next two days passed in much the same way as the first. Fitz did his best to engage her in conversation, though it usually ended in a quarrel. She was free to walk in the garden as she wished, and treated as an honoured guest within the house, soon discovering that Amberly was a lovely place to live.

She asked Fitz if she might go riding, and after some thought he agreed, though said she must be accompanied by two grooms at all times.

'I do not care to ride with a groom plodding on behind me,' she said, annoyed by the stricture. 'I have been used to riding alone at Dorling.'

'Ah yes,' he said, 'I believe it is a fine estate, Corinna. Do you intend to live there or shall you reside in London?'

'I shall spend some time at Dorling, for I have many interests there. We are trying to improve the land and thus the yield by new methods of irrigation and husbandry.'

'Few ladies of my acquaintance are interested in such things,' Fitz said. 'You must talk to my bailiff before you leave us, Corinna. He has many ideas on the subject that might interest you.'

'What interests me most is when you intend to let me leave,' Corinna snapped. For a while she had been happy to talk to him as they strolled in the fine gardens, but at the mention of her leaving she was once more aware that she was merely a prisoner here. 'Just how long do you intend to keep me here, sir?'

How much longer could he hope to keep Corinna here against her will? Glancing at her that evening as she sat reading a book she had discovered in his library, Fitz thought that she seemed outwardly content. Yet he knew that she must be seething inwardly over her enforced stay at his home. Indeed, he was not sure why he had continued to hold her here. The past three days had been both a torment and pleasure to him. He had not imagined that seeing her every day in such quiet domesticity could bring so much satisfaction. Indeed, without her this house would seem empty, as would his life, for she had come to mean too much.

At first it had amused him to tease and mock her, but of late he had discovered that he wanted her to smile at him in her own special way. When she laughed it was such a joyous sound, though rare enough. Was it because of what he had done that she sometimes looked so sad – or was it because of the way she had suffered at her husband's hands? He was to blame on both counts, for he knew that if he had not seduced her she would never have married that monster.

Corinna looked up and caught him watching her. 'Why are you staring at me like that, Fitz? What are you plotting now?'

'I was thinking that you were beautiful,' he replied. 'You seemed so serene sitting there – like the Madonna.'

'You will have it that I am fat and now you liken me to a middle-aged matron,' she said in a mood somewhere between laughter and temper. 'But I do not mind. Say what you will, for it is no matter to me. You will grow tired of this jest and then I shall be able to go home.'

'Supposing I said that I did not want you to leave me.'

'I should not believe you,' Corinna said. 'For some reason it amuses you to play this game but . . .'

He rose to his feet and walked towards her. Instinctively she rose to meet him, a flicker of apprehension in her face. He thought she might try to run from him, but she made no attempt to resist as he took her into his arms. For a long, tense moment he gazed down into her eyes, watching as they seemed to become brighter, to widen with surprise and anticipation, and then he kissed her. The sensation was as nothing he had ever felt before, his desire fiercer and more needful than he had experienced with any other woman. Even that fateful night in the summer house had not been like this. His kiss deepened, became hungrier as he felt the heat engulf him, her body pressed close to his, melding with his in mutual passion.

'I do not know what power you have over me,' he whispered huskily. 'Only that I am mad for you, that I would dare anything to have you . . .'

'No! You must not,' Corinna cried and wrenched free from his embrace. 'I cannot . . . I cannot . . .' She was trembling and his brows furrowed as he looked at her. Was she afraid of him?

'What is it, my love?' he asked huskily. 'Surely you know I would not hurt you. I may have said things that seem to threaten, but it was merely mockery.'

Corinna turned away from him, her shoulders stiff as she tried to reconcile her feelings and the fear that had spread through her as she sensed the hunger in him. A part of her was crying out for his kisses, for his loving, but another part of her recoiled from the very idea of such intimacy, from the humiliation she had suffered so often.

'You don't understand,' she said in a choked voice. 'You do not know what he did to me . . . the vile way he abused me, the things he said as he vented his spite on me . . .'

A shiver ran through her as she felt his hands on her shoulders, his lips warm against the nape of her neck as he kissed it lightly. 'I am not your late husband, Corinna. I would not hurt you the way he did. I care for you more deeply than you realize. Do you not remember how good it was between us that night? I know I seduced you, but you gave yourself to me so warmly, so sweetly . . .'

'Do not!' she cried and wrenched from him again. Tears were trickling down her cheeks as she turned and gazed into his face. 'Please, I beg you, do not remind me of what might have been. I loved you then, perhaps I love you still, but he has ruined me. I am not fit . . .' With a cry of despair she fled from the room in tears.

'But I love you, Corinna. What he did means nothing . . . We can erase it from your mind – only trust me . . .' His words fell upon the empty room as she fled without looking back.

Corinna heard him but she was too distressed to listen, running up the stairs and along the landing to her own room.

Fitz stared after her, then, cursing himself for his impatience, turned away to strike his fist against the wall in frustration. He was caught in a trap that he had helped to forge. If he had behaved as he ought when they were both young . . . But it was useless to repine. Corinna had been badly scarred by her late husband's bestiality and it might be impossible to repair those scars.

The game Fitz had been playing no longer seemed amusing. He must allow Corinna to leave Amberly if she wished. He had no right to hold her here – had never had the right to bring her here against her will. At first he had been angry, bitter that she had wanted him dead, but then he had realized that, deep down, his reasons for bringing her here had been very different.

He had tired of being on the town, of the constant round of pleasure that had dominated his life for the past five years. He wanted a wife and children to inherit the fortune he had built up since he came into his estate. And there was only one woman who could fill the empty, aching need inside him.

Corinna stared at her face in the dressing mirror. Her skin was blotched with the stains of her tears. She had bathed her face with cold water when the storm of emotion had at last passed. Years of despair and misery had come out as she wept; for too long she had bottled her unhappiness inside her, knowing that if she once gave way she would become little more than her husband's whipping boy. She had had to be strong if she wanted to survive. Her defiance had built a wall of ice about her heart, protecting her from Sir Keith's spite and shutting out all feeling, but the feelings had gradually been creeping back since Uncle Henry had carried her off with him, and now they were in full flood.

She knew that she might never be able to forget what her husband had done to her, but the love she felt for Fitz had melted the ice and she could no longer shut herself away from the truth. It might be that she would never be able to respond to his love-making, but she knew that she must try. She must take that step forward or her life was finished.

It was by now quite late. The house had been silent for a while, the servants having retired to their beds. Corinna looked at herself in the mirror for a moment longer and then picked up the candlestick that stood on her dressing chest. She knew that Fitz would be in his bedchamber, which was at the far end of the landing and up a tiny flight of stairs. It was now or never. If she could not find the courage for what she needed to do, then she might as well retire to Dorling Hall, for she could not bear the thought of meeting him in company and knowing that it was hopeless.

She went out into the hall. Only one or two candles were still burning, the others having been extinguished for the night. Her heart was beating wildly as she walked the length of the hall. What would Fitz think of her for coming to him at this hour? Her courage ebbed and flowed as she walked up the stairs to the small landing that led to his apartments. At the door, she almost turned and fled, but to do that would be to seal her fate. Fitz had spoken of his feelings for her. They might not be as deep as her own for him, but they were surely sincere. He wanted her as his mistress, and, suddenly, she wanted very much to be the woman he desired.

She knocked on the door. There was silence for a moment, but then, as she was about to turn away, the door opened and he stood there dressed in a cherry-red and black striped dressing robe. He stared at her for a moment, his eyes thoughtful, understanding, as he measured the courage it had taken for her to come to him, and then reached out and drew her into the room, his eyes intent on her face.

'If you have come to appeal to my better nature, I have reached my decision, Corinna. This was a cruel trick to serve you and—'

'No,' she whispered and put a finger to his lips. 'Please let me speak, Fitz. I must say it now or I may never have the courage.'

'I am listening.' His expression was that of a man who expects to hear the worst and somehow that made her laugh, softly, huskily.

'No, no, my dear, it is not so very terrible. I have told you something of what I suffered with my husband, but I daresay you may imagine what I cannot bring myself to tell you. Suffice it to say that I believed I could never bear a man to touch me in that way again.'

'Corinna, I should not have—'

'Hush, dearest. You make it more difficult, and indeed

it is hard enough. I have come here tonight to ask you to help me. *He* made me afraid to laugh or love. If I stroked a dog he would have it cruelly put down, sometimes in front of me. He once had a young groom beaten for daring to smile at me. I had to smother all feeling, all need, just to survive . . .'

'Corinna, forgive me . . .'

'You were not to blame for his insanity,' she said, her eyes glowing in the pale light of the candle she still held. 'I have forgiven all the rest, for you were right to say that I gave myself to you willingly. You should not have acted as you did, nor should I have allowed it, but all that is past. What matters now are our present feelings for each other. I care for you and I believe that you care for me sufficiently to help me become a woman . . .'

'I care for you more deeply than you can guess.'

'Then help me,' she whispered in a voice caught with emotion. 'Teach me how to behave, Fitz, the way a woman behaves with her lover. I am afraid that I cannot . . . that I have nothing to give . . .'

'You have everything to give,' he murmured huskily. 'You are so beautiful, so full of spirit and warmth. You think that you cannot love because of what he did, but once you let go, once you trust, it will be as second nature to you.'

'Oh, Fitz, I am so lonely . . .' Her voice broke as the tears threatened to overwhelm her, and suddenly he understood her suffering with more clarity than words could ever say.

'My darling.' He reached out and took the candle from her, setting it down on a chest of drawers, and then he stroked the side of her face with the tips of her fingers. 'You are so lovely, so clever and brave. I adore you, want you so very much.' He felt her tremble and smiled for he sensed it was fear of emotion, fear of failure rather than of him. 'Do not fear me, Corinna. I shall do nothing that frightens or hurts you. We shall discover the pleasure of touching, of being close to each other, and the rest will come in time.'

'Fitz,' she whispered and then she was in his arms, being

kissed tenderly and yet with such suppressed hunger that it
sent tingles through her body. He took her hand and led her
to the bed, gazing into her eyes and touching her cheek again.
'Show me everything. Teach me. I want to be whole again,
to love as others do . . .'

'First we shall undress you,' he said and turned her round,
unhooking the back of her bodice. He kissed the nape of her
neck, making her tremble, but this time she was not afraid.
This was Fitz and she had loved him for such a long time.
He helped her slip off her bodice and then the skirt of her
gown. In her petticoats and fine linen under-bodice she looked
fragile and vulnerable, her flesh smooth and white, enhanced
by the soft light of the candles. 'You are so lovely, my darling,
and no, I do not think you fat. You are perfect, as perfect
as you always were in my dreams.'

'Do you dream of me?' she asked, surprised. 'I dreamed
of you so often. It was the only way I could bear my life.'

'I have never ceased to think and dream of you, my love,'
he murmured against her throat. He pushed her fine silk
chemise lower, revealing her breasts, which he kissed, the
tip of his tongue circling her nipples and making her moan
with pleasure. 'But no dream could be as wonderful as this,
having you here in my arms.'

She arched her back as the desire ran hot in her and she
realized that all her fears had been groundless. She was not
encased in ice; she was not afraid of him or what he would
do to her. This was so different to those nights of humiliation she had endured that it seemed another lifetime, and she
another person. The past was merely a bad dream and she
would forget it. 'Oh, Fitz, I love you . . .'

'I love you, my darling,' he replied. 'But we must go
slowly. We have been denied for so long. I would have this
right between us.'

Corinna was swept back through time, the years between
falling away as if they had never been. She was a young girl
with her first lover, and they were about to make love for
the first time. His mouth, tongue and hands were everywhere

on her body, stroking, caressing, and lavishing tenderness upon her. She knew that he would not hurt her, and she allowed him to do what he would, following his lead trustingly, instinctively, wanting the pleasure he was giving her to go on and on, as it did seemingly for ever. And then she was gasping, crying out as the waves of delicious sensation broke over her, making her body arch towards him, the feeling so intense that it was only when it was over that she realized he had not penetrated her.

'Fitz . . .' She turned to him, touching his face, her fingers moving into his dark hair, stroking him, grateful for the release he had given her, the easing of that dam of pent-up emotion inside her. 'We did not . . . I mean, you did not . . .'

'Hush,' he murmured, kissing her. 'I wanted you to understand the beauty of loving, that it can sometimes be unselfish – giving rather than taking. My pleasure came from yours, though another time it may be different.'

Tears were on her cheeks as she buried her face against his warm, moist skin and let him stroke her hair, lulling her to sleep like a child. And sleep she did, for some hours, waking to find him lying beside her, leaning on one elbow looking down at her, a smile on his lips.

'How are you this morning, my love?' he enquired. 'You slept like a babe.'

'I have not slept like that for years,' she said and blushed as one eyebrow quirked at her. 'I feel rather foolish . . .'

'Why?' He pecked at her nose, then kissed her, cutting off her reply. 'You have nothing to feel foolish about, my love. You are perfect, deliciously warm and womanly, an angel.'

'I was so awful to you.'

'Yes, you were.' His laughter was soft with an underlying joy that made her heart race. 'How often I have wished to put you across my knee and spank you these past weeks, Corinna. No wonder I was driven to the desperate act of abducting you.'

'Did you really believe that I had conspired to have you murdered?'

The smile died from his face as he considered this. 'For a while I thought it likely. After all, you had good reason to hate me. I had ruined your life, and I believed that a dying man would tell the truth, but I was a fool. I should have known he hated me.'

'Why?'

'He was a rogue and a criminal, Corinna. He knew that I was on the verge of exposing him, that once I did he would be ruined, and he wanted me dead. He might have paid someone to do his dirty work, but he fell out with the man most likely to accept the commission and had him taken as a highwayman. I cannot say why they quarrelled, but I know it was he who laid the information. Who can tell why thieves fall out? It was probably over the price paid for a stolen jewel or some such thing.'

'Was he really such a rogue?'

'Yes. I know that he gave useful information about the whereabouts of wealthy friends, who were later robbed, and that he handled stolen goods. Do you doubt my word?'

'No, of course not. It is just that he seemed so much the gentleman . . . so pleasant.'

'It is often so. Appearances count for little.'

'Yes, that is true. Sir Keith seemed a gentleman before . . .' A little shiver went through her. 'But he changed when he knew . . .'

'That you were having my child?' She nodded and his brow creased in a frown. 'The child died, I believe.'

'I miscarried after he had beaten me.'

Fitz put his arms about her, drawing her close. 'I am so very sorry, my love. So very sorry . . .'

'We shall not speak of him again,' she said and he held her away from him as he heard a new note in her voice, surprised to see the look in her eyes was one of mischief. 'I have wasted too much time, Fitz. We have but begun my lessons. I think you should teach me some more.'

'You are an apt pupil,' he said, catching her mood. 'I shall be delighted to continue your education.'

Corinna laughed as he bent over her, his lips brushing hers teasingly, making the desire flare to life inside her once more. She had wondered if it could happen again, feared that it might not, but again she discovered her fears were groundless as she was swept away by the hot passion between them. This time she was not so passive, for she had discovered that it was as good to touch as to be touched, and her fingers explored the satin hardness of his back. His skin was smooth to the touch and there was but a sprinkling of dark hair on his chest and arms, and also a little dark arrow leading down to the throbbing heat of his masculinity.

This time he did not hold back and she learned that the act of love could be more fulfilling than she had realized, taking her to new heights of pleasure as their bodies fit together in a sweet rhythm of desire.

She cried out as he spilled himself inside her, then lay with his head against her breast, his hand continuing to stroke her thigh as she lay quivering beneath him.

Again she wept for pleasure, but this time they did not sleep. In a while they loved again, Fitz seeming as if he could never have his fill of her. Then, at last, he told her that she must return to her own chamber for the moment.

'We must have a care for your reputation, my love.'

'It matters not,' she replied. 'I think it was lost when I came to your house when you were ill, and if not soon after.'

'But I would not have the servants gossip about the lady I adore,' he said and smiled at her. 'Go and ring for your maid. We shall talk later, Corinna.'

'We may talk as often as you please,' she said. 'I am your mistress, or your lover, call it what you will. Nothing else is important. I daresay there will be some gossip, but we shall survive it.'

'I care naught for the gossips, but I do care what is said of you.'

Corinna laughed as she dressed and left him. She walked back the way she had come, wondering if she might meet one of the maids, but was fortunate enough to reach her own room without incident. She was smiling as she threw off her things and got into her own bed. Fitz was right; it would not do to shock the servants too much, and she knew Rose would be here with her breakfast at any moment.

Fitz had said they needed to talk, and perhaps it would be best to clear the air on certain matters. She was not quite sure how to conduct the kind of relationship they intended, for she had never expected to be any man's mistress. Had she been unmarried it would have been frowned upon in society, but as a widow she had more freedom. Her father might think it a further shame upon his name, but she would try to keep it from him. Anne would probably leave her. Corinna was certain she would not approve.

Corinna smiled as she stretched her arms and legs, feeling relaxed and as light as air. She had not felt this good in an age. She was still smiling when Rose brought in her tray.

She spoke pleasantly to the girl and asked her to set it on the table near the window, then got up and went over to sit in the sunshine that had begun to filter through the opened curtains. Glancing out, she saw that Fitz had gone riding. She thought that she would tell him she might like to accompany him one morning. It was ages since she had gone out in the early morning, but it could be pleasant. Hardly anyone would be about and the stillness was very appealing. No doubt Fitz had gone out so that the air would clear his head and allow him time to think.

Life would be different for both of them in future.

But Corinna had misjudged Fitz in assuming he needed time to sort out his thoughts. He was feeling on top of the world, his plans for the future already formed. There were no doubts in his mind. He knew exactly what he wanted from the future and he had made up his mind to speak to Corinna on his return. She might take some persuading, but he was sure that she would soon see that he was right.

So deep in thought was he that he was not aware of anything untoward – nor did he see the rope that stretched across the narrow path he followed through the trees.

Ten

Corinna waited expectantly for Fitz to return. He had said they would discuss the future that morning and she had imagined he would not be long delayed by his ride. Yet by the time luncheon was served she had seen no sign of him. She asked the butler if he knew where his master had gone, but he was unable to say; he knew only as much as she did herself.

'I am sure I have no idea, ma'am,' he told her with a straight face. Harris was aware, as was everyone else below stairs, that his master had spent the night with this lady. He was neither shocked nor surprised, for it had been expected. The marquis had had several ladies in his life before this, but none of them had ever been brought to this house. No one knew the circumstances of her being brought here, for none of the house servants had accompanied them from London. It had been something of a mystery, which was now solved. If the marquis had abducted the woman he loved, then it was none of Harris's business, though it was much whispered about by those of a lesser order. Harris thought himself above such things, though he missed nothing. 'It is often his lordship's habit to visit his tenants, and he may have been delayed if there is a problem. The marquis is a conscientious master, ma'am.'

'Is he a good master, Harris?'

'Yes, my lady. I believe he has made many improvements since his father died. The late marquis was a man of . . . uncertain temper, who often quarrelled with those who served him. However, his lordship was very fond of him and much upset when he died.'

'And when was that?'

'Five years and some months.'

About the time they had first met, Corinna thought. Perhaps that might account for his waywardness at the time. It occurred to her that although she felt so much a part of him and he of her, she really knew so little of him, of the man inside, the man she had only glimpsed from time to time.

'Very well,' she said. 'I shall need only a light meal for the moment, but his lordship may be hungry when he returns.'

She ate some bread and butter and cold meat and drank tea afterwards in the parlour, feeling restless as the afternoon wore on and Fitz did not return. What could be keeping him? He must have discovered something seriously wrong to make him stay away so many hours. Surely she had not mistaken him. She was certain it had been his intention to return so that they might discuss the future.

For a few moments she wondered if he had regretted what had passed between them the previous night – but then why should he? Their loving had been very satisfactory for both, and she knew he had derived as much pleasure from it as she had. In any case, it would be a simple matter for him to detach himself from her in a few weeks if he cared to, and something told her that such an eventuality was not in his mind. He had spoken to her of love and of sharing their lives. She knew that such relationships could last for many years and that some couples remained devoted to one another. Of course, there was no real reason why they should not marry. Fitz had no wife . . .

Corinna shut off that thought before it could take root. She must not expect more than Fitz was willing to offer. As yet he had made no mention of marriage, denying it was in his mind when she accused him of wanting to marry her fortune. But of course they had been at cross purposes then, both angry and blaming the other. How foolish they had been, she thought, smiling to herself.

Yet when the light began to fade from the sky and Fitz had still not returned, she was uneasy. Had he gone off to visit a friend because he did not wish to face her? Was it possible that he regretted the intimacy between them? Surely not! He had seemed so genuine, so loving . . .

After the time for supper had come and gone, she summoned Harris and asked him if his master was given to unexplained absences.

'Not to my knowledge, ma'am,' he replied. 'I would not have expected it while there was a lady staying.'

'Does your master often have ladies staying?'

'Mixed company,' he assured her. 'This visit was . . . forgive me . . . unusual, my lady.' He gave a little cough behind his hand. 'But of course you were ill when you arrived.'

'Yes. I am a little concerned, Harris. Do you think we should consider making a search?'

'Should we not leave it until the morning? His lordship might be with one of his tenants or perhaps chanced to meet an acquaintance.'

'I think you should organize a search now. It is possible that he met with an accident.'

'His lordship is an excellent horseman, my lady.'

'I am aware of that – but my mind is uneasy. I believe his lordship meant to return after his ride. I would prefer it if the search began now.'

'If you wish it, my lady.'

Corinna could see that he thought she was making a fuss for nothing, but she had begun to feel very uneasy. When Harris returned later to tell her that men were out searching but as yet no sign of the marquis had been found, her stomach began to tie itself in knots. What could have happened to him?

'You will continue the search nevertheless,' she said. 'Just in case his lordship is hurt.'

Harris inclined his head and went away, clearly thinking she was a foolish woman – or perhaps that she was being given a message she did not understand. Could it be that Fitz had chosen this way to tell her that he regretted what had passed between them? Surely not. Her imagination had begun to conjure all kinds of fearful things and she was filled with a growing dread.

After a sleepless night and two visits to his room, which was empty, she began to wonder if he had simply ridden off and left her. The thought was extremely painful and she could not believe him capable of such cruelty – and yet where had he gone? If he had met with an accident there must surely be some sign of it. His horse had not been found wandering, nor was there any sign of his injured body – so where was he?

The question was not answered that day or the next. By now even Harris was beginning to look slightly uneasy, for extensive enquiries in the area had brought no answers.

'If his lordship had had an accident, his horse would have been found wandering,' he said, hoping to relieve her mind. 'Horses often return to their stables, ma'am, that is why I did not think it likely that a riding accident had occurred.'

'So do you believe his lordship has ridden off to meet someone?'

'He may have heard of a cockfight or a bare-knuckle contest somewhere,' Harris said. 'Gentlemen enjoy these things and are often carried away by the excitement.'

Not if the woman they professed to love was waiting! Corinna was torn between anger and worry. She feared that something had happened to Fitz, but it was clear that his servants believed she was being given the brush-off. She could do nothing here. Besides, she might hear news of him in London.

'I shall return to London immediately,' she told the butler. 'Meanwhile, you will continue the search here and I shall see what can be learned in town.'

'Yes, ma'am,' Harris replied. 'Do you wish to take your things with you?'

'I have almost nothing of my own here, as you are aware,' she replied. 'Thank you, but I wish to leave immediately and shall not delay for any reason. Please have the carriage

brought round at once. I shall write a letter to the marquis
– should he return and ask for me.'

'Yes, ma'am.'

Corinna was very angry as she saw his assumed look of
servility. It was clear that he believed she was no longer of
any importance in the house. She felt as if she would like
to scream at him for his lack of anxiety on behalf of his
master, but knew that she must retain what dignity she could.
After all, it was possible that he knew more of the matter
than she did.

Within half an hour, Corinna was seated in the marquis's
carriage and on her way to London. She had a nagging fear
that something terrible had happened to Fitz. And yet, if
there was truly no sign of his horse, it became more likely
that wherever he was he had gone there of his own free
will.

'So you have returned,' Anne said and kissed her cheek.
'You look tired, my dear. I hope the situation at home was
not as bad as you feared?'

Corinna hesitated, remembering that Fitz had told her Anne
believed she knew exactly where she had been. She had not
asked for an explanation at the time, for she had been too
angry, but now she saw what must have happened.

'You had my message?'

'Yes. I do hope your friend is recovered.'

'Yes, much better,' Corinna said, then shook her head.
'No, this will not do. I shall not be a party to this deception.
The truth is that I was abducted by Fitz Lanchester, Anne.
I lied to you that evening for I had no headache and I went
to his house. When I got there I was told he was desperately
ill, but as I bent over him he seized me and made me his
prisoner.'

'Corinna!' Anne was shocked. 'Whatever did you do? How
did you escape?'

'It was not quite like that,' she said and explained, leaving
out only the details of their night of passion. 'We made up

our differences and I was then his guest. And then he rode off and simply disappeared.'

'Disappeared?' Anne was puzzled. 'I do not understand you. What could have happened? Did he meet with an accident?'

'That was my first thought, but searches have been made and nothing has been found. His butler thought that he might have gone off to watch a prize fight or some such thing.'

Anne looked puzzled. 'I must admit that that surprises me, for he always seemed so considerate. Is he often given to such behaviour?'

'No, not that anyone can recall.'

'Then it is unlikely he did so,' Anne said sensibly. 'If things were as you say between you . . .' She took a deep breath, then looked Corinna in the eye. 'I have often thought he might care for you deeply, Corinna. If that was the case, and from his recent behaviour I would think it likely, then he would not simply ride off and leave you. If he decided to finish the relationship he would tell you.' Her no-nonsense manner was reassuring, because Anne did not say things merely for effect.

'You are right,' Corinna said, feeling better than she had for some days. 'It has been much on my mind, for Harris made me feel that I was causing a fuss over nothing. And yet in my heart I have never believed that Fitz would choose to end our friendship in that way.'

'No, I do not think that he would dream of doing so. So what will you do next, my dear?'

'I must make enquiries, discreetly. Someone may have seen him or heard of him . . .'

'Yes, it is awkward, for no one knows that you were with him.'

'No, and I should not care to have it known in the circumstances.'

'Perhaps I could go to the marquis's house. His servants know me and I could ask if anything is known.'

'Yes, that might be better,' Corinna said. 'Leave a

message that I would like the marquis to call on me when he returns. In the meantime we shall see if there is any news of him.'

'He means a great deal to you, does he not?' Anne looked at her intently, reading the truth in her face. 'You are in love with him, my dear.'

'Yes,' Corinna admitted. 'I have always loved him, though for a time I believed I hated him. I . . . I think he cares for me. We had fought our way through to an understanding. If he could just walk off and leave me without a word . . . But no, I will not allow myself to believe that. He would not have used me so ill.'

'I do not think it,' Anne told her. 'Something must have happened to him, Corinna. I think you should hire an agent to make discreet inquiries. We can only do so much ourselves, and one of those Bow Street Runners – you know the men I mean, I daresay.' Corinna nodded. 'Well, I have heard that some of them undertake private commissions. I believe I know of one such person. Would you like me to ask him to call on you?'

'Yes, please, I think I should,' Corinna said. 'But you will deliver my message to Fitz's house first and we shall give it a few days. If there is no reply I shall employ an agent to discover what has happened.'

A week passed, during which Corinna heard nothing of Fitz. No one had seen him, nor had they heard of his disappearance. She made no mention of it herself for she realized that it might seem odd if she were too particular in her enquiries. After another three days of restless frustration, she could wait no longer and asked Anne to request the agent she had heard of to call upon them. It was that very same day that a man came to the house asking for her, and she admitted him thinking it might be the agent, feeling a little surprised when the marquis's valet was shown into the parlour instead.

'Forgive me for disturbing you, Lady Dorling,' he said.

'But I was most concerned about his lordship. Knowing that you were in the country with him and his having disappeared . . .'

'So you have heard at last.'

'From his lordship's nephew, Mr Tobias Stephens, milady. He called to see his uncle in the country last week and was told he had gone off somewhere, and so he came up to town looking for the marquis. It was the first I had heard of it, and to be honest I was anxious straight away. It isn't like his lordship, ma'am, and that's a fact.'

'I am glad that you show some proper feeling,' Corinna said. 'Harris appeared to imagine I was making a fuss for nothing and because of that I have wasted time, though I am about to set an agent to look for him.'

'I am relieved to hear it, my lady. I was about to do the same, though Mr Stephens seemed to think it might all be for nothing.'

'Have you any idea where he might have gone?

'His lordship's friend is in the country at the moment. Mr Rowlands – I believe you know him. It is just possible he might have gone there, I suppose.'

'Mr Rowlands returned to town just yesterday,' Corinna told him. 'I saw him last evening and he has not heard from Fitz. Indeed, he asked me if I had seen him myself and if he had recovered from his injury.'

'Ah, I see.' Reed nodded his head. 'It appears that we have a mystery, my lady.'

'Has your master enemies that you know of?'

'There may be some, though I do not know them. His lordship did not mince his manners, my lady. Some accuse him of arrogance, though it is merely his way. He does not suffer fools lightly, and if he takes something into his head there is no gainsaying him. I daresay there may be some who wish him dead . . .' He looked as if he would say more, but when Corinna pushed him he shook his head. 'It would be wrong of me to raise suspicions when I don't know the truth of it, ma'am.'

'Yet you have thought of something. Will you not confide in me since we are to be together in this?'

'Mr Stephens . . .' Reed shook his head again. 'He is the marquis's heir, you know. I imagine he might sometimes think of what he would inherit if my master should die without issue.'

'Surely not!' Corinna was shocked at the idea. 'What kind of a man is he?'

'He looks as if a puff of wind might blow him away . . . but I have thought him a sly creature.'

'Indeed?' Corinna frowned. 'Then he will bear watching. Very well, Reed, I shall start this investigation. I wish I had spoken to you when I first returned to London. We must hope the trail has not gone cold, for too much time has elapsed.'

'You were in a difficult position, ma'am.' Reed hesitated. 'As to what happened that night – I did try to tell his lordship that you had helped him, but he was too angry to listen.'

'With good cause, perhaps,' she said and smiled wryly. 'I see you know more of my secret than I would care to be known generally.'

'You may rely on me for discretion, my lady. I believe you have my master's welfare at heart and that is my one concern.'

'Thank you,' Corinna said. 'I shall confess that I am very worried. Something has happened. I do not know what, but I shall leave no stone unturned in trying to find him, as the saying goes.'

'I thought it would be best if someone other than Mr Stephens were to organize the search for his lordship.'

Corinna nodded. She sensed that Reed suspected the marquis's nephew of being less than trustworthy, though whether or not he had anything to do with Fitz's disappearance was another question. Never having met the gentleman, she had no idea if Reed was right to be suspicious or not. But she was soon to discover for herself that the valet had reason enough to at least wonder.

Tobias Stephens introduced himself to Corinna that very evening. He had asked to be made known to her and was clearly an admirer from the way he held her hand, bowing over it gallantly. He was an attractive man with pale blond hair and blue eyes, and he oozed charm, his manners elegant and gracious.

'The most beautiful lady in the room,' he said. 'As soon as I saw you I knew that I must meet you, ma'am. Forgive me if I presume, but I believe you to be on good terms with my uncle – Lanchester.'

'We know each other,' Corinna said and felt a tingling sensation at the nape of her neck. Something in his eyes made her wary, though his manner was one of polite concern. 'Yes, I believe you might say we are friends.'

'Then perhaps you may have some idea of where I might find him.'

'I had heard he was in the country, is that not the case?'

He gave her an odd look, which made her think he knew that she had been recently staying at Amberly herself. 'I fear he has gone missing, odd as that may sound. I have come to town to see if I may discover his whereabouts.'

'Yes, I knew that he had gone off somewhere,' Corinna said. 'For you may know that we were together shortly before he left Amberly.'

'Yes, Harris told me you were worried about him. He thought Lanchester had merely gone off with friends, but it seems odd, do you not think so, ma'am?'

'Yes, very strange,' she replied. 'One does not normally go off without a word when one has a guest staying.'

'No, indeed.' Tobias Stephens looked suitably anxious, but Corinna understood at once what Fitz's valet had meant by having his doubts concerning this man. 'I believe you have already employed an agent to search for my uncle, ma'am.'

Now how did he know that? She had given strict instructions that the investigation was to be kept secret. Corinna wondered but allowed nothing of her thoughts to show as she answered him.

'Yes, I was worried, and as you say, we are good friends. I must admit that I am concerned over his disappearance.'

'Then perhaps we should work together,' Tobias said. 'I am going down to Amberly in a few days, Lady Dorling. I thought perhaps you might care to accompany me.'

'I am not sure . . .'

'You think it would be improper? But of course I meant your companion to accompany us, and your maid.' He smiled at her, seeming almost too sure of his powers of persuasion.

Corinna's instinct was to refuse instantly, but then in a moment she realized it was what she wanted. If Fitz should return to Amberly from a pleasure jaunt she would have something to say to him, but if he was in some trouble then she must be at hand, in case he needed her.

'In that case, I accept willingly,' Corinna said and smiled. Fitz's valet had put her on her guard and she was proof against this man's charm, but he would be better watched than left to his own devices. 'It is most kind of you to invite me, sir.'

'I hope we shall be friends,' he said and inclined his head to her. 'I shall call upon you tomorrow to make further arrangements.'

'I shall expect your call, sir.'

Anne came up to her as he walked away. 'So that is the nephew,' she murmured softly. 'I think Mr Reed was right; he is altogether too pleased with himself.'

'He knows I have begun a search for Fitz and he wants us to accompany him to Amberly at the end of this week.'

'Did you say we would go?'

'Yes, I thought it prudent to keep an eye on him. And besides . . .'

'You do not know what to do with yourself while you wait for news.' Anne gave her an understanding look. 'I think the marquis must have had some kind of an accident that morning, my love. I know the agent you employed has decided to concentrate his search within a few miles of the Amberly estate. We must hope that he discovers Lanchester's whereabouts.'

'I pray that he does, and that Fitz is safe.'

Corinna had become increasingly anxious as the days passed, and now the worst dread of all had begun to haunt her. Supposing Fitz was dead. Sir Maxwell Everard had wanted to kill him. It was possible that others might feel the same way, and perhaps one of them had already succeeded.

She did not know how she could face the future if that were the case. She would have nothing left to live for . . .

Corinna insisted on taking her own carriage to Amberly this time. She meant to have her own servants about her and she sent word to George Reed, asking if he would care to accompany them. He came to see her as soon as he received the message.

'Thank you for asking me, my lady,' he said. 'I am doing little good here in town and I would like to join the search for his lordship if I may.'

'It is possible that a strong arm may be needed at some time,' Corinna told him. 'I do not care for Mr Tobias Stephens, though he has been perfectly pleasant and courteous to me – but I believe, as you do, that he is sly.'

'He is altogether too anxious to make himself at home in his lordship's property,' Reed told her with a frown. 'As he has a right to, of course, if his lordship . . .' He broke off as he saw the flash of pain in Corinna's eyes. 'Forgive me, my lady, but we have to face the facts. It is possible that his lordship met with a fatal accident.'

'Yes, I know,' Corinna's voice held a sobbing breath. She had faced the fact but found it too hurtful to speak of, even to him. 'But we shall not give up hope, Reed. I intend to carry on the search until I have proof that he is dead.'

'That might take years, ma'am.'

'Then it will take years. I have no intention of abandoning him to his fate.'

Reed's eyes crinkled in a smile of approval. 'I believe his lordship was more fortunate than he knew, my lady.'

'Well, that is for the future,' Corinna said. 'I am glad that you are to accompany us. I shall feel safer so.'

If Tobias was put out when he learned that his uncle's valet was to accompany them, he gave no sign of it. In fact, he seemed to be pleased and said that he would be grateful for any help in finding his uncle.

His eagerness to find Fitz struck Corinna as being a little odd, until she realized that he could not claim the fortune that would be his unless the marquis was found to be dead. Fitz's disappearance meant nothing, and seven years would need to pass before he could be declared legally dead. Unless he wished to wait, Tobias must provide sufficient proof of his uncle's death.

It was an unkind thought and Corinna tried to put it from her mind. For herself she could find no fault in the young man's attentions. Indeed, he was so attentive that she feared he had ideas concerning her that she would find alarming if he pressed them. Did he imagine she might find him acceptable as a lover? From the way he held her hand whenever possible, and certain looks he gave her, she had begun to think that he felt a certain passion towards her. And that made her uncomfortable.

A very different Harris greeted Corinna on her return to Amberly. It was clear that he had become anxious about his master and did everything he could to make amends, even going so far as to apologize to her in private.

'You were right and I was wrong, Lady Dorling,' he told her. 'There has been a development just yesterday.'

'A development?' Corinna's heart began to beat wildly. 'What do you mean? Have you news of Lanchester?'

'His horse has been found, ma'am,' Harris said. 'It was discovered limping and taken by a farmer to his own stables. There is evidence of damage to the front legs of the beast, just above the fetlocks, as if it might have stumbled over something. One of the grooms thought the scars looked as if they might be rope burns.'

'Rope burns . . .' Corinna shivered as one of her worst nightmares came to mind. 'You mean the horse was brought down by a rope pulled tight across its path?'

'Yes, ma'am,' Harris replied and looked awkward as she gasped. 'This is my fault, ma'am. Had I taken you seriously, a more intensive search might have brought this to light sooner.'

'You thought I was making a fuss over nothing, and indeed there were moments when I thought it myself,' Corinna admitted, deciding that nothing would be gained by placing blame. 'I hope you will keep me informed of anything that comes to light, Harris. I am very worried about his lordship.'

'Yes, ma'am.' He cleared his throat, a slight colour in his cheeks. 'George Reed is a good friend of mine.'

'Yes, I see.' She smiled wryly, realizing that the butler now knew more of her history than before. 'I thank you for your apology and we shall forget any difference of opinion. May I ask how this new information came to light?'

'It was the agent from London, ma'am – the one as you set on the case.'

'Then he has already earned his money.' Corinna felt the first flickering of hope. 'If his lordship is to be found, I believe we can trust Mr Jones to do what is needful.'

'He seemed a very determined character,' Harris told her. 'A search of the area where the horse was found has been going on since yesterday, ma'am, and we hope for news shortly.'

'That is all we can do – hope and pray.'

Corinna's prayers were not sufficient to bring news that day, nor for several days after. Herbert Jones reported to her in writing every other day, but it was not until they had been at Amberly for almost a week that she received a letter containing the first glimmer of hope.

> *I have this minute heard something that may be of interest. It involves a journey of some twenty miles, and I am about to embark on it. My hopes have been raised of finding news of his lordship, but may come to nothing. You will hear as soon as I have certain news.*

Corinna could barely contain her excitement. She showed the letter to Anne and then to Reed, and then decided that it must be shared with Fitz's nephew. He read it slowly, frowning as he handed it back to her.

'The man gives no clue as to what his news might be. The fool might have told you whether the outlook was good or bad.'

'I imagine he did not want to raise our hopes too much,' Corinna said. 'But at least this gives us some hope.'

'Yes, it does,' Tobias replied. 'I can see that you have had your expectations raised, Corinna. I wish that they may not be dashed. It would grieve me to see you hurt. You must know that I have a great regard for you.'

'You have been courteous and generous in allowing me to come here,' Corinna replied. 'I thank you for that and hope we may be friends.'

From the expression of frustration in his eyes, she guessed that friendship was not what he had in mind, but if he hoped for more he would be disappointed. She did not exactly dislike him, but she was not sure he was to be trusted.

'I had believed we were already friends,' he said with a sulky twist of his mouth. 'We must hope that this agent of yours does not keep us waiting too long for news.'

'I just pray that it is the right news,' Corinna replied. Yet she was afraid that it might be the worst, for if Fitz had been deliberately brought down by some evil person, what more might have been done to him?

She did not voice her thoughts, for she considered that

to do so might make them happen. Instead she prayed that Fitz would be returned to her, and that they might yet find happiness together.

Eleven

'Yes, we do have a gentleman who meets with the description you have given us,' Brother Aslom said. 'He was in a bad way when one of the brothers picked him up on the supply wagon and brought him in to the monastery, and he is still weak. I think he would have died had he not been found. What did you say his name was?'

'The man I seek is the Marquis of Lanchester,' Herbert Jones replied. 'Has he not told you his name?'

'The poor man does not know it himself,' Brother Aslom replied and shook his head sorrowfully. 'For more than a week he lay close to death, and we prayed for his soul, but then he rallied and came to himself. He is a very strong man, for he had been wounded in the shoulder not long before this further attack was made on him.'

Herbert knew a surge of excitement, for this fitted with what he had been told. 'What was the nature of the attack?'

'We do not know exactly, for he cannot tell us, but he was badly beaten and robbed of his possessions. He had only his breeches when we took him in; his clothes, valuables and boots had been stolen.'

Herbert made a note of this in his book, ready for the report he would send to Lady Dorling. 'Is it possible that I might see him?'

'Yes, I see no reason why not, for he is working in the gardens with the other brothers. He asked to be allowed to earn his keep and we saw no reason to deny him. He is not yet strong enough to leave us, but the sunshine and the company helps him, and we believe he will grow well again.'

165

Herbert followed the monk into the garden as he was bid, his keen eyes instantly picking out the man who did not belong there. It was obvious that this was a man who came from the upper classes, and his description was very like that he had been given, despite the bruises on his face. He seemed relaxed in the sunshine and was laughing at something one of the brothers had said to him, and then he turned and saw that a stranger was amongst them. His eyes narrowed, and he seemed wary, his guard raised as if expecting trouble of some kind.

'Forgive me for intruding upon you, Brothers, sir,' Herbert said, wondering at the flicker in the tall man's dark eyes. 'I have come here in the hope of finding a man I have been looking for these past weeks, and I hope that he I seek may be you, sir.'

'Who are you?' the tall man asked, his dark gaze sharp and distinctly suspicious. 'I do not know you – do I?'

'I have been told that you know no one, sir,' Herbert answered. 'I am employed by a lady – Lady Corinna Dorling – to find you if I can.' Again there was a flicker in those dark eyes but the man's expression remained blank. He either did not recognize the name or he was a fine actor; at this moment Herbert was not certain which to believe. 'Does the name mean nothing to you?'

'Should it mean something?'

'I had hoped it might. I have been told that you do not know your own name, sir – but the lady is most anxious about you and I thought she might mean something to you.'

'I do not recall the name. But you have not told me yours – or the name of the man you seek.'

'I am Herbert Jones, sir, lately of the Bow Street Runners, gone into business for myself. The gentleman I seek is Edmund, Lord Fitzroy, Marquis of Lanchester.' He watched carefully for the flicker but there was none this time, though he was beginning to believe this man capable of controlling his emotions, of giving nothing away. 'Does the name mean nothing to you?'

The tall man shook his head. 'What proof have you of your identity or that you are employed by this lady?'

'I have a letter of contract,' Herbert said. He reached into his pocket, saw the other flinch and shook his head. 'Forgive me, sir. Believe me, I mean you no harm. I have only your good in mind.'

'Show me the letter.' It was handed over and read, then returned. 'Clearly you are who you say you are, but I have reason to be careful, as Brother Aslom may have told you.'

'But surely it was robbers and thieves who set upon you, my lord?'

'Who knows?' The tall man's brows arched. 'What do you plan to do now that you think you have found the man for whom you have been searching?''

'It is my intention to write to Lady Dorling, perhaps to have someone come here to identify you.'

'May I ask you to wait for a day or so, sir? I wish to give this some thought – and then perhaps I shall return with you to . . .'

'Amberly, my lord,' Herbert supplied as was expected. He was not convinced that this man, who he firmly believed was the marquis, was truly suffering from loss of memory. He was giving a good performance, but there was too much pride, too much arrogance for a man who had no knowledge of his standing in the world. In his opinion the marquis was playing a deep game. 'That is the name of your family seat.'

'Indeed,' Fitz replied, knowing that Herbert was suspicious and cursing him for being altogether too intelligent. It had been an easy matter to deceive the good brothers, though he had felt some remorse, for they had been kind to him. Indeed, but for their nursing he would surely have died. 'I am indebted to you for finding me, sir. I must ask you not to send your letter. One day soon we shall return to Amberly by post-chaise. I would wish my whereabouts to remain a secret until then, if you please.'

'Very wise, my lord,' Herbert said. 'It is always wise to be careful when one is not certain of one's enemies.'

'Do I have enemies?' Fitz asked. 'Perhaps you have sussed them out, Mr Jones.'

'I might have some idea, sir,' Herbert said and touched the side of his nose with his forefinger. 'We may perhaps have time to discuss this in the morning . . .' He hesitated, then said, 'You won't be giving me the slip, sir? I've known some to do it, though they was fly coves on the run from the law.'

'You have my word that I shall not,' Fitz said and smiled oddly. 'I rather think it would be a waste of time, for you would no doubt find me again. Indeed, I think we may deal well together, Mr Jones. You may perhaps be of further use to me in this matter.'

'Ah, that's what I had hoped, my lord,' Herbert said. 'For whoever it might be, your lordship certainly has an enemy and that person wants you dead.'

'I had hoped we might have heard something by now,' Corinna said as she sat in the front parlour, embroidering the corner of a handkerchief. The long French windows overlooked smooth lawns and a drive leading between tall trees, which she now knew led out eventually to the main road. 'Mr Jones has always been so punctual with his letters.'

Anne reached for her hand and pressed it. 'Do not be anxious, my dear. I am sure it is not bad news or we should have heard by now.'

'But it is almost a week. A journey of some twenty miles does not take that long. It would have been an easy matter for Mr Jones to return and tell me . . .' She broke off as she saw a light carriage bowling up the drive. 'Someone is coming. I wonder . . .'

The chaise had come to a halt and one of the grooms had jumped down to open the door. A man got out and Corinna recognized him at once as her agent. He was followed a moment later by the tall imposing figure of the man she had longed to see. Her heart gave a great leap of joy and she was on her feet, her needlework falling unnoticed to the floor as she hurried from the room. She was in the hall as the two men entered, but she halted as Fitz turned to look at her, his face expressionless.

''Fitz!' she cried. 'What is it? What is wrong?'

'Excuse me, your lordship, allow me.' Herbert Jones came bustling past him. 'Lady Dorling, may I ask you to identify this gentleman, please?'

'Identify? But he is Lanchester, the man I asked you to find.'

'I suspected as much,' Herbert said with a satisfied look. 'However, I fear his lordship cannot for the moment recall his own name. He suffered a terrible accident, which has led to this unfortunate loss of memory.'

'Fitz cannot remember . . .' Corinna felt a sense of loss mingled with relief. She had wondered why, if he was still alive, he had not made an attempt to contact her and why he had stared at her so oddly, but this explained everything. 'Oh, my poor darling, how sorry I am for all that has happened.' She walked towards him, a smile on her lips. 'We have all been so anxious about you, dearest.'

'Forgive me, ma'am. Would you mind telling me who you are?'

'I am Corinna – Lady Dorling.'

'And our relationship is . . .'

'Close friends,' Corinna replied hesitantly for she could not claim more in the circumstances. 'I was staying here when you disappeared. I returned to London a few days later, but came down when the search was begun at the invitation of your nephew, Mr Tobias Stephens.' She thought something flickered in Fitz's eyes but could not be sure.

'Thank you for explaining, ma'am,' Fitz said, showing no emotion whatsoever. 'You will forgive me if I excuse myself for the moment. I have been unwell and the journey was tiring. I would like to retire to my rooms – if someone could show me where they are, of course.'

'I shall do that, my lord.' George Reed had been standing discreetly in the background but now came forward. 'I'm

169

Reed, your valet, sir, and it is my job to take care of your lordship. If you will place yourself in my hands we'll soon have you shipshape again, sir.' His eyes moved disapprovingly over Fitz's borrowed apparel, which was ill-fitting and, in his valet's opinion, entirely unsuitable to a man of his importance. 'Once you have your own things about you, you will feel more the thing.'

'I daresay,' Fitz replied and now there was the merest glimmer of a smile about his mouth. 'You must bear with me, Reed, but for the moment I do not know what the thing is . . .'

'Just so, sir.' Reed nodded to Corinna reassuringly. 'Now don't you worry, ma'am, we'll soon have his lordship back to his normal self now that we've got him home.'

'Thank you,' Corinna said. She watched as Reed led his master upstairs, talking all the while. She could only hope that Fitz would recover his memory very soon. But at least he was here, he was alive, and for that she would be eternally grateful.

'Doesn't know his own name?' Tobias stared at her in shocked disbelief. 'That's hard to swallow, Corinna. Bit of a sham if you ask me. Lost all memory? Seems unlikely to me.'

'I cannot imagine why you think that Fitz would lie,' Corinna said. 'There is simply no reason for him to do so.'

'It's a rum go, that's all I can say. As for this story of his being attacked . . . Strange, don't you think? Where did it happen, did he say?'

'He can have no memory of it,' Corinna reminded him. 'We know only what the monks surmise from their observations. He was attacked, beaten and robbed . . .'

'Why, if he had died his body might have lain unnoticed in a ditch and no one would be the wiser,' Tobias said and looked annoyed. 'The rogues might have left him his signet ring.'

'What difference would that have made? The monks were unlikely to know him from his ring.'

'It bears his crest,' Tobias said but looked cautious, as though aware of having struck a false note. 'Well, I suppose we must think ourselves fortunate that he was not killed.'

'Yes, of course. I thank God for it.' She could not help but rejoice in her heart, even if Fitz's cold look had struck a chill note.

What had made him look at her that way? He had seemed angry, wary – as if he did not trust her. Very much the way he'd looked at her the night she had gone to his room and he had made her his captive.

The devil was in it, Fitz thought as he glanced at his image in the dressing mirror. He was once again a man of fashion, his borrowed clothes consigned to perdition by his outraged valet. But how could he restore the life he had once known? So much of it seemed now to have been a sham, an empty existence. His short stay amongst the Brothers had shown him that he had no use for his former life – but how could he go forward when there were so many doubts in his mind?

His plan depended on being able to keep up the pretence of having lost his memory, and it was proving increasingly hard to do so with Reed's sharp eyes watching his every move. Difficult to deceive a man who had always been more friend than servant. And then there was the question of Corinna. The hurt in her face had been plain to see earlier, but that might be an act and he dare not reveal the truth to her for fear that she had been in league with whoever had tried to have him murdered. After all, he had only her word for it that she had not persuaded Everard to try and kill him.

Reed seemed to have fallen under her spell, for he was full of praise for her, and had lost no time in telling him that it was only due to Corinna that he had been found.

'She was worried about you from the start, sir,' Reed told him as he laid out the clothes he assumed his master would wish to wear. 'Harris admits he thought you had gone off for private reasons, but she instigated a search almost at once. She then returned to London, and after discovering there was no sign of you there, hired the agent who found you.'

'Then I must be grateful to her, must I not?'

Reed gave him a puzzled, slightly disapproving look but made no further comment. Fitz knew himself rebuked; he had been subjected to his valet's silences before and understood them. He was tempted to confide in the man, in whom he had perfect confidence, but despite his need to believe Corinna, he remained cautious. Better to keep his own counsel for now.

Fitz's loss of memory was not entirely false, for when he had first come to his senses at the monastery, he had been truly unable to recall who he was. His memory had returned to him gradually, and he had soon realized that his life was in danger. The attack on him had been deliberate, for it was his habit to ride in the same direction of a morning, and in the first few moments before he fell he had seen the faces and heard the voices of the men who attacked him. Whoever his enemy was, it could serve no purpose to reveal his hand just yet.

His fear was that he would discover that Corinna was mixed up in it all. Half of him denied it vehemently, and yet there was still Everard's confession on his deathbed. To lie at such a time was a desperate thing. But if he had not lied, then it meant that Corinna was false. To believe that would rob him of all hope of a future.

The memory of their night together had returned to him with all the others as he began to recover his strength, and it hurt him to believe that she could give herself to him so sweetly and yet conspire against him. Surely it was not so! What reason could she have for wanting him dead? No reason, surely. And yet the thought tormented him, twisting in his mind like a maggot.

Perhaps he would tell her the truth, swear her to silence concerning the true state of his mind. But still the doubt lingered and he smothered the desire to go to her, take her in his arms and tell her of his love and need. He would wait just a little longer.

He became aware that Reed was speaking to him, talking about his nephew, telling him that he had come down with Corinna.

'Tobias – here?' he said without thinking, and frowned. 'What brought him, I wonder. He dislikes the country . . .'

'Just so, my lord,' Reed said and smiled his satisfaction.

Fitz realized that he had made a slip, but it had been a vain hope to keep a secret from the man who knew him so well. 'You are a sly dog, Reed,' he said. 'But I daresay you will keep my secret.'

'Certainly, your lordship. You will need to be constantly on your guard, sir. It might be as well to employ someone to watch your back. Whoever tried to murder you might decide to have another go.'

'Yes, that is my fear,' Fitz replied. 'The reason why I have decided to keep up the pretence for as long as I can. At the moment only you and Jones know the truth.'

'Good man, Herbert Jones,' Reed said with a nod of his head. 'I trust him, sir. With the two of us on the alert you should be right and tight. Trust us to look out for you, my lord. I shouldn't care to have Mr Stephens step into your shoes, and that's a fact – begging your pardon for any slight on your lordship's nephew.'

'Thank you. Your sentiments are appreciated, Reed, and echo my own.' Fitz hid his smile of amusement. He had been taken unawares by the trap laid for him, but it was not likely to happen again. From now on he would keep his eyes and ears open. 'I should not like to discommode you for the world, my dear fellow.'

Reed gave a snort that hid his laughter. He was glad to have his master back to his usual self, and couldn't wait to see the back of that sly fox who had been lording it over them for the past few days.

'Lady Dorling, I wished to speak to you on a matter of importance.'

Corinna turned as she heard the voice of Tobias Stephens, her brow creasing as she caught a note of urgency. 'Is something wrong, sir?'

'It is merely that I wished to speak to you . . .' He hesitated, clearly ill at ease. 'Of my feelings. Now that Lanchester has returned and . . . I wanted to make it known that my regard for you has grown during the time we have spent together. I wanted, in fact, to ask if you would do me the honour . . .'

'Forgive me,' Corinna said swiftly. 'If you mean to ask me to walk in the garden I shall accept, for it was in my mind to go out as you spoke. It is such a lovely day and the garden is looking very fine, do you not think so?'

'Yes, very fine.' He scowled at her, for his intention had been very different as she well knew. Her swift intervention had saved him from making a fool of himself, but it did not prevent him from feeling angry. 'I shall not keep you from your walk, ma'am. Please excuse me.'

Corinna sighed as he turned and walked from the room, the picture of hurt dignity. She was aware that she had angered him, that perhaps she had soured their relationship. He had clearly been about to ask her to marry him, and she had wanted to spare an embarrassing moment for them both, but he was not grateful to her – far from it.

Sighing, Corinna went out into the garden. She had turned down more than one young man during her stay in London, and there really was no way to spare their hurt feelings.

She was walking in the rose garden when Fitz came up to her a little later that afternoon. She turned her head to look at him and smiled as he suited his pace to hers, clearly intending to join her in her walk.

'It is a pleasant afternoon, is it not?'

'Very pleasant. We are fortunate in the summer this year, I think.'

'Oh yes, it has been fine for some days now.' Corinna bent to smell the delicious perfume of a dark-red rose. 'That particular rose has such a lovely scent, and you have a beautiful home and garden, sir. I have enjoyed my stay here, but I should think soon of returning to London.'

'Should you?' Fitz had wondered how best to approach the subject of their situation and she had just given him his opening. 'You must forgive me, ma'am, but I do not quite know what we are to each other.'

She laughed softly. 'You are not the only one, sir. We are in somewhat of a coil in the circumstances. We have not always been on the best of terms, but I believe we had reached an understanding before your accident.'

'Indeed? What kind of understanding?'

Corinna's cheeks felt warm. It was an embarrassing situation, but honesty would be best in the circumstances. 'The kind that many ladies and gentlemen find together. I must tell you that we have been lovers, sir. Both in the past and again recently.'

'And are we in love?'

'My own feelings have recently become much warmer,' she replied and stopped walking, looking up at him. 'This is so difficult for me, Fitz. I have been wracked with anxiety for you, yet I was not sure that you had not left me deliberately.'

'Had we quarrelled then?'

'Many times,' she said with a rueful laugh. 'But we had fought our way through the bitterness and anger, and it seemed that we might be happy together.'

'Were we to have married?'

'That is something I cannot tell you. You had not spoken of it, although something . . . But no, I shall not claim what I cannot know. We made love the night before . . . the accident, if it was an accident. I have been told that your horse showed signs of rope burns to its forelegs.'

Fitz raised his brows at her. 'You think it may not have been an accident?'

'In truth I do not know,' she said and frowned. 'You once told me that you might have enemies, and I have feared that someone wanted you dead, though I do not know who that person might be.'

She was so beautiful and seemed so sincere, so honest – how could he doubt her? He had almost made up his mind to confess his secret when he saw a man walking towards them and recognized him as his nephew, the heir of Amberly.

'Good afternoon, Uncle,' Tobias said. He had apparently recovered from his pique, for his manner was smooth and pleasant. 'I saw you both from the windows and came to join you. I am glad to see you back and hope that you are feeling better.'

'And you are my nephew, I presume,' Fitz replied, his expression giving nothing away. 'My late sister's boy, so they tell me.'

'You have no recollection of me, sir?' There was a flicker of something in Tobias's eyes but it was quickly hidden. 'It is strange that you should have no memory at all.'

'Yes, very odd,' Fitz agreed. 'I do not know how it may be – though I must admit that some things have come back to me since my return. Not faces or people, but the house and the estate. I seem to know my way about by instinct.'

'Then no doubt your memory will return in time, Uncle.'

'I have every hope that it will do so,' Fitz replied. 'I believe you do not generally reside at Amberly, Tobias. To what do I owe the pleasure of this visit?'

'I came with Lady Dorling – to help in the search for you. Naturally I was concerned when it seemed that you had disappeared without trace.'

'Then I am indebted to you for your concern,' Fitz murmured silkily and in a way that made Corinna glance at him with sudden suspicion. 'I must, of course, always be pleased to welcome family to Amberly – but was there anything in particular you wished to see me about?'

A nerve flicked in Tobias's cheek. It was not a month since he had asked Lanchester for the money to pay a gambling debt and been refused. Would he remember that, or was it truly forgotten with all the rest?

'There is a small matter of business,' he said. 'But it will keep until another time.'

'Speak to me this evening before dinner.'

'Thank you.' Tobias cleared his throat. 'I shall probably return to London soon – what are your plans, Lady Dorling? May I be of service to you at all?'

'You are kind to think of it,' Corinna replied. 'I am not quite sure of my plans as yet, but—'

'Corinna has accepted my invitation to stay for a little longer,' Fitz put in before she could finish. 'Of course, you are also welcome to stay if you wish, Tobias.'

'Thank you, but I have business in town. And now I shall leave you to continue your walk together. Uncle . . . Corinna.' He inclined his head to them, turned and walked back to the house.

'What do you think of my nephew?'

Corinna was surprised by the question. 'I do not know, Fitz. He can be charming but . . .' She shook her head and would say no more, though he raised his brows to encourage her. 'It would be wrong of me to express an opinion. I hardly know him.'

'Very wise,' Fitz said and looked thoughtful. 'I too shall reserve judgement for the moment.' He smiled at her. 'You will accept my invitation to stay?'

'Yes, if you wish it, for a few days, and then I must leave you. I never intended to stay in town beyond the season. I should go home to Dorling Hall. There are matters needing my attention . . .'

'Yes, of course. But we must meet if we are to continue our relationship.'

'It would not be fair to either of us until you have recovered your memory,' Corinna said. 'In time, perhaps . . .'

'Yes, I agree that it is awkward. I was not suggesting that we should take up where we had left off, merely that I wished to know you a little better.'

'Of course, that is also my wish,' Corinna said and smiled. 'I must tell you that what happened between us was very sudden. We have a long and painful history, Fitz, and it has taken much heart-searching on my part – and I daresay on yours – to arrive at a place where I no longer feel bitterness towards you.'

'Have I harmed you in the past, Corinna?'

'I was harmed by your impulsive actions,' she said and explained briefly what had passed between them, claiming nothing that was not true or just and leaving out much that she might have said. 'But I have forgiven the past. It is over and now I wish only to make sure that the future is better for both of us.'

'You are very forgiving.'

'I have learned to forgive,' she replied. 'Once I believed I hated you – but when I thought you might be lost to me for ever I was devastated. Yet I make no claim on you, Fitz. You owe me nothing.'

'You are as generous as you are beautiful.' He wanted to confess to her that his memory was intact, but realized that she would only be hurt by his distrust of her. Once again impulse had led him astray, and now there was little he could do – except court her. He reached for her hand, carrying it to his lips and placing a light kiss in the palm. How could he have doubted her? He saw now that he had wronged her in his thoughts. 'I think that I love you. Will you allow me to fall in love with you, Corinna?'

'Perhaps it is best that we go slowly. Only time will tell if our feelings for each other were but an impulse or true love.'

'Then you will stay with me for a while?'

'Yes, I shall stay.' She smiled and he reached out to touch her cheek with his fingertips.

'I shall try to become worthy of you.'

'Now do not promise too much,' Corinna teased. 'I know you for a sad scamp and would not have you change drastically.'

'But I shall and must if I am to deserve your love,' he said earnestly. 'Shall we go into the house now? I think that it has turned cooler of a sudden. We may have a storm . . .'

Watching from one of the upper windows of the house, Tobias frowned as he saw Fitz laughing and playing court to Corinna. Damn him! How had he managed to survive the attack on him? Any other man would surely have died. Jealousy and anger twisted and turned inside him like a worm. Clearly the widow was attracted to Lanchester, and just as obviously she would not be interested in his nephew. Beautiful women liked power and money, and Fitz had both, while he, Tobias Stephens, the heir to Amberly, had nothing. Even the small fortune he had inherited from his father had long since been spent. He was deeply in debt and his only hope of recovery was in the fortune that would be his if his uncle were to die.

He had believed that it would be a simple matter to spring the trap on Lanchester, employing a set of rogues that would do anything for money. They had betrayed him, robbing Lanchester as he lay unconscious from the beating he had received, but leaving the job unfinished. It was likely that the marquis would not have been identified if he had been found dead, and that meant Tobias could not have inherited for several years.

It was clearly useless to employ the rogues again, particularly as Lanchester would be on his guard for the moment. Nor did Tobias dare to risk suspicion falling upon him. He must be careful or he would be caught in his own trap this time.

Had Lanchester really lost his memory, or was he merely playing a long game? Tobias could not be sure. He had decided to put Lanchester to the test by asking him for a loan. It had been refused in no uncertain terms last time, but if his uncle had truly lost his memory he would not know how often he had helped Tobias out of trouble in the past and might be more inclined to give him the money he needed.

Twelve

'Forgive me, Nephew, but am I in the habit of lending you money?' Fitz asked when confronted by Tobias in the library that evening. 'I have no objection to it providing that it does not occur again. You must understand that I do not approve of gambling money you do not have, sir.'

'Yes, of course,' Tobias said, swallowing his pride. One day this would all be his and then he would do what he damned well liked! 'I am sorry to ask, but it is either borrow money or sell my entire estate. I cannot think you would approve of that, sir.'

'No, I should not,' Fitz agreed. 'Have you thought of staying at home and investing in the new agriculture? My bailiff tells me I am an advocate of the new methods. You might become a prosperous gentleman farmer if you chose, and then you would have no need to come cap in hand to me.'

'I did not imagine you would care to see your only relative employed in such activities, sir. After all, I am your heir.'

'Only until I have a son, I believe,' Fitz reminded him. 'If my memory returns I may marry quite soon, and then I imagine you may find that you are no longer in line to inherit my fortune.'

Tobias hardly knew how he managed to keep from striking out in his frustration. 'Then I must congratulate you, sir, and I shall try to follow your advice. That is, if you will help me this time . . .'

'I shall give you a draft on my bank,' Fitz told him. 'But

this is the last time, Tobias. Do not come to me again for it will avail you nothing.'

'Of course not, sir. I shall not be so foolish in the future.'

'Then we shall forget this interview,' Fitz said and offered his hand. 'Let us shake on it and be friends.'

Tobias shook hands, accepted the note from his uncle and thanked him. 'This is very good of you, sir.'

'We shall say no more of it,' Fitz told him. 'Do you still plan to return to London in the morning?'

'Yes, sir. I must settle my affairs, and then I shall go down to the country.'

'Good. See that you do,' Fitz said and nodded. 'We should not keep the ladies waiting.' His eyes flicked to Tobias's face. 'Have you any plans for marriage in the near future yourself?'

'The lady I had hopes of has the prospect of a richer prize, I believe,' Tobias replied, affecting an air of regret and hurt feelings. 'Had things been different . . . But I have nothing to offer her.'

'I see . . .' Fitz frowned but did not push the matter. Tobias seemed to be implying that he might have had hopes of Corinna. He was an attractive young man, after all, and it was possible that she had encouraged him at some time in the past. Once again, Fitz found himself torn with doubt, but he suppressed it as they went into the drawing room and found Corinna with her companion. 'Corinna . . . ma'am . . . I hope I find you well.'

'I am Mrs Anne Crabtree,' Anne told him kindly to save him the pain of searching for a lost name. 'I am Lady Dorling's companion, but you do not know me well, though we have met at various affairs.'

'Thank you for telling me, ma'am,' Fitz said and smiled at her. 'It is pleasant to meet you again.' He turned to Corinna and saw that she was puzzled by something. 'You look beautiful this evening, Corinna.'

'Thank you.' She came forward and he kissed her cheek. 'I thought you looked tired earlier, Fitz, but you seem more yourself this evening.'

'I thank you for your concern, Corinna. I confess that I am feeling better now that I am home again.' He signalled to Harris to pour the champagne. 'I thought we should celebrate my return. I hope you will join me in a toast – perdition to our enemies!'

Corinna and Anne raised their glasses at once, Tobias more slowly. Fitz noticed his nephew's pained look and wondered. He would not like to suspect his late sister's only son of wishing him harm, but it looked as if Tobias felt the toast a bitter pill to swallow.

It was a devil of a coil, for even if he could prove to his own satisfaction that his nephew had been behind the attack on him, what was he to do about it? It would go against the grain to have him arrested and put on public trial, and yet murder was such a foul thing. Besides, he knew that he had made more than one enemy over the years, and it would be uncharitable to suspect Tobias without proof. All he could do was be on his guard and wait.

Corinna heard the thunder and saw the forked lightning hurtle towards the earth. She stifled a scream for it was immediately outside her window and, foolish though she knew it to be, storms had always frightened her. She decided that she would go downstairs and find a book to read in the hope that it would take her mind from the storm. She slipped on soft slippers, pulling on a heavy brocade robe that covered the fine silk of her night chemise. Then she picked up a chamber stick and, shielding the candle flame with her hand, went out into the hall, walking softly along the deeply carpeted passage to the top of the stairs.

Only a few candles were still burning, making the large hall shadowy and dark in the corners, and she paused at the foot of the stairs to light a branch of candles that had gone out from her own. Hearing a slight sound behind her, Corinna was in the act of turning her head when something struck her from the side and she stumbled, falling to the floor. Everything went black around her, and the next thing she was aware of was someone bending over her. Then a strong, pungent smell was making her feel she wanted to sneeze and her head snapped back as her eyes opened.

'Thank God,' Fitz said. She blinked as she saw that he had been holding a burning feather quill under her nose. 'I was afraid you were badly hurt. You must have fallen down the stairs. What on earth were you doing wandering about at this hour, Corinna?'

'It was the storm,' she said and sat up. She placed a hand to her head as she felt the pain swamp her and lay back against the cushions once more until the dizziness passed. 'I think I must have banged my head – it hurts rather a lot.'

'I noticed some blood as I carried you here. I shall bathe it for you in a moment,' Fitz said. 'Did you faint or miss your step?'

'I do not remember.' Corinna blinked, struggling to remember for a moment. 'But surely I was at the foot of the stairs. I had stopped to light the candles there . . .'

'You fell at the foot of the stairs – not down them?'

'Yes, I think so . . .' She gazed up at him in bewilderment. 'I do not remember what happened after I bent to light the candles . . .'

'It was the blow to the head,' he said. 'It affects the memory sometimes. I have learned that to my cost.'

'Yes, of course. At least I have not forgotten who I am,' Corinna said. 'But what were you doing down here, Fitz?'

'I could not sleep,' he said and smiled oddly. 'Unlike you, I thrive on storms, Corinna. I love to watch them; they fascinate me – especially over the sea. That is a truly magnificent sight.'

'Not if you are at sea and caught in a storm.'

'Very true,' he agreed, his mouth quirking at the corners. 'I would not have thought you would be afraid of a little storm, Corinna.' She had so much courage and it touched him to discover that a storm made her vulnerable.

'Perhaps that is because you do not know me well,' she replied and managed to sit up properly without going dizzy.

'Is that a brandy decanter I see on the table, Fitz? A small glass would oblige me, if you please. I am feeling a little shaky.'

'Of course,' he said and went over to the table. He carried the tray to a little table next to the sofa, poured a generous measure into a glass and then handed it to her. He then soaked his kerchief in water from the jug that accompanied the decanter, kneeling down beside her and turning her head so that he could see the wound. 'Your head is cut – this may sting, but it will cleanse the wound. After I have bathed it I shall apply a little brandy to cleanse it of infection. Whatever caused you to fall, you must have banged your head very hard.'

'It certainly feels as if it has been split open,' she said and suppressed a cry of pain as he applied the spirit to the back of her head. 'You do not make a good surgeon, Fitz.'

'Forgive me if I hurt you. It was not intentional.'

'I am aware of that. It was very foolish of me to be so careless.'

She sipped her brandy. 'I think I prefer this as a drink to a cure for a cut head.'

Fitz laughed. 'Well, I have done now. You did not wish me to send for your companion and raise the house, I presume?'

'No, indeed, I should not want that. It was fortunate for me that you were not in your room. I might have lain there all night.'

'You might have been very ill – or died,' Fitz said and felt a rush of emotion as he realized that he would have been devastated had that happened. He had been kneeling on the floor beside her to bathe her head and now he suddenly took her hand, his expression very strange in the candlelight. 'Will you marry me, Corinna?'

'Fitz!' She stared at him in shocked surprise. 'This is very sudden. I had not expected it.'

'I feel that you are important to me,' he said, choosing his words carefully for he must appear to regain his memory piece by piece. 'I believe I love you – and I do not want you to suffer any more accidents. If you were with me you would not need to go wandering about in the night because there happened to be a storm.'

Corinna laughed, delighted by the absurdity of his proposal. 'I do not know that it is a sensible idea for marriage, Fitz – but I must admit that I find it appealing.'

'Marriage to me or having a companion in a storm?' he asked, laughter in his eyes.

'Both,' she said promptly and they both laughed. 'You will make my head ache, Fitz. Worse than it already does, I mean.'

He leaned towards her, kissing her forehead. 'Forgive me for hurting you, Corinna – in all ways.'

'The past is past,' she told him. 'We had already decided that, my dear. Yes, I shall marry you – if you are quite sure that is what you want.'

'I should not have asked if it were not.'

'Supposing you regret it when your memory returns?'

'My memory is coming back little by little,' he said and took her hands, helping her to rise and holding her as she swayed slightly. 'You are quite safe, my darling. I have you.'

'If you changed your mind, I would release you,' she said, gazing up at him. 'But we have wasted too many years already, Fitz. When you were missing I knew that my heart would break if you did not return safely, and that is why I am prepared to marry you despite your loss of memory. I know that I love you. My only fear is that you will think I have trapped you into this – that you might have wanted only to make me your mistress.'

'I am not the young fool I was when I hurt you the first time, Corinna. You have told me what I did and the consequences – and that you have forgiven me. Even if I did not love you, my honour would demand that I ask you to be my wife. However, it is because I do love you that I ask and for no other reason.'

'I would not marry you for the sake of your honour or my

own,' she told him. 'But for love – that is another matter.'

'So you will have me despite all my faults?'

'Perhaps because of them,' she admitted.

'And will you teach me how to behave as a gentleman ought?'

'I do not imagine I should find it easy to change you. Besides, I love you as you are, Fitz.'

'Then we shall marry – and soon. I want to look after and cherish you, Corinna.'

'Do you wish to marry in town or here?'

'That is your choice, of course, though my own preference would be for a quiet wedding here. We may invite our friends to a ball in London before the wedding if you wish.'

'That is an excellent idea,' she said. 'I must return to town to order my bride clothes in any case. And truly, I ought to pay a visit to Dorling. I must not neglect the estate, for it is a sacred trust placed in me and I must abide by it.'

'I would not want you to neglect your duty, Corinna. Yet I hope you do not mean to keep me waiting too long.'

'For just as long as it takes to have the banns read, I imagine.'

'We shall be in church to hear them this weekend,' he promised. 'Are you ready to return to your room now, my love? Or would you rather sit here with me for a while longer?'

'I think the worst of the storm is over,' Corinna said. 'But I should be glad of your arm to walk upstairs, Fitz. My head aches quite shockingly.'

'I cannot understand how you came to fall so hard if you were at the foot of the stairs.'

Corinna looked at him as she took her arm. 'I wish I could remember. There was something when I was lighting those candles, but irritatingly it will not come to mind.'

'Do not try to remember if you cannot,' Fitz said. 'It will come in time.'

'Yes, I am sure of it,' she said. 'It hardly matters now.'

'Providing it does not happen again.'

Fitz smiled as he spoke, keeping his thoughts private. His first reaction on finding Corinna slumped on the floor was that she must have fallen down the stairs. However, having bathed the wound to the side of her head, he now had his doubts. He could not be certain, of course, but he suspected that she had been struck a blow to the head by a heavy instrument.

'Tomorrow I shall ask the doctor to call on you,' he told her. 'I should like him to look at your head, Corinna.'

'I am sure there is not the least need.'

'I would like to be sure no real harm has been done,' Fitz said. 'Foolish, you may think, but to please me.'

'To please you?' She stopped at her door and smiled at him. 'Of course, if you wish it, Fitz. I shall not ask you to stay with me, dearest. I would rather like to sleep.'

'Goodnight then, my love,' he replied. 'I shall see you in the morning.'

He saw her inside the door, then frowned as he walked to the end of the hall and up the stairs that led to his own apartment. She would be safe enough now, for he did not think another attempt to harm her would be made that night. It was a most unpleasant suspicion to harbour, but he was very much afraid that someone had tried to kill Corinna that evening, and that if he had not come out of the library when he had, that person might well have succeeded.

Why should anyone wish to kill her? Fitz could think of only one reason, and that left a sour taste in his mouth. From now on, he would have his nephew watched closely.

Alone in her room, Corinna retired to bed, her thoughts a mixture of happiness and the vague doubt that lingered at the back of her mind. Something had happened just before she passed out, but it was as if a curtain had descended in her mind and she had no idea of what it was that had caused her to fall.

Tobias had hidden himself in the shadows as his uncle came from the library. Had he realized that Lanchester was about he would not have seized his chance to strike Corinna down, and cursed his ill luck that he was unable to finish the work. Given time, he would have carried her body to the lake and disposed of it, hoping that it would remain caught in the reeds for long enough for him to be far away by the time it was found.

He was still shaking when he emerged from his hiding place and hurried back to his own bedchamber, knowing that he had come close to being caught. The attack on Corinna had been reckless and unplanned, a chance he had not expected to come his way. Had it succeeded, Lanchester's plans for marriage might have been postponed indefinitely, giving him plenty of chance to dispose of his uncle.

He would do it properly next time, he thought, though after this evening's fiasco he did not dare to move too soon. Hidden in the shadows, he had heard a few words of the conversation between his uncle and Corinna as they went upstairs, passing within a few feet of where he stood, shivering and in fear of discovery. Fortunately, they had been too wrapped up in each other to suspect their words were overheard.

It seemed they were to marry sooner than he had imagined. That was a nuisance, and meant he must act sooner rather than later. His mind worked furiously as he thought about how best to bring about the death of his uncle.

For the moment he could think of no solution that would not carry a huge risk of discovery. Perhaps it might be easier to get rid of Corinna . . . He must think more carefully before making his move this time. One more false step and he might find himself at the end of the hangman's noose.

A shiver ran down his spine and, back in his bedchamber, he poured himself a large brandy and drank it all in one go. That was better! He had stopped shaking and could think more calmly now. He was not suspected so far. He would take his leave in the morning as planned, and think about what he would do next.

*   *   *

Corinna spent three days in town, choosing the style and material for her wedding gown, and for other gowns she might need. On the evening of the third day, she took her farewell of Fitz, for it had been decided that he would remain in town to take care of business that had been neglected and join her at Dorling Hall in ten days' time.

'I shall escort you home to Amberly,' he told her with a last, lingering kiss. 'And then we shall be married, my darling.'

'In truth, I cannot wait,' she said and smiled up at him. 'I do not wish to be parted from you now, Fitz, but we both have business that will not wait.'

'That is the weight of responsibility,' he replied and touched her cheek. He felt a sudden urge to say that he would accompany her to Dorling, but hesitated and the moment was lost.

'And I am glad that you take yours seriously. I had imagined that you spent your time in idle pursuits like most of the gentlemen I know.'

'Far from it. I am far too busy with other matters,' Fitz laughed and touched a finger to her lips. 'No, I shall not tell you, my sweet, for I do not think you would approve. And indeed, I have decided that it is time for me to leave my adventures behind and become a responsible man. I may even take my seat in the House when some cause moves me.'

'Politics?' Corinna raised her eyebrows. 'I have never seen you in that guise, Fitz, but I shall not quarrel with it if you choose to take up a position. Tell me, are you for Mr Pitt or Fox?'

'Fox is well enough when he's sober, but I think Pitt the better man.'

'Fitz!' she upbraided him. 'I daresay Mr Fox drinks no more than any other gentleman.'

'He is a rapacious gambler,' Fitz said with a frown. 'Hardly surprising, one may say, considering that as a small child of perhaps six years or so he was given a handful of guineas and told to hazard them at the tables.'

'I have heard that tale before,' Corinna confessed. 'Is it really true?'

'He boasted of it once when in his cups,' Fitz said with a wry smile. 'I believe it, for I call him a gambler and a lover of wine, not a liar.'

Corinna laughed and struck him on the arm with her fan. 'You had best mind your tongue, my love, or you will find yourself fighting another duel.'

'I have done with duels,' Fitz said and suddenly drew her close so that she could feel his body heat and the beating of his heart. 'That is why you see before you a reformed man. I want to live as long as God intends and spend my old age with you, Corinna.'

'I am glad to hear it.' Her eyes brimmed with love as she gazed up at him. 'Do you wish to stay with me tonight?'

'Nothing would make me happier,' he said. 'But we shall not shock poor Anne. Impatient as I am to make love to you, my darling, I can wait a little longer for my happiness.'

'Then I shall bid you goodnight,' she said and kissed him once more. 'We have an early start in the morning.'

Fitz let her go reluctantly and they parted, she to go upstairs to her bedchamber and he to walk home. He walked slowly, deep in thought, though not so lost that he was unaware of the shadow some way behind him. He smiled and sang the words of a love song softly to himself.

His shadow went everywhere with him these days. Tomorrow he would see the other members of the Lords of Reform and tell them that his buccaneering days were over. He had enjoyed his adventures, brushing shoulders with rogues and the scum of the gutters in his efforts to help bring comfort to those most in need. However, in his heart he had always known that his behaviour was that of a reckless youth, riding out to tilt at straw giants. Yes, he had done good things, but there were other ways. He had complained often enough that the government was ineffective and did not concern itself with social problems, believing that the sword was mightier than the pen. Now he saw that perhaps he and others of like minds might do more for the people they championed by making the laws rather than flouting them.

It was time he grew up, assumed the responsibility that was his by birth, made his appearance in the House and attempted to right the wrongs that he perceived.

Thirteen

'You will not need me for much longer,' Anne said to Corinna as they sat together in the drawing room at Dorling Hall. 'I believe I must begin to look around for another position.'

'I shall be sorry to part with you,' Corinna said and wrinkled her brow in thought. 'I shall not be often at Dorling Hall, I imagine, though it must continue to be run exactly as if I lived here. I was wondering whether it might not be a good idea for you to live here in my stead, Anne. You could keep a general eye on things and write to me if you thought it necessary – and of course we shall visit from time to time.'

'You are so generous,' Anne said and fumbled for her kerchief. 'But I should feel that I was your pensioner. I must have time to consider . . .'

'Yes, of course,' Corinna said at once. 'But you have seen how much there is to be done here, Anne. I have excellent servants and they are to be trusted implicitly, but there are things that only the mistress – or someone in her place – can do.'

'Yes, I do see that,' Anne replied and then blushed. 'I did not mean to tell you this just yet, Corinna. However, I have received a proposal of marriage . . .'

'But that is wonderful! Of course you must forget my offer at once. I am very happy for you, Anne.'

'You may recall Mr Thomas Rush? He is Lord Rush's cousin and some years older than I – but so charming and kind.'

'And when are you to be married?'

'Well, I have not yet given him my answer,' Anne replied. 'It happened the day before we came down to Dorling, and I needed time to consider. I was not sure whether I wished to marry again.'

'Mr Rush is an excellent man,' Corinna told her, then kissed her cheek. 'You must do as you wish, of course, Anne – but I think it would be just the thing for you.'

'Yes, that is my opinion,' Anne replied shyly. 'I received a letter from him today. He is coming down tomorrow and asks if I will receive him. I thought you would not mind.'

'Of course not,' Corinna replied at once. 'I am delighted for you, and I wish you every happiness.'

'Then I shall receive him in the small parlour,' Anne replied looking happier than Corinna had seen her. 'I had never expected to receive such an offer and surely would not have done so had you not taken me to London with you.'

'I am pleased that things have turned out so well for you.'

Corinna got up and walked over to the window to glance out at the garden. It was a lovely day and the sunshine was tempting her outside.

'I think I shall go for a little walk. Will you come with me, Anne?'

'Yes, certainly,' Anne said and jumped to her feet. 'We must make the most of this lovely weather for I fear it will not last much longer.'

Corinna left Anne to entertain her suitor the next morning and went out to cut some roses. She would be leaving Dorling in two days and she had noticed some rather lovely blooms the previous afternoon. She might as well pick them now, for she would not be here for some months to come.

She bent to snap the stem of a wonderful dark-red rose; it had the most gorgeous perfume and was her favourite. She was thinking that she would ask the gardener to prepare some cuttings for her to take to Amberly when she heard a footstep on the gravel path and looked up, her heart beating faster.

Her eyes narrowed in surprise, as she saw not the man she had hoped might have come early but his nephew. What had brought Tobias here?

'Corinna, forgive me if I startled you,' he said and she saw that he was agitated. Something untoward must have happened to cause him to be in such a state. 'I am the bearer of terrible news.'

'What news?' She felt a lurching sensation in her stomach as she saw his grave expression, starting towards him, her hand outstretched. 'Please, you must tell me.'

'My uncle has been shot in the back while out riding,' Tobias told her, and took her arm to steady her as she near stumbled. 'Forgive me, but I know no other way to tell you. Besides, time is of the essence. He is very ill and calling for you. I brought my carriage and came straight away to fetch you. You will come, ma'am?'

'Yes, yes, of course.'

Corinna was trembling, her heart thudding in her breast. She had no thought of refusing his offer, no thought of anything but Fitz lying near to death. She must go to him and with all speed.

'Who has done this terrible thing?' she asked.

'I shall tell you as we go,' Tobias promised. 'My uncle has many enemies, ma'am. I fear that one of them has been awaiting his chance. I was afraid of this after the last time. I warned him to have a care but he would not listen, and now I fear we may lose him . . .'

'Oh no!' Corinna gave a sob of fear. She saw his carriage drawn up waiting and hesitated. 'I must go in and tell Anne where I am going.'

'That has all been taken care of,' Tobias said. 'Indeed, she told me where I might find you. She will pack your things and have them sent on to Amberly. But of course, many of your bridal clothes have already arrived there.'

'My bridal things . . .' Corinna smothered a sob. Would

she ever have reason to wear them? 'Oh yes, thank you. Yes, I shall not stay for anything. Anne will know what to do. It was only to save her from worrying that I thought to delay.'

'I knew you must think as I do,' Tobias said with a small smirk that Corinna was too distressed to notice. 'I have placed a cloak inside the carriage for you, and a few items you may need on your journey.'

'You are kindness itself,' Corinna said and gave him her hand as he assisted her into the carriage. He climbed in beside her and immediately the vehicle launched off, the horses quickly gathering momentum as they sped away down the drive and Corinna was thrown against her companion. 'Pray tell the coachman to take care. I would not have us overturn, sir.'

'Oh, he is an excellent driver,' Tobias replied. 'Have no fear, Corinna. You are perfectly safe with me. I shall take good care that nothing happens to you.'

Corinna felt a tingle of alarm. His expression was too gleeful, too excited to ring true. Suddenly she suspected a trap – a trap into which she had walked like a fly into the spider's web.

'No! This is wrong!' she cried. 'You have tricked me. Fitz has not been shot. You lied to me. You are abducting me . . .'

'That is very true, I am afraid,' Tobias said and laughed. 'I never thought that you would fall for it so easily, Corinna. I had three men waiting to seize you had you refused – but you came so trustingly.'

'I must have been mad,' she said, regretting the terror-driven impulse that had compelled her to go with him. 'I was warned not to trust you, sir.'

'By Reed, I imagine.' Tobias grabbed her arm as she lunged at the door. 'No, I should not advise that, my dear Corinna. If you threw yourself from the carriage while we are travelling at this speed you would either break your pretty neck or your head. That would not suit me, ma'am. You are the bait only, not the prize.'

'What do you mean?'

'I would have wed you if you had allowed me to make my offer, and then Fitz might have lived for a few years longer – providing there was no sign of another heir. Had you betrayed him, he might have sunk back into his reckless ways and I should have been saved the trouble.'

'What do you mean – his reckless ways?'

Corinna sat back against the squabs. He was right about the certainty of terrible injury if she threw herself from a speeding carriage, and her attention was caught. This was not a simple abduction to force her to marry him; it was a plot to lure Fitz into danger.

'Has he not told you about his little band of adventurers? Like Robin Hood, they ride out to right the wrongs of the poor, taking from the rich whenever possible to give it to guttersnipes.' He sneered at her. 'You look shocked, my lady, as well you may. It is ridiculous, is it not? A band of grown men acting like overgrown schoolboys!'

'How do you know all this?'

'Because I have my spies, too. I know my uncle has his, and I took a leaf from his book. I have waited for a chance to kill him, but there is always a shadow – that damned agent you hired, Corinna. I can never hope to get near Lanchester. So I shall bring him to me.'

'And what good will that do you?'

'He will pay a huge sum for your ransom or I shall have him killed. Indeed, his death may be preferable. I shall not do the killing myself. I am not such a fool – though had the chance presented itself, I had considered it. No, I have found a man who will do it for me. He is an ex-Runner as it happens, turned sour by the way he has been treated by gentlemen he has worked for in the past. I shall appear to arrive after he has despatched both you and my uncle, and then I shall kill him. Naturally he does not know that, and expects me to pay him a large sum of money.' He was looking so pleased with himself that Corinna felt sick. How could she plead with such a man?

The answer was of course that she could not – but what could she do? She might seize her chance for escape, should it come, but was that the best way of dealing with this dangerous man? She did not imagine she was in any immediate danger from him, for he clearly needed her as the bait to draw Fitz in. At least she knew what he intended and perhaps, if she was clever, she could find a way to warn the man she loved.

'Your plan will not work,' she said, pleased that she had succeeded in shocking him out of his complacency. His gaze narrowed as he looked at her. 'Fitz will not walk into a trap. He is not as impulsive as I.'

Tobias stared at her thoughtfully. 'He is in love with you. He will come when he realizes you have been snatched from under his nose. Oh yes, he will come – and when he does . . .'

Corinna shivered as she saw his smile. She had suspected him of being false beneath his charming manners, but never had she imagined that he could be this evil. What a fool she was to have walked so tamely into his snare! But she had thought only of Fitz, her fear that he might die overriding all thought of herself.

'Then we shall wait and see,' she said, giving a creditable impression of being much calmer than she truly was. 'May I ask where you are taking me, sir?'

'A house I have borrowed for the purpose,' Tobias said. 'It is near to being a ruin, but I daresay you will not mind that. I have prepared a couple of rooms, and providing that you do not make trouble for me, you shall be treated well enough until it is time.'

'Am I supposed to thank you for that, sir?' Her eyes flashed with the temper she could not conceal.

'I could make you grateful to me, Corinna. If you would be nice to me I might even wed you myself. You would still have the title you want and the money – merely a different bridegroom.'

'I would prefer to die,' Corinna said and, seeing his eyes

narrow with anger, sat back against the squabs and closed her eyes.

She would no doubt have done better to smile and plead for his favours, but her pride would not allow her to beg. Nor would she take the alternative he had offered. If Fitz was to die then she would be glad to die with him. However, she knew her lord too well to imagine that he would walk as tamely into the web as she had, and she must be ready for whatever happened.

If there was something she could do to help in their escape, she must do it. For now she needed to think.

She was aware that the man sitting beside her was staring at her even though her eyes were closed. No doubt he had expected her to behave very differently. If he had thought she would weep and beg, then he did not know her. She had been taught to endure by a master in the art of torture, and if Tobias imagined that she was subdued by his threats then he was much mistaken.

Corinna had no intention of allowing him to have his way, but for the moment there was little she could do. She thought about the reaction at Dorling Hall when they discovered she had disappeared, for no doubt Tobias had lied about having told Anne that he was taking her to Fitz. Would Anne alert Fitz immediately or would he know nothing until he arrived at Dorling Hall?

And what of the ransom note? Corinna's mind turned over the questions one by one, but could find no answers. All she could do was be patient and bide her time.

'But she would never have gone off like that without a word to me,' Anne cried as she was informed that Corinna's basket had been found in the rose garden, but that no other sign had been discovered. 'She knows that I would worry.'

'One of the gardeners saw her get into the carriage, ma'am,' the butler told her. 'He says she went willingly, that she was not forced in any way, and seemed in a hurry to leave.'

Anne stared at him, torn between distress and disbelief.

'It is just so unlike her. I cannot believe that she would . . .' She broke off as the housekeeper came in carrying a silver salver on which lay a sealed letter. 'You have something from Lady Dorling for me?'

'It is addressed to whomsoever is concerned for the where-abouts of Lady Corinna Dorling,' the housekeeper said in hushed tones. 'I brought it to you, ma'am, you being her companion and his lordship not here.'

'Thank you,' Anne said and took the letter with trembling hands. She broke the seal, which was unknown to her, and read the brief note inside, then gave a cry of alarm. 'Lady Dorling has been kidnapped! This is a ransom note for twenty thousand pounds . . .'

'That is a huge sum,' the housekeeper said, her face turning pale. 'However could it have happened – right here and in broad daylight?'

'She must have been tricked in some way,' Anne said. She stared at the note in dismay. 'What are we to do? The Marquis of Lanchester must be informed at once. Yes, yes, I must write to him. He will know what to do, I am sure. A groom must ride for London as soon as I have addressed my letter. Lanchester will—'

'Did I hear my name?' Anne looked up and gave a cry of mingled anguish and relief as she saw his tall figure stride into the room.

'Thank God you are come, sir,' she said. 'We were not expecting you until the morning.'

'My business was finished in town and I could not stay away longer,' Fitz said. 'Why all the long faces? Where is Corinna?'

'She has been abducted,' Anne told him and handed him the letter. 'I was just about to write to you, for I do not know what to do, sir. This is terrible, terrible! My poor Corinna. How can it have happened, and right under our noses?'

'Tell me exactly,' Fitz commanded. Faced with Corinna's companion in a state of near hysteria, he could not afford to let his own feelings hold sway. 'Did anyone see her taken?'

'One of the gardeners,' Anne said, her voice rising. 'He said that she appeared to go willingly, but I know she would not have left without telling me where she was going unless she was tricked. I know she would not!'

'I agree,' Fitz said, his expression grim. 'If she went without a struggle she must have known her abductor – and believed whatever excuse he gave her for needing to leave so abruptly.'

'Do you think . . .' Anne began and then hesitated and blushed. 'It is impertinent of me to suggest this, sir, but your nephew struck me as being of a sly nature.'

'Yes, I think you have hit upon the very one,' Fitz agreed, his gaze hard and fixed upon her in a way that made her shiver. 'If Corinna went off so hastily she must have believed . . .' He swore under his breath as he remembered the reckless way she had come to him when he was ill after the duel. 'She must have believed that I needed her.'

'Yes, of course,' Anne said. 'If she was told that you had been injured in some way . . . She was near out of her mind with worry when you were wounded in that duel – and again when you disappeared. Since two attempts have been made on your life, why should she doubt it when your nephew told her that a third had occurred?'

'Tobias can be charming when he chooses,' Fitz said grimly. 'I believe he may have had a hand in the last incident, for I observed his manner when we met afterwards and thought it false.'

'Oh!' Anne stared at him in surprise. 'Then you . . .' She broke off in embarrassment. 'Am I right in thinking that you did not truly lose your memory, sir?'

'Forgive me, yes,' Fitz replied with a wry twist of his mouth. 'When I first came to my senses I could remember nothing of the attack or who I was, but the memories returned within hours. I kept up the pretence because I was not sure who my enemy was at that time. Indeed, I have no proof even now – but I suspect Tobias. He has wasted the small fortune his father left him, and I believe he covets mine as well as the title.'

'That is wicked,' Anne said, looking upset. 'To try to murder you . . . And now he has taken Corinna. What do you think he means to do to her? Will he release her for this ransom, do you think?'

'I very much doubt it,' Fitz said, an angry gleam in his dark eyes. 'If it was he who took her – and she would not have gone with a stranger so willingly, I think – then he knows she would denounce him. No, he must kill her and me if he is to be safe, for I shall never rest while he lives. No doubt he hopes to lure me into his trap, and Corinna is the bait.'

'He is truly an evil man and deserves to be punished,' Anne said, her face quite pink. 'But what will you do, sir? Do you know where he intends to take her?'

'The note says that we must wait for further instructions,' Fitz said. 'But my nephew has not been as clever as he imagines. I know that he has been spying on me, but I do not think he has noticed that he is also constantly watched. I have a fair idea of where he may have taken her – and I have no intention of sitting here and waiting for him to pull the strings.'

'But what shall we do?' Anne cried as he turned to leave. 'Supposing another note is sent here?'

'Then you may send it to me,' Fitz said and smiled at her. 'I shall leave one of my people here to watch over you, and he will act as our go-between. I shall not tell you not to worry, dear lady, for I know that you must be anxious for Corinna's return. I shall tell you only that I have defeated more evil minds than my nephew's and I hope that I shall bring Corinna to Amberly very soon. If you receive no news in three days, you should make the journey there and wait to hear from us.'

Anne could do nothing but agree. She was distraught and wished that she might do something to help her friend, but she knew that the marquis would do all that was possible. All she could do was wait.

*   *   *

Corinna looked around the room in which she had been locked. It had once been furnished in a luxurious manner, but the bed hangings were now dusty and faded, the drapes at the window fraying into holes. A fire had been lit at some time to take the worst of the damp from the room, and the bed had been aired with a hot brick in a warming pan. However, there was no denying the desolation of the house itself.

She had seen from her window that the drive was choked with weeds from years of neglect, and that the roof had in some parts fallen in on itself. Clearly the mansion ought to be pulled down, for it belonged to the Tudor era and had been left to decay, perhaps because the upkeep was beyond its owner.

How could Fitz possibly find her here? She had hoped that she might be taken to a house not far from her own estate, but they had travelled for some hours, arriving as it was growing dark. She had seen only one servant when they arrived: a man of surly countenance and shabby apparel. He had been waiting at the house, unlike the three rogues who had followed the carriage on horseback.

Tobias had obviously not intended her to run away. Even had she managed to run from the carriage when they stopped to change horses at a posting inn, she would have been caught very quickly and then she might have been drugged. It had seemed best to let her captor imagine that she was subdued, so she had made no attempt to run when she was bundled from the carriage and brought to this room on the first floor. At least she still had her wits about her. Her natural caution told her it would be better to wait until the early hours of the morning when, hopefully, the guards set to watch her might have grown sleepy and careless.

She went to the window and looked out. There were no trees close enough to enable her to climb out and escape that way, and the window had been nailed up to cover that method of escape. Tobias had obviously been planning this for some time – perhaps from the moment she had refused to let him speak to her of his feelings.

She remembered the night of the storm, when Fitz had found her unconscious at the foot of the stairs and thought she had fallen. She had never been able to recall what had happened as she bent to light that candle, but now she thought she knew. Was she to have been killed then, or merely abducted? Tobias had taken a risk, for if he had been seen he would have been unmasked.

Was he the one who had paid those rogues to attack Fitz as he was riding? It seemed likely that he must have been. Reed had suspected him of being eager to step into Fitz's shoes, and it must have shocked him when his uncle returned in reasonable health and promptly announced his intention of being married.

She went over to the bedroom door and tugged at the handle, but it was securely locked. She needed some kind of weapon to pry the lock open – or something hard and heavy with which to attack whoever came to bring her supper. A brief search of the room told her that neither was available. It seemed that she was a prisoner until help came. Yet she would not wait idly for rescue, knowing that Fitz was to be lured to his death. She must find some way of hoodwinking her captors before Fitz came. After all, it would take some hours for a letter to reach him in London. She surely had at least a day in which to work out her plan.

Aware all at once of the demands of nature, she looked under the bed and discovered a thick china chamber pot. At least she would be able to relieve herself and . . . A little smile came to her eyes as another thought occurred to her.

Tobias filled his glass with the rich red wine and held it to the light, admiring the colour. It was the best Madeira he could buy and he intended to have much more of it in future. Once he had his hands on Lanchester's fortune he would spare no expense for his own comforts. He enjoyed good living and liked to indulge himself – and he liked to gamble. It was unfair that Lanchester should have all that money and he barely enough to keep body and soul together.

It was also unfair that Corinna should love his uncle and not himself. He had admired her from the first moment he set eyes on her, and the thought of bedding her had lived with him for a while. Well, he had her at his mercy now. He smiled unpleasantly. He had left her alone while she was quiet in the carriage for fear that she would cause trouble, but now she was safely locked up with no hope of escape there was no reason why he should not indulge himself a little.

What did it matter if she screamed and fought him? No one would hear her – no one but the bullyboys he had employed to help him kidnap her. The man he needed most had not yet shown up, but he would surely be here by morning. The lure of the huge sum of money he had offered would draw the fool here, and Lanchester might arrive by the next evening. All the threads would then be in place for the double murder – three by the time he had finished, he thought, drinking the rest of his wine. He felt very pleased with his own cleverness. The promise of all that money and power was going to his head. It made him hard, a throbbing heat in his loins as he thought of Corinna upstairs.

She was there; his for the taking. And he was in just the mood for a little rough stuff. It would not be the first time he had raped a reluctant woman, like the maidservants he had tumbled without a thought for anything but his own pleasure. Corinna had insulted him too often and it would give him pleasure if she struggled. He would enjoy seeing her humbled; a few well-aimed blows and she would lose that superior manner of hers that he found so infuriating. It would be amusing to teach her a lesson or two.

Picking up his candlestick, he started for the stairs. His head was slightly muzzy from the wine, but he still had the urge and the power to show that bitch just who was the master now.

Corinna heard the slow, heavy tread of a man's footsteps. She had begun to think they meant to starve her, but perhaps this was her supper on its way now. She reached out behind her to the chamber pot she had used earlier, touching its reassuring solidity with her fingertips. Someone was going to be very, very sorry before she was finished!

She tensed as the key was inserted in the lock and then turned. Should she attack at once or wait until the man was right in the room? As he entered, she was surprised to see it was Tobias himself rather than one of his henchmen. There was no sign of a supper tray. He seemed to sway slightly as he stood looking about him, and she realized then that he had been drinking.

'Do you mean to starve me?' She went on the attack immediately, sensing that he had come for some purpose. 'I have eaten nothing since this morning.'

'It will do you good to go hungry for once,' Tobias snarled. His eyes narrowed as the fuzziness in his head cleared and he saw her properly for a moment. 'Why are you standing over there?'

'Did you expect to find me sleeping? Is that why you came – to attack me when I was defenceless?'

'Shut your mouth, bitch,' he muttered. 'I've come to teach you a few manners; a lesson you will not soon forget.'

Corinna had heard those words many times before, but from a master in the art of cruelty, not a drunken sot. Her fingers sought out the pot behind her, her mind working quickly as he advanced towards her. She willed herself to stand still, to let him come to her so that the surprise would be all the greater. He was smiling in that superior way, imagining her helpless, perhaps expecting her to beg for mercy. But never once in the terrible days and nights of her marriage had she begged, and she would not start now.

Tobias hesitated. Something in her manner had got through to him. She ought to be frightened, weeping. He had wanted her to weep as he inflicted hurt on her, because she had wounded his pride, made him feel a fool. He wanted to humble her, but she was defiant.

'I see you do not realize what I mean to do,' he said and

205

then began to tell her word for word the humiliation he intended to inflict, laughing and nodding like a fool as a trickle of saliva ran from the corner of his mouth. 'Oh, yes, I shall have you on your knees yet, my proud beauty – and on your back.' He laughed as though he were very clever. 'Why don't you try to run away? His eyes narrowed in sudden suspicion. 'What are you hiding behind your back?'

He was very close to her now. She would never have a better opportunity. Corinna's hand fastened around the thick handle as she jerked the pot and swung it around, tossing the contents into his face. The urine went into his eyes, stinging them, blinding him as he stumbled back, clutching his face in shock, horror and sheer disbelief that she had done something so unexpected.

'You filthy bitch!' he cried, infuriated by her unexpected attack. He clawed at her, but his eyes were stinging too much to see properly and he yowled like a scalded cat, stumbling about the room as she neatly avoided his clumsy lunges. Then she was out of the room – for in his confidence he had forgotten to lock the door – and was starting down the stairs. 'Bones! Mick! She's escaping! Get the bitch! I'll make her pay for this if it's the last thing I do.'

Corinna reached the bottom of the stairs before the first rogue rushed out of a room to the right and made a grab at her. She avoided him and ran straight into the arms of a second. He was a great brute of a thing and caught her, circling her with his massive arms and swinging her off her feet as she struggled and screamed at him to let her go. He flung her over his shoulder, holding her across her backside as she kicked and pummelled at his back, screaming.

'Hold her, hold the bitch!' Tobias called as he came down the stairs. The top half of him was soaking wet and it seemed that he had tipped a jug of water over himself in an effort to remove the contents of the chamber pot. His face was red, his eyes painful as he struggled to see the woman who had humiliated him. If he had hated her before, his feelings were twice as bitter now, and it was all he could do to keep himself from ordering her immediate death. 'She has to be taught a lesson – bring her into the parlour, Bones.'

'Put me down!' Corinna demanded and, at a sign from Tobias, was unceremoniously dumped on the floor at his feet. She fell with a bang, winded and stunned, gazing up at him. He aimed a kick at her, which she avoided as best she could, but took on the shoulder. 'You deserved what you got, sir. No gentleman speaks to a lady as you did.'

'You are a harlot and a slut,' Tobias said and spat at her. 'I would kill you right now if I did not want to make sure of Lanchester. It may be necessary for you to write a letter begging him to come to you.'

'I shall never do that,' Corinna said scornfully. 'You may do your worst, sir. I shall not have a hand in luring Fitz here . . .' She broke off as loud noises came from the hall; there was a shout, a scuffle, and then a single shot. Alarm registered in Tobias's eyes. He motioned to the man called Bones.

'Go and see what's going on,' he ordered, then bent down and caught hold of Corinna's arm, dragging her to her feet and holding her in front of him, as though using her to shield his own body.

Had Fitz come for her? Corinna's heart gave a wild leap of joy, followed by fear. He must not walk into a trap for her sake!

Fourteen

'B e careful!' Corinna cried, and then felt Tobias's left hand close over her mouth, his right arm about her throat, making it impossible for her to either struggle or speak, for he was crushing her windpipe, squeezing the breath out of her.

She tried to break free, but he had her tight and she could do nothing. She heard more sounds from the hall, a muffled groan and then silence. Oh God, had that wretch hurt Fitz? If he was dead . . .

Corinna stopped struggling as she saw a man enter the room. It was Bones, but he had a pistol to his head, his arm twisted up behind his back, his eyes bulging with obvious terror. Relief swept through her as she saw who held the pistol, but fear for him still raged inside her.

'There are others,' she managed to gasp before Tobias tightened his hold, hurting her, silencing her.

'My men are dealing with them,' Fitz said. But this was a man she had never seen, his eyes like black diamonds glittering with a cold anger. 'If he has harmed you he will pay for it, Corinna. Believe me, he will pay.'

'I'll kill her if you come a step closer,' Tobias said and jerked his arm so that she could not breathe and sagged against him. 'How the hell did you know where to find me?'

'Kill her and you will die seconds after her. Loosen your hold, man!' Fitz smiled oddly as the other obeyed. 'I have many eyes, Tobias. You made so many foolish mistakes. I have been watching you since the last attempt you made on my intended bride's life – and you will pay for all your sins at the end of the hangman's rope.'

'I'll take both of you with me,' Tobias cried. 'Her first and then you.' He smiled as he saw a face he knew behind Fitz. 'Your men have forgotten my ace card, Uncle. I think I win the trick. Kill him! Kill him now, Ringer!'

A man stepped forward, coming past Fitz into the room. It needed only a glance at his misshapen nose and ear to see that he had been a prize fighter at some time in his life. He looked fearsome and Corinna was terrified as she saw the wicked pistol in his hand. He would kill Fitz and it was all because of her.

Desperation gave her strength. Tobias had slacked his hold on her a little. She suddenly brought her elbow back sharply into his ribs, and at the same time kicked down on his ankle with the heel of her shoe. Taken by surprise, he gave a scream of rage and let her go, half pushing her so that she stumbled over the hem of her gown in her effort to move away from him.

'Protect yourself, Fitz,' she cried, staring up at them from where she lay. Then Ringer was bending over her, holding out his hand to her. His smile was encouraging, reassuring, not at all as if he meant to kill her, and yet she could not trust him. She scrabbled away from him, looking to Fitz to see why he did not act. 'He means to kill us both – and you, sir, if you are his assassin. He told me so!'

'It is all over,' Fitz said and pushed hard on Bones's shoulder so that he was forced down into a kneeling position. 'You were always a fool, Tobias. Did you really imagine it was so easy to deceive me? Take over here, Ringer. I shall deal with my nephew myself.'

'Don't kill me, sir,' Bones begged as a different pistol was held to his head. 'I was only doin' a job. I'll work fer you if you let me go. I never killed anyone in me life.'

'Take him to join the others,' Fitz said with a jerk of his head. Corinna watched as Bones was hauled to his feet and made to walk from the room, his head bowed, the pistol trained relentlessly against it. 'I can manage here. Corinna, come here to me, my love.' Fitz's pistol was aimed at Tobias's heart, but for a moment his eyes flicked to her anxiously. 'Has he harmed you? Has he . . .'

She was on her feet now. She moved towards him, trying to keep clear so that she did not block his view of Tobias, but for just one moment Fitz was distracted, and in that instant, his nephew took a tiny pistol from his coat pocket. Corinna saw it, screamed and moved instinctively to put her own body in front of Fitz's. The shot echoed in her ears and she felt the ball thud into her shoulder, and then she was falling, falling into the void.

She neither saw nor heard what happened afterwards. Two shots were fired above her unconscious form; one going wide, the other finding its mark.

'It will not be the first time I've taken a ball out of someone's shoulder, my lord,' Reed said as Fitz hovered anxiously at his back. 'Might I suggest that you go away and leave this to me, sir?'

'You may suggest whatever you please,' Fitz growled. 'Just don't expect me to take any notice. Remember, it was me you took the ball out of last time, and I know how it hurts.'

'If you would prefer to call out a surgeon . . .'

'In these parts?' Fitz swore loudly. He knew there was no alternative, but he was terrified that she would die. 'Wouldn't know where to look for one. You'd best do your worst, man, or she'll bleed to death.'

'I assure you that is not the case,' Reed replied patiently.

'If your lordship could spare a moment . . .' Herbert Jones was at the door behind him. Fitz looked at him impatiently. 'Mr Reed will look after her, sir, and this needs your attention.'

'I'll be back,' Fitz barked at his long-suffering valet. 'If you let her die . . .' But he held back his threat and went to see what his agent wanted. Reed would do all he could, and he was as skilled as most surgeons. 'What is so important that it can't wait?'

'Your nephew is conscious and asking for you, sir.'

'It's a pity my shot didn't kill him,' Fitz muttered.

'You aimed slightly too high, sir,' Jones told him bluntly. 'A pity that, if you don't mind my saying so, your lordship. If he was dead it would be an easy matter to dispose of the body as it were – but what are we to do with him now?'

'Reed will attend to his wound later,' Fitz said. 'Let him suffer. It is only a matter of time until he finds himself at the end of the hangman's noose.'

'He is threatening to expose certain activities of your lordship's,' Herbert said with a little cough. 'Might it not be better to get rid of him in another way?'

'Smother the runt?' Fitz asked. 'I'll break his neck if he threatens me with blackmail.'

'No doubt your lordship can refute his claims that you habitually meet and consort with rogues of all kinds, sir.'

Fitz quirked an eyebrow. 'It seems Tobias isn't quite the fool I took him for – so what are we to do with him? I won't be a party to murder. Had my shot killed him that is one thing; to do murder is another. I've done nothing wrong, you understand, but it would cause a damned scandal if word of my, shall we say, slightly reckless activities got out . . .'

'Just so, sir. I had thought your lordship might send him on a long holiday to the West Indies. He may die of a fever there as many do, or he may make his fortune and become a better man.'

'Would he consent to that alternative?'

Jones smiled. 'I daresay any man would take transportation over a hanging, sir. They will plead any cause for it in the courts – but I was not suggesting that we ask the young man's permission.'

'Do what you want with him as long as it is not murder.' Fitz looked over his shoulder. 'Is that all?'

'What of the men he employed?'

'Give them a few guineas and send them off,' Fitz said.

211

'I doubt they bear enough of a grudge to bother what becomes of their paymaster.'

'They will run for their lives,' Herbert predicted and grinned. 'Right you are, sir. You can go back to your lady now – a very brave lady from what I hear, sir.'

'She is a damned fool,' Fitz muttered, his face working with emotion. 'Why did she do it? Answer me that.'

'The fair sex are a mystery, my lord; there's not a man living knows how to work out what goes on in their heads. I daresay she thought she was saving your life, sir.'

'At what cost to herself?'

Fitz felt the knife of grief cut deep. He would far rather be dead than forced to see Corinna shot down in front of him, to know that her life hung in the balance.

Leaving Herbert to sort out the fate of his nephew, Fitz went back into the bedroom. Reed was gripping something bloody with a pair of tiny forceps. He looked up with a smile of triumph and dropped the ball and instrument into a basin on the table by the bed.

'There, my lord; it wasn't so very bad, was it?'

'How should I know, since Herbert conveniently took me out of your way?' Fitz went to stand by the bed, gazing down at the woman he loved. She looked very pale, her eyes closed, the lashes fluttering on her cheeks. As he watched, a little moan escaped her. 'Did it come out clean – no shattering of the bone?'

'Very little, my lord. I think we have been lucky.'

'Will she take a fever?'

'I imagine she may,' Reed said. 'I have done my utmost to protect her, sir, but these are not the best of circumstances.'

'This blasted house,' Fitz snarled. 'It is not fit for pigs, let alone a delicate lady.'

'Not so very delicate, my lord. I imagine she has suffered worse.'

'You mean the scars on her back?' Fitz shook with the force of his emotion. 'Her husband did that to her, Reed. He beat her with a cane because she defied him – beat the child out of her deliberately. I had no idea. When I knew . . . if he hadn't been dead, I should have killed him. He was a vindictive beast.'

'Indeed, my lord. Any man who can inflict that sort of pain on a lady does not deserve to live.' He laid a hand on Fitz's shoulder for a brief moment. 'I must finish my work and then she should sleep.'

'I thank God for you and your potions, Reed,' Fitz said. 'I think she would have died if you had not been here.'

'Perhaps,' Reed replied with a slight smile. 'My purpose in life is to serve you and my lady, sir. I have none other.'

Fitz nodded. 'Get on with it then; I'll not interfere. When you've done I'll sit with her.'

'As she did with you that night, sir.'

'And I served her ill for it,' Fitz said with a rueful look. 'You have no need to remind me. I know that I have been less than careful of her in the past. If it is granted to me I shall make amends in future.'

'Just so, my lord.' Reed smiled as he bent to his task once more. He knew his master of old and his temper. He was given to thoughtless rages at times, and many called him a rogue, but there was none more loving in his heart. He prayed the lady lived, for if she died, his master would know no peace.

Fitz sat by Corinna's side until dawn, when Reed managed to pry him away for long enough to shave him and wash Corinna. It was not fitting that Reed should do such intimate tasks for her, but there was no one else, although Fitz had sent word to her companion and it was hoped that help was on the way. If fortune favoured him, her ladyship's maid would take over from him before she even realized what was happening.

As yet she was still unconscious, and the fever that he had feared was upon her. He bathed her in cool water, settled her pillows and longed for the comforts of Amberly. It appeared that the sheets on the bed were the only ones to be found in the house. All the water had to be carried from an outside pump that had seen better days. The kitchen was naught but a ruin, and the water had to be heated over a fire in the parlour, which did not help Reed in his efforts to care for his mistress.

When Fitz came back to the room, he motioned to him to lift her from the pillows while he forced a little of the fever mixture he always carried in his baggage into her mouth. She moaned and some of it dribbled down her chin, but he noticed with satisfaction that she had also swallowed.

'At least she still lives, sir,' he said encouragingly as Fitz's face worked with his emotion. 'And I believe she is a strong and determined young lady.'

'But she suffers,' Fitz said and his hands curled into fists that he smashed together in his anguish. 'It should be me, Reed. I want it to be me. Let me feel her pain; let me die in her place if need be.'

'Now that is foolish, sir,' Reed scolded as if talking to the boy he had first taken in hand as a young man. It had been Reed who had comforted him after his father's death, Reed who had gone with him to the West Indies and watched as the spoiled youth became a man. 'You must be strong for her. She will need you when she starts to recover. You must be here for her, to help her.'

'If only there was something I could do!'

'If you really wish to be of help . . .' Reed drew a breath as his master looked at him. 'We need more wood for the fire, sir. It would also be of use if someone were to go to the village and see if there is a doctor to be had.'

'I sent Herbert Jones to see if he could find someone an hour ago,' Fitz said. 'There are few provisions here. We need food and wine, and other things. Herbert is the man to find them if they are to be had in the district. I'll chop the wood myself. At least I can be of some use there.'

Reed smiled oddly as his master went out. It was a menial task, and one that the Marquis of Lanchester would normally not consider, but it would do him good – work some of the aggression out of him. And it left Reed free to get on with the essential job of looking after Lady Dorling.

Fitz felt the axe slide into the dry wood, watching as it fell into logs that would burn well on the parlour fire. It gave him some satisfaction doing a job that he would never ordinarily have thought of doing. He could feel the ache beginning in his shoulders, for despite his strength he was not used to such work. He was glad of the pain; it helped to ease the fear inside him.

Corinna had looked so vulnerable in that bed. He knew what pain was, how it sapped even the strongest man's vitality, and his heart ached for what she must suffer even if she lived. Damn Tobias! Would that he had killed him. He almost regretted allowing the rogue his life. He had deserved to die at the rope's end like the wicked wretch he was – and yet murder was a foul thing. He did not think Corinna would approve if he had told them to kill the rogue.

Oh, God! What was he to do if she died? He did not think that he could bear it. His life would have no meaning; his plans for the future would be worthless.

He looked at the pile of kindling and realized there was probably enough for a month. Surely they would not be forced to stay in this pigsty for so long! He wanted to take his love back to Amberly, where she would have every comfort, but she could not be moved until her wound had begun to heal.

The day dragged on, the hours seeming to pass so slowly. Fitz divided his time between sitting with Corinna and performing some of the necessary tasks about the house. Herbert had returned with a country doctor, who examined Corinna, looked grave and commended Reed on his work.

'Your man knows as much as I in the treatment of such wounds, sir,' he told Fitz before he left some twenty minutes later. 'I have given him some powders that may help with the pain if she wakes, but there is little we can do except pray for the poor lady.'

Fitz ground his teeth, kept his hands at his sides when he would have liked to shake the fool until his teeth shook. Catching Reed's look, he controlled himself with difficulty and asked the man to see himself out.

'Mr Jones will pay your fee, sir.' His temper exploded as the physician clattered down the stairs. 'Damn him! He might as well have stayed at home for all the use he was.'

'The powders will help when her ladyship wakes, my lord.'

'She will wake? Promise me!'

Reed saw that he was in agony, almost to the point of breaking.

'We shall need some hot soup, sir,' he said. 'I believe Mr Jones managed to find us some provisions. If you could get the kitchen range working it would be a help.'

'The kitchen range?' Fitz stared at him blankly. 'I have no idea how the damned thing works.'

'I do not think it beyond your powers of deduction, sir.'

Fitz glared at him. 'You will be telling me to scrub the scullery floor next,' he muttered.

'Cleanliness is a blessing,' Reed replied, hiding his desire to smile at his master's outrage. 'Of course, if you can't manage the range I am sure Mr Jones might know what to do.'

'I can manage,' Fitz said and went out. If he did not know better he would think that he was being given jobs to do to keep him out of Reed's hair.

Between them, Fitz and Herbert managed to clear out the collected dirt and debris from the old range, which included sweeping the chimney with a brush Herbert had discovered in one of the cupboards. He concentrated on scrubbing out the ovens, while Fitz swept the chimney, a task that left him with black hands and arms.

'I thought there were climbing boys for this,' he muttered, tasting the soot on his tongue and spitting it out in disgust.

216

'Indeed, sir,' Herbert agreed congenially. 'Poor little devils. Their masters often light a fire under them to make them climb, but as it is we don't have a boy and if you want this range to work without smoking us all to death . . .'

'I shall have to do it, shan't I?' Fitz gave him a rueful grin and stuck his head up the wide chimney again. This time he dislodged a bird's nest, which fell down on him, covering him in dried muck, feathers and twigs. 'I think it is clear now.'

'Well done, my lord,' Herbert said. 'You look rather black, sir. You had best go and wash your head in the yard – can't go up to see her ladyship like that.'

Fitz gave him a look meant to kill at six paces and went out into the back yard. He had to pull water from the well, because the ancient pump had broken and would need to be mended before it could be used again. He filled a bucket and sluiced himself, stripping his shirt off. At least he had a clean one in his saddle pack – Reed had seen to that. He straightened up, looking at the backs of his knuckles that had rubbed raw while he was attacking the neglected chimney.

What was it Jones had told him about masters lighting a fire under their climbing boys? Over his dead body! It would never happen again in his houses. There should be a law to stop such wickedness and he would do what he could to see the practice was stopped.

He drew more water, thinking he might as well take it and save one of the men from coming out to fetch it later. Herbert had just begun to make a chicken broth and cook some bacon for their supper. The menial tasks were all he was fit for, so he might as well make himself of use.

'You should not be doing that, my lord,' a woman's voice said and he glanced up to see Anne Crabtree. He was at the back of the house and had not heard her carriage arrive. 'Is there no one else to do such tasks? It is as well that I thought to bring Corinna's maid and some of the menservants with me. We shall soon have this place looking more the thing, I promise you.'

'Thank God you have come, ma'am,' Fitz said, going towards her. He was conscious of being naked to the waist and slung his wet shirt over him. 'Forgive me, I have been cleaning the chimney . . .'

'My goodness!' she exclaimed. 'What are things coming to? I never heard the like – nor saw it, either. How on earth did you come to be here, sir?'

'You received my message – that Corinna is hurt?' She nodded. 'We dare not move her until her wound starts to heal. I know this place is not fitting, but we must make the best we can of it.'

'For that you may rely on me,' she said. 'Mr Jones asked me to see you first, my lord – but I should like to be taken to Corinna now if I may.'

'Of course. My man has been looking after her. Reed is an excellent surgeon, though he has never been trained to it. He removed the ball from her shoulder and has cared for her since. She might not now be living if it were not for him.'

'She told me how good he was when you were ill,' Anne said. 'Well, I am glad to be here, for it seems you need me. I thought to bring some linens with me, and more goods are following. We must do what we can to make this place habitable, sir.'

'It is hardly that, ma'am, but with your help must improve.'

'Oh, you will be surprised what a few extra pairs of hands may do,' Anne said. 'Though I can see your people have done their best.'

'We need a woman's touch.'

Anne smiled and turned back into the kitchen. If that broth was to be edible, it was clear that she must take it in hand as soon as possible.

Fitz sat by the bed, his eyes half closing as drowsiness crept over him, but they were wide open in an instant when he heard Corinna's faint cry. He got up and bent over her, gazing down as he saw her eyelids flicker. And then she had them open and was gazing up at him, a puzzled expression in their azure depths.

'My lord?' she whispered. 'Where am I? Have I been ill?' She licked her bottom lip. 'My throat is so dry. May I have some water?'

'Yes, of course, my love,' he said and took a glass from the table beside the bed. Lifting her gently, one arm about her shoulders, he held the glass to her lips but would only let her sip it. 'Reed says you must not have too much at a time.'

'Is Reed here? Am I at Amberly?'

'No, Corinna. This place is called Wintering Manor, and it is a crumbling ruin far from anywhere, I fear. Do you not remember how you came to be here?'

'I was brought . . . by Tobias,' she said, her voice little more than a croak. 'A sip more of water, if you please, and then I would sleep.'

'Yes, of course.' He gave her the water and then laid her back against the pillows, bending to place a soft kiss on her brow as her eyes closed. She sighed and a smile touched her lips for a moment.

Fitz remained staring down at her for a few moments, and then he became aware that he was crying, tears falling down his cheeks and wetting her face. He had not cried since he was a boy and his pet dog had been put down because it had the mange.

'Oh, Corinna,' he said, his voice catching. 'Corinna, I thought you were going to die. Thank God . . . Thank God . . .'

'And Reed, my lord,' Anne said as she came into the room and heard his cry. 'I think your man has saved her life. When I arrived, I feared that she might never recover.'

'I can never repay him,' Lanchester said.

'He would ask for nothing but to serve you,' Anne told him with a gentle smile. 'You are as a son to him, my lord.'

'Such devotion deserves reward, and shall have it,' Fitz

said in a choking voice. 'She is sleeping peacefully now. I shall leave her – but you will call me if . . .'

'You will be sent for when she is able to see you,' Anne said. 'You should rest now, sir.'

'Perhaps. You have made me redundant,' he said and smiled oddly. 'I have no more jobs to do.'

'Why not go for a ride?' she suggested. 'When you return, we may have good news for you.'

'Yes, it would be good to take some exercise.'

He inclined his head and went out. If Corinna continued to improve they might be able to leave soon, and he had business that must be attended to at Amberly. Their wedding had been planned for a week's time, but it must be put back for some weeks, until Corinna was well enough to enjoy it. Amberly was but three and a half hours' hard riding. He could be there and back before nightfall.

Corinna would probably sleep most of that time, and she would want the attentions of her maid when she woke. He could be there and back before she realized he had gone.

'I thought Fitz was here,' Corinna said as she looked up into the face of her companion. 'Was I dreaming?'

'No, indeed, my love,' Anne told her with a smile. 'He has sat with you every night since you were hurt so badly. I sent him off because he was in need of something to do.'

'Oh . . .' Corinna felt a sense of disappointment. She had dreamed so pleasantly of Fitz and wished that he might be here with her. 'My shoulder is quite sore.'

'I imagine it is very painful,' Anne said. 'The doctor left some powders for you to take if you were in pain – shall I mix one for you?'

'It will make me sleep,' Corinna said. 'I want to be awake when Fitz comes to visit me.'

'Shall I go down and see if I can find him?'

'Would you mind?'

Corinna lay back against her pillows as Anne went out.

Her dream had been so sweet. She and Fitz had been walking in the rose garden at Amberly, and he had picked a rose, presenting it to her with a kiss. Now she had woken to a strange bedroom, a fearful pain in her shoulder and no sign of Fitz. Where was he – and why had he left her when she needed him?

In another moment she knew that she was being unfair. She had others to watch over her and he must have many things to do without sitting in this stuffy room.

She closed her eyes but the sweet dreams had gone and now she was haunted by frightening memories. She knew that Tobias had shot her. He had meant to kill Fitz, but she had thrown herself in front of him, foolishly some would say, but she had acted instinctively to save the man she loved.

Where was he? She needed him here to banish the shadows from her mind. The pain was so bad that she hardly knew how to bear it, and she felt the tears trickle down her cheeks, though in an instant she had dashed them away.

Anne returned looking upset. 'Forgive me, Corinna. When I sent Lanchester out for a ride I thought to give him an hour's relief from his anxiety, but it seems he has ridden over to Amberly and taken Mr Jones with him. It will be nightfall before he can return to us.'

'Oh!' Corinna sighed. 'The pain is very bad now. Perhaps I should take one of those powders.'

'I am certain you should, my love,' Anne said. 'I consulted with Reed and he insists that you must be kept quiet and peaceful for another day or two.'

'Was Reed here with me at the start? I seem to remember him helping me.'

'He did everything for you at the beginning. Your maid and I have tended you since we came, but it was Reed who saved your life.'

'Thank him for me,' Corinna said. 'Ask him to come and see me tomorrow. I shall feel better then.'

Corinna was not destined to feel better by the morning.

By the time Fitz returned from Amberly, bringing with him several more servants and some comforts they desperately needed, Corinna was once more in the grip of a fever.

When he learned that she had woken and asked for him, he was distraught and would not leave her throughout that night, sleeping briefly in a chair and waking fitfully each time she cried out. The fever seemed even worse than before, and Fitz sent for his own doctor to come from Amberly, but by the time he arrived it had begun to wane.

Corinna woke again to see Fitz bending over her, tenderly bathing her forehead with a cool cloth. She smiled up at him and caught his hand. Thankfully, her shoulder no longer felt as if a burning iron was thrust into it, but she was very weak, her lovely hair lank with sweat.

'So you have come back to us at last,' Fitz said as she looked at him. 'You frightened me, Corinna. I truly thought we had lost you this time. Even Reed had begun to lose hope.'

'I am sorry to have worried you all,' she said and let her hand lay in his as he sat on the edge of the bed, looking down at her anxiously. 'It was very foolish of me.'

'It was foolish of you to throw yourself in front of me,' Fitz told her. 'Very brave, but very foolish. I wish you will not do such a thing again.'

'Are you likely to be attacked often?' There was a faint gleam in her eyes and Fitz smiled in relief. It seemed that she had come back to him at last. 'I must make a note of your instructions, my lord. I should not like to be at odds with my husband.'

'Oh, Corinna, my love,' he said, his voice breaking on a note of laughter mixed with tears. 'I see that you have not changed.'

'Would you have me chastened? Afraid of my own shadow?'

'You know that I would not.' He bent to kiss her brow. 'Will you have some broth if your maid feeds it to you? We have been making the damned things for days, but you would swallow hardly a drop while in the fever.'

'I should imagine not,' she said with a show of spirit. 'I cannot stand broth. I will take a little clear soup if you please, or a coddled egg.'

'Not broth?' Fitz looked amused. 'After our friends have gone to such trouble to make it for you?'

'You can eat it for me,' she said and reached for his hand, her eyes moving over his face. 'You look tired to death, Fitz. Have you been keeping late nights?'

'You might say that,' he replied with a wry grin. 'I was obliged to visit Amberly and set our wedding back a month.'

'And why did you do that?' She struggled up on to her elbows. 'I shall be perfectly well in a few days.' But even as she spoke she knew it was a lie. Her head was going round and round, and she felt as weak as a newborn lamb. 'At least, a week or so will serve.'

'You will do as the doctor tells you, my love,' Fitz said. 'I cannot go through all this again. It was far worse than being ill myself.'

'I am feeling much better,' she declared. 'At least my shoulder does not feel so painful now.'

'I know exactly what you are going through, my love,' he said ruefully. 'I have been shot more than once and it never gets any easier.'

Corinna lay back against her pillows. It had taken more effort to try and raise herself than she had imagined. She closed her eyes for a moment, taking her time to recover. When she opened them again, Fitz was still sitting there looking at her.

'When did you recover your memory?' she asked. 'Did it come back all at once?'

'Recover . . .' Fitz had not realized what he was saying, and for a moment he was lost for words. 'Ah yes, I see . . .'

'You didn't lose it at all, did you?' Her eyes flashed accusation at him. 'You were pretending all the time. I wondered more than once, for you did not behave as a man struggling to remember who and what he was, but I could not see why you did not tell me the truth. Obviously, I realize now that you were trying to keep it secret from Tobias – did you not trust me to keep your secret?'

'It was better that you did not know.'

Corinna's gaze never left his face. 'Why? Because you thought I would accidentally betray you or . . .' Her eyes widened and suddenly the colour left her face. 'Did you think that I might be involved with the person who had set upon you?'

He remained silent, for how could he answer her at such a moment? 'This is not the moment to discuss these things, Corinna. You know I love you—'

'Do I?' she asked, a touch of bitterness in her voice. 'How can I be sure, Fitz? Love and trust go hand in hand. If you believed that I might betray you – indeed, that I had plotted to have you killed after that night, that night I believed so special to us both – then you do not love me.'

'That is ridiculous,' he said. 'Why should I have come here if I did not love you? Why has it near driven me mad all this time you have been so ill?'

'I do not know,' Corinna replied. The ache about her heart was more painful than her shoulder at its worst. 'I have a headache and I need my maid to do certain things for me. Please go away now, Fitz. I want to be alone with my maid.'

'But you must know how much I love you!' There was a cry of despair in his voice. 'Corinna, I swear that I love you. It is true that for a while I wondered. There was Maxwell Everard's testimony – and then I was attacked again. I did not know who was my enemy and . . .'

'You thought it might be me,' Corinna said. The tears were stinging her eyes and she did not know how long she could keep them back in her present state of exhaustion. 'Please go away, Fitz. I shall send someone to tell you when I am ready to see you again.'

Rebellion flared in him. How could she be so cruel as to dismiss him when he had suffered so much agony for her sake? She must know that she meant everything to him. She must!

Fifteen

It took all of Fitz's willpower to keep from going to Corinna's room again that day. He sat alone in the parlour that night, brooding over the rift between them. He was tempted to drink too much of the fine wine he had brought with him from Amberly, but refrained. Getting drunk would not solve this problem. Indeed, he was not sure how it could be done. Corinna had the right to be angry, for he had not shown either trust or love towards her.

It was useless to try and explain that he had not been thinking clearly when he first recovered his senses, or when he returned to Amberly. The attack on him, so close to his own estate, had given him cause for much reflection. He had always imagined himself invincible, and to discover that he was as vulnerable as any other man had made him wary. He ought to have known that his enemy was not Corinna, for she had given herself to him so completely. Indeed, in his heart he had known it, but he had chosen to hold back, and though he had regretted it later, he had done nothing.

It was his own fault and it all came back to the same thing. Had he gone to Corinna's father in the first place, she would never have suffered an unhappy marriage, and none of this need have happened. What could he do to make amends? Would she ever forgive him?

Fitz was a man of action, and yet he knew that in this instance only patience would help his cause. Somehow he must win Corinna's love back. How he was to do that was a mystery, but it must be done, for he could not imagine his life without her.

'Why will you not see Lanchester?' Anne asked, looking puzzled. 'Surely the poor man does not deserve to be kept at a distance after all he has done? He suffered terribly when you were so ill.'

'It will do him no harm to wait until I feel well enough to receive him,' Corinna said, a sharp note in her voice. 'Did you know he lied to us about losing his memory, Anne?'

'Yes, he told me that at Dorling. I had suspected it before then and I asked him. He told me his reasons at once, which I understood perfectly.'

'But he might have told me. Surely he must have known that I would not betray him.'

'Intentionally, of course you would not,' Anne replied in her calm, gentle manner. 'But you might have done so without thinking. Remember, my love, Lanchester was not himself. He feared another attempt on his life. One cannot always think clearly in those circumstances. I for one am glad that I was not told, for I could not have been sure to keep his secret.'

Corinna looked at her reproachfully. 'You are defending him, Anne. I had thought you would take my side in this.'

'But of course I am on your side. However, I see no point in prolonging a quarrel over such a little thing. Will you throw away your chance of happiness for one mistake?'

'There have been many mistakes,' Corinna said crossly. It really was too bad of Anne to side with Lanchester! 'I have already forgiven him several times.'

'Then you may do so again. Love is forgiving, Corinna. I do not think it would be possible for a man and a woman ever to be happy together if *she* could not forgive. Men are careless creatures, my dear. They are impatient, hasty and often hurt one when they do not mean to – but if the love is there, we forgive them. That is the nature of marriage.'

'Was it that way for you?' Corinna looked at her curiously,

for she knew that Anne always held that her husband had been the best of men.

'Yes, of a certainty. We quarrelled quite dreadfully when we were young. I was hot-tempered then . . .'

'You – hot-tempered?'

'Yes, indeed,' Anne said and laughed as she saw Corinna's look of disbelief. 'I have grown older and wiser, and when my husband died I realized that I had been so lucky. It is not given to every woman to have such love. Yes, we disagreed – heatedly at times. He hurt me once or twice, but always he was sorry and he meant it. I daresay I may have hurt him unintentionally.'

'You are so much better than I,' Corinna said and smiled as Anne shook her head. 'Oh yes, you are – but you may be right. Fitz may stew for a while, for he deserves it, but I daresay I may forgive him in the end. You will not tell him I said that?'

'No, of course not,' Anne promised. 'I would not dream of betraying a trust – but I am glad that you are feeling more yourself, my love.'

'Yes, I do feel much better,' Corinna said. 'My shoulder is still very stiff, but the first terrible pain is easing, and I am not so tired. If I feel as well in the morning I shall get up and come downstairs.'

'Are you sure you feel able? The doctor advised at least ten days in bed, Corinna.'

'The doctor is an old woman,' Corinna replied. 'The summer is racing by and I want sunshine for my wedding, not rain and cold – that is if I decide to marry Fitz, of course.'

'Of course,' Anne replied hiding her smile. 'Very well, I shall leave you to rest now. Let us hope it is a nice day tomorrow and then you may sit in the garden.'

A chair had been placed for her in what had once been the rose garden; she had a parasol to hand and a book of poems, as well as a jug of restorative lemon barley water on the table next to her. It was the second day she had been out of bed and she had made her way here alone, refusing all offers of help.

Corinna was not sure why she was still keeping Fitz at bay. She had spoken to him since she began to leave her bedchamber. Her manner had been polite but cool, the barrier between them almost as much of his making now as her own. He had said nothing more of his feelings, nor had he asked her how she felt, merely saying that he was glad to see her so far recovered. She could not help regretting the rift between them.

The sun was warm on her face as she sat with her eyes closed, drowsing in the sunshine, and she woke with a little start as she felt something wet touch her hand. When she looked down, she saw that a young sporting dog, hardly more than a puppy, had come up to her and was licking her hand.

'Hello, little fellow,' she said and stroked its soft head, smiling as it wagged its tail and put its front paws on to her lap. 'Well, aren't you the friendly one? It is nice to meet you. What is your name?'

'He is called Rupert, after a gentleman who was good to me once,' Fitz said as he walked up to her. 'Is he annoying you?'

'No, of course not,' Corinna said, feeling a cold spurt of fear. 'Don't hurt him, please. I like him . . . You won't hurt him, will you, Fitz?'

'Of course not. Why should I? He's going to be a good gun dog. Besides, I've never harmed a dog in my life.' His eyes narrowed as he looked at her. 'Why did you imagine I would?'

Corinna blushed. Why had she thought for a moment that Fitz might hurt the dog merely to punish her for her coldness? It was unkind of her and showed a lack of trust. Momentary perhaps, but real for all that. Perhaps Fitz's decision not to tell her the truth had been little more – a moment of hesitation, which should be forgiven for both their sakes.

'It was foolish of me, but . . .' Her eyes filled with tears as the memory swept over her. 'My husband had all my dogs and horses put down because I wouldn't . . . I wouldn't tell him if you were the father of my child.'

'Good God!' Fitz stared at her in horror. 'How could a man do that to you? If he were here I would thrash him to an inch of his life and then string him up by his ankles to let the crows eat him alive.'

'Fitz!' Corinna said and then laughed at the absurdity of his statement. 'You would not . . . could not do such a thing. You might think it an excellent idea, but you would not do it.'

'To a man who hurt you the way he did? It's hardly punishment enough. I might do worse if I could think of it in time.'

'No, Fitz. You might thrash him in anger. I do not think you would do so in cold blood.'

'Why do you say that?'

'Because . . . Reed told me that you aimed high to avoid killing Tobias. You could easily have killed him had you wished.' She looked at Fitz curiously. 'What have you done with him? He isn't dead, is he?'

'I imagine at this very moment he is enjoying a sea voyage to the West Indies,' Fitz said grimly. 'Perhaps *enjoy* is not precisely the right word. He will have to work his passage as best he can, and when he gets there he will have to work to pay for his new life. If that does not make a better man of him, I do not know what will. It is a hard life out there but also a good one.'

'You spent some time there, I believe.'

'Yes. The opportunity was given to me at a time when I needed something to fill my life. I took it and came home a much richer man. If my nephew uses his opportunity well he may end up the same – or he may drink himself sense-less and die of a fever. The choice is his.'

'Let us hope he stays there and causes you no more trouble, Fitz.'

'He knows there is nothing but a hangman's noose waiting for him here. If he returns to England I shall not hesitate. I saw him before he was taken off to the ship, and I think he understands me somewhat better now.'

Fitz had arranged himself on the grass at her feet, Rupert lolling over him and panting in delight as his tummy was rubbed with firm, gentle fingers.

'You will spoil him,' Corinna remarked. 'He will not be fit for work if you continue to make a fuss of him.'

'I have decided that he is far too soft for a working dog,' Fitz said and smiled at her. 'I shall give him to you, Corinna. You shall have him for your own, since he has taken a liking to you and you to him.'

'I have not dared to love an animal since . . .' Corinna swallowed hard, conquering her emotion. 'Thank you. That is the nicest gift you could possibly give me, Fitz.'

'You shall have many others when we go home,' he said and smiled up at her as she reached down to stroke the dog and had her face licked enthusiastically. 'I shall be glad to be at Amberly, for you can be properly cared for there, my love. Everyone has done their best in the circumstances, but they have had much hardship to bear for our sakes. This old place is not fit to live in and should be pulled down.'

'Reed told me he had you chopping wood and sweeping the kitchen range,' Corinna said, a wicked light in her eyes. 'I confess I should have liked to see that, Fitz.'

'I daresay you might have found it amusing to see me covered in soot and bird muck,' he said with a mock scowl. 'It was my first attempt and, though successful, I assure you it will be my last.'

'Did you know that climbing boys are ill-treated?' Corinna asked with a frown. 'There is much poverty in our country, and many people live terrible lives. I saw it for myself in that hospital I visited. I shall do what I can to help those in need, Fitz. You will not object, I hope.'

'It is an interest we may share. I am thinking of taking my seat in the Lords, Corinna. In the past I have done . . . various things that may have righted a few wrongs, but it may be best if I try to work through the law in future rather than against it.'

'What do you mean?' She opened her eyes wide.

Fitz hesitated, and then he told her. He told her about the young girl he had first rescued and taken to a bawdy house because there was nowhere else he could take her apart from the workhouse.

'I felt as if I were sealing her fate,' he admitted honestly. 'But she did not wish to be a servant, for she said the mistress would work her to death and then throw her into the streets. I discovered later that she was with child and that was why she would not ask to be a servant. Fortunately, the woman I gave her to is decent enough. She helped her when the child came, had it adopted, and then . . .'

'But it is still wrong,' Corinna said. 'Wrong that there is no hope for a girl like that. We should have places where they can go to be helped – schools and nursing for their children.'

'Most of them never see their children. They are sold or given to the workhouses. Some miscarry because of ill treatment by their pimps. Or the mothers die of the pox . . .'

'It breaks my heart. Can nothing be done to help them?'

'There are those who try,' Fitz assured her. 'My friends and I have managed to close some of the worst of the houses where girls are forced to work against their will, but I doubt it will ever be ended. Brothels are as old as mankind, and will always exist in some form. For myself, I believe it would be best to have some form of control over them, so that there are strict rules and the girls are well cared for – much as Mrs Rose does for her girls.'

'That does not make it right, Fitz.'

'I can see that we shall have much to discuss of an evening,' he replied with a smile. 'But you must accept that we can only do so much, my dearest. The streets of London, and of every large city for that matter, are filled with poor wretches. Many of them only get through their miserable lives because they drink gin until they have no feelings left.'

Corinna shuddered. She had known what it was to suffer pain and humiliation, but she had never been starved, cold and alone with nowhere to sleep but the street.

'At least we can help the children,' she said. 'At the hospital I visited with Mr Selby, I saw the good work they were doing. Surely more places of that kind could be set up if people of like minds would help.'

'Selby is a good man,' Fitz agreed, 'and there are other hospitals and homes being built or refurbished – but there is only so much that can be done by philanthropists. You must know that Mr Jonas Hanway, besides giving us that wonderful thing the umbrella, has done much good for poor children. He has already put successful appeals before parliament that have led parishes to keep records of the poor, and through him there are children living in the country who must surely have died had they not been sent away from the poverty of their homes. Yet despite his work, and that of others, much more needs to be done. There must be changes in the law, in education and taxation, so that the lower classes have a chance to improve their own lives rather than relying on thievery or charity. And that will take a great deal of persuasion, my love.'

'It might take more than a man's lifetime.'

'Yes, indeed, I would think that very possible,' he said and smiled at her. 'But to strive for the impossible is interesting, is it not?'

'Yes, I think it would give purpose to a man's life.' Corinna smiled at him and ruffled the dog's soft coat as it pawed at her skirt. 'I think this scamp wants to finish his walk, Fitz. Take him as you intended, and then join me in the parlour for tea. I think we should make plans for returning to Amberly, and our wedding. Our guests will be imagining all kinds of things . . .'

'I was happy to receive an invitation to your wedding,' Robert Knolls told Corinna as he was shown into the small back parlour at Amberly where she sat at a pretty writing desk, making a start on correspondence that had been long neglected. 'And Angela is very excited about meeting you.' He turned and beckoned to a young woman who was hovering somewhere behind him. 'Come, my dear. There is no need to be nervous.'

'No need at all,' Corinna said and stood up to greet her father's wife, who was tiny and pretty and looked fragile. She was carrying a beautiful wickerwork cage in which four yellow canaries were twittering as they hopped from one perch to another. 'How lovely. I used to have birds when I was a girl.'

'So your papa told me,' Angela said. 'These are my own present to you, Lady Dorling. Robert has something more valuable, but . . .'

'Nothing could be more welcome to me,' Corinna said and took the cage from her, looking at the pretty creatures for a few moments and then setting the cage where its inhabitants could see the garden and feel the warmth of the sun. 'So beautiful, and I shall love to hear their whistling. I shall have a large aviary placed outside my window so that they may go outside while the weather is mild. Thank you very much, Angela. I am very glad to have your gift, and to welcome you to Amberly.'

The girl blushed but looked pleased, coming to sit beside Corinna on the little gilt-framed sofa near the window. 'Were you writing your letters when we arrived? I love to write letters, but best of all to receive them. Especially when my friends have been somewhere exciting.'

'Then perhaps we shall become correspondents,' Corinna said. 'Writing letters to my friends is one of the chiefest joys of my life, Angela. Tell me, what else gives you pleasure?'

'Oh, I like to walk on fine days, and to read poetry. I love music, though I am an indifferent exponent.'

'Do not believe her,' Robert said with a fond smile. 'She plays the spinet very well.'

Angela blushed and shook her head. 'But my greatest joy is looking after my son,' she said. 'He is so wonderful – isn't he, Robert?'

'Yes, m'dear,' he replied. 'You will give me your opinion when you see him, Corinna. I believe he has my eyes.'

'Has he been taken to the nursery?'

'Yes,' Angela said. 'I wasn't sure if you would want to see him. He was crying when we arrived and you have been ill . . .'

'I am much better now. May I see your son, Angela? I should so like to. I lost my own baby . . .'

'Oh, poor you,' Angela said with ready sympathy. She jumped to her feet at once. 'Do come and look at little Bobby and tell me if you think he is the spitting image of his father.'

'I am sure you were wrong to doubt her,' Corinna told her father when they were alone later that afternoon. 'The child is very like you, Father – and Angela is a sweet girl. Her flirting is innocent, I am convinced of it.'

'I daresay you are right and I am a jealous fool,' he said ruefully. 'Whatever the truth, I shall bear it. I learned my lesson well, Corinna. Angela will never suffer my anger as you did. I only wish I could go back and reverse what I did to you.'

'The birds were your idea, were they not?' Corinna smiled as a hot red colour surged in his neck. 'It was your way of telling me how sorry you were for the threats you made.'

'I would never have carried them out. I might have raged and threatened, but I could not have done it.'

'My husband did,' she said. 'He fed the carcasses of my dogs and horse to his hounds and made me watch. And a week later he beat me until I lost my child.'

'I never knew that . . .' Robert looked at her in horror. 'No wonder you could never forgive me.'

'But I have,' she said. 'I have found happiness, Father. Tomorrow I shall marry the man I adore, a man who loves me, as he has proved many times. I have finally put the past behind me.'

'I have no doubt that Lanchester is a decent man. They tell me he does a fair bit for charity. A friend of yours – Mr

Selby, I believe – told me in confidence that Lanchester is on the board of several hospitals for foundlings. I have agreed to help fund one of the newer ones they are setting up. Angela was upset when she heard how some children are treated so ill, and she begged me to contribute, so I have.'

'I like your wife more and more,' Corinna said. 'I hope you will both visit with us whenever you can spare the time.'

'So I can forgive myself then?'

'Yes,' she said and kissed him on the cheek. 'Tomorrow you can give me to the man I love, Father. It is the start of a new life, and everything begins from then'

'You made a beautiful bride,' Fitz said when they were at last alone in their bedchamber, their guests having dispersed or retired for the night. In the morning they were to set out on their wedding trip, first to Fitz's house in Cornwall and from there to France. 'I was very proud of you, my love.'

'And I of you,' she said and reached up to touch his cheek with her fingertips. 'I love you very much, Fitz – but I hope I have not cheated you. Seeing my father with his new son this past couple of days has made me think that perhaps I have not been fair to you.'

'What do you mean?' His expression was grave as he looked down at her and saw that she was anxious.

Corinna gazed up at him, her eyes shadowed with doubt. 'I have wondered – I am afraid that what *he* did to me may prevent me from giving you a child. If that were so I should indeed have wronged you, for you must want an heir, Fitz.'

'For a moment you frightened me,' he said and laughed softly. 'If it is given to us to have a child – son or daughter – I shall rejoice. But if it is true that we cannot know that happiness I shall not blame you, nor shall I wish that I had married someone else.'

'Are you sure, Fitz?'

'Perfectly sure,' he replied and bent to kiss her, first on the bridge of her nose and then on the lips. Light at first, his kiss deepened to passion, and in another moment he picked her up in his arms and carried her to the bed, where he lay her gently amongst the silken covers. He sat on the edge of the bed, his hand stroking her cheek and then tracing the line of her throat to the sweet valley between her breasts that were scarcely hidden by the thin material of her night chemise. 'I love you and only you, Corinna. You are my wife, my world and my love. I want to be with you for the time that is allotted to us. I shall be faithful . . .'

'Even when I grow fat and ugly?'

He laughed as he saw the mischief in his eyes. 'Even then – but I do not think you will ever be ugly, my darling.' He bent over her, his lips teasing hers as he began to kiss her again. And then he was there beside her on the bed, pulling her night chemise over her head so that her lovely body was open to his hungry gaze. 'How could this ever be ugly to me?'

Fitz bent his head, his lips and tongue lavishing adoration on every part of his body as he moved steadily from her throat, her breasts, her naval and then the moist centre of her femininity.

Corinna gave a start of surprise and then a little moan of pleasure as his tongue invaded her and she felt sensation so sweet that she could only writhe and whimper as he worked his magic on her. And then he was naked as she, his flesh pressed closed to hers as he held her to him, and they began the slow, sensuous dance of love.

Again and again that night they loved as one, finding pleasure that neither of them had ever known before. In the end they slept, entwined in each other's arms long after dawn had broken. The servants crept past their door and did not disturb them, though Rupert grew impatient and seized his chance to invade their paradise and jump on the bed, licking their faces until they woke.

'Thank you, that will be quite enough of that,' Fitz said and groaned. 'Did I really give you this animal, Corinna? I must have been mad. I suppose I shall have to get up and take him for a walk or he will lick me to death.'

Corinna laughed for he was merely teasing her, and she knew him to be a man she could respect, trust and love without fear.

Corinna stood in the gardens of the French chateau, gazing down at the wooded slopes through which she could just catch a glimpse of the sea. It looked very blue in the sunshine, and the day was extremely warm. She wondered if the heat explained her recent moment of faintness. She gasped as it came over her again, and for a second she swayed unsteadily, pressing her hand to her forehead as a slight moan escaped her.

'Is something wrong?' Fitz had been throwing sticks for Rupert to retrieve, and now he came back to her, looking at her in concern. 'Are you feeling unwell?'

'I was faint for a moment,' she said. 'But it is passing now. I shall be well enough soon . . .' But before she could finish her sentence the ground came zooming up to meet her and she would have fallen had Fitz not caught her in his arms.

She came round a few seconds later as he carried her back to the chateau where they were staying with friends of Fitz's, gazing up at his anxious face as he lay her gently on a chaise longue and knelt beside her.

'Oh, how foolish of me,' she said. 'I daresay it was the heat. It is exceptionally warm today, Fitz.'

'No, it is not particularly warm,' he corrected her. 'This is early October, Corinna, and the weather is pleasantly warm. It was not the heat that made you swoon, my love. I have noticed that you seemed a little quiet for a couple of days now.'

'Yes, that is true,' she admitted. 'I have felt a little unwell.'

'I shall have the doctor sent for immediately,' Fitz said and stood up. 'Stay where you are until I return, Corinna, and then I shall carry you upstairs.'

'I am sure I can walk. I am much better now.' She sighed and lay back as she saw his frown. They had been married for six weeks now, and she knew better than to go against him when he was so anxious for her sake. It was as if their love, having come to them so much later than it might, had made him overprotective of her. He was afraid of losing her because she had become too precious to him.

Fitz returned within a very few minutes, telling her that someone had been dispatched to bring the doctor to her, and then he lifted her carefully in his arms, carrying her upstairs to the luxurious suite of rooms that were theirs for this visit. After laying her gently down, he summoned her maid to make her comfortable and then went downstairs to await the doctor.

Corinna lay gazing up at the beautifully painted ceiling of her bedchamber. The chateau was luxurious beyond imagining, its furniture gilded and painted, its upholstery of the finest silk brocades. The gentleman who owned it had vast estates in the West Indies, and it was there that Fitz and he had become friends. Count Henri Lefarge was a rich man and his wife Marianna was a lady of both French and West Indian descent. They had three children, including one very beautiful daughter, her skin the colour of pale coffee.

Corinna had made friends with Marianna and invited her to visit with them at Amberly in the future. She had fallen in love with their daughter, Julie, and it had increased her own longing for a child threefold. Fitz had declared he would not mind if they could not have children, but for Corinna it was the one thing needed to seal their happiness.

She had wondered if the sickness she had endured on two separate mornings, and now this faintness might be a sign that she was carrying a child, but she had not dared to hope or to mention the possibility to Fitz.

She closed her eyes, trying to block out the hope that had begun in her mind. She must not let herself hope for something that might never be. After her miscarriage she had been warned that she was damaged inside and that it would be difficult and perhaps impossible for her to bear children in the future.

Opening her eyes when the doctor entered, Corinna saw that he was a young man, and when he spoke she realized he was English.

'I am Doctor Robinson, here on holiday with my friends. I was delighted to be of service when I heard you were taken ill. If you would like to tell me exactly how you have been feeling, Lady Lanchester – and then perhaps I may examine you.'

Fitz had hovered in the doorway, but now he turned aside, giving her some privacy with the doctor. She explained her sickness and the faintness, and also that she had miscarried some years earlier. The doctor listened, nodded his head and then asked if he might lift her night chemise to examine her stomach.

'Is it what I hoped?' she asked when he had finished his work.

'There is no evidence of a malformation or disease,' he told her with a smile. 'I cannot be perfectly sure at this early stage, Lady Lanchester, but I imagine your hopes are more likely than illness.'

'Thank you . . . We were not certain it would be possible for me after the way I lost my child.'

'Would you like to tell me more details about your miscarriage?'

Corinna told him everything and saw his shock. 'I was warned that it might be difficult for me to bear a child to its full term, sir.'

'Yes, indeed, I can see why that might be the case. However, I think you should not let it overshadow your thoughts, Lady Lanchester. It may be best if you rest in the later stages of your confinement, but until then I see no reason why you should not live as you usually do. No horse riding, of course.'

'No, certainly not,' she agreed. 'Do you think it would be safe for me to return to England?'

'Not just yet. I should like to examine you again two weeks from now. If I think it safe then, I shall discuss it with Lord Lanchester. You will need to travel in easy stages, for too much jolting might be dangerous in the early months.'

'Thank you,' Corinna said and then asked anxiously, 'You will not worry him too much? He is overly concerned for me already.'

'I shall reassure him that you are a strong, sensible young woman, and that he ought not to worry unduly,' he promised as he left her.

However, downstairs in the parlour, he confided to Fitz that he was anxious concerning Lady Lanchester's ability to carry her child full term.

'She is a strong, sensible lady, but her past history means that she may miscarry, sir. I would not advise you to count on a living child, for you may be disappointed.'

'My wife is my main concern,' Fitz told him. 'If she would do better to remain here until after the birth we shall do so.'

'Well, I shall visit her in two weeks,' the doctor said. 'After that, I advise you to find another physician for her. I return home to England at the end of this month. However, there is a man in Paris I could recommend if you decide to stay here until the birth.'

'I would be grateful for his name,' Fitz said. 'I would take no risk where my wife's health is concerned.'

'Very well, I shall visit in two weeks, and in the meantime I shall confer with Monsieur D'Artois.'

Fitz thanked him and went back to the bedchamber where Corinna lay, her eyes closed. He bent over her, kissing her forehead, a terrible fear clutching at his heart. If he were to lose her now . . .

She opened her eyes and smiled at him. 'Do not look so worried, dearest. I am feeling much better. I shall get up in a moment and come down to the parlour.'

'Are you sure you ought?'

'You must not fret for a little faintness,' Corinna told him. 'It means nothing. Marianna visited me a moment ago. She told me that she had a terrible time with her first child, though the others were nowhere near so much trouble. She

241

has promised me something that her grandmother told her about when she was married. She says it will help the sickness and the faintness will pass in a week or two.'

'I love Marianna and her family dearly,' Fitz said. 'But she is not a doctor. Doctor Robinson is to consult with a physician in Paris who knows a great deal about ladies with a delicate constitution in such matters. I think perhaps we shall stay here in France until we are sure it would be safe for you to travel, Corinna.'

'But do you not have business at home? We have been away for more than six weeks already, Fitz.'

'My business can wait,' he said and bent to kiss her. 'If it becomes necessary for me to return, I shall leave you here and come back as quickly as possible.'

'If that is what you want,' Corinna said and took his hand. 'I do not want to lose our child, Fitz.'

'And I do not want to lose you.'

'Oh, you need not be concerned for me,' Corinna promised. 'I am as strong as a horse. Only wait and see – I shall be up and about in no time at all.''

In that she was proved right. By the time Doctor Robinson returned to examine her again, the faintness was gone and the sickness merely a memory. She had begun to feel really well, and was full of energy.

'Clearly you are very strong, and sensible,' the doctor told her. 'I believe my earlier fears were unnecessary. I shall tell your husband that he may safely take you home if you so wish, providing that you travel slowly and in easy stages.'

Corinna thanked him for his advice. When Fitz came to her afterwards, she told him that she wanted to go home at the end of that week. He was reluctant at first, despite having received the doctor's advice that it would do no harm, but Corinna's pleading persuaded him.

'If it is what you want, my love,' he said and kissed her.

'I think I should like to be at Amberly for the birth of our son,' she told him, and smiled as his brows raised. 'Marianna told me that it is always a boy when you feel as unwell as I did at the start.'

'Well, we shall see,' Fitz replied.

He was haunted by the doctor's warning that they must not hope too much for the birth of a living child, though he had said nothing of it to his wife. Corinna was so happy, and he knew that she would be devastated if she were to lose their child now.

Sixteen

There were but two weeks to go to the predicted birth of her child, and thus far Corinna had remained perfectly healthy if one did not count swollen ankles and a back ache that had caused her some sleepless nights. Angela was visiting with her, for she was three months into her second pregnancy, and they enjoyed each other's company.

'I know the last weeks are the worst,' Angela told her as they sat together in the parlour with their embroidery. 'One feels so huge and it is difficult to see one's feet.'

Corinna laughed. 'I feel so ungainly. I am sure I must waddle, though Fitz says that I look beautiful.'

'That is because he loves you,' Angela said and patted her stomach. 'Robert is much the same now, far more affectionate and considerate than he was the last time. Indeed, he almost drives me mad. If I rested as often as he would have me, I should have months of inactivity. I have tried to tell him that I am having a child, not a terrible illness, but it is to no avail. He will have it that I am delicate and I am not at all!'

Corinna smiled. 'You are very right, Angela,' she agreed. 'Sometimes I am hard put to keep my temper. Fitz behaves as if I was made of glass and would break if he touched me.'

'Well, at least he has gone to London for a few days.'

'I had great difficulty in persuading him that he should,' Corinna said. 'He was reluctant to leave me, but I told him he would be back in plenty of time for the birth.'

'How long did the doctor say?'

'About two weeks – why?'

'I would say it might be a little sooner,' Angela said. 'You have been so fidgety of late and you can scarce sit still – that is usually a sign that the birth is imminent.'

'Then I hope it will happen before Fitz gets home,' Corinna said. 'At least it will save him the pain of suffering while I am in labour.'

'Yes.' Angela smiled at her sympathetically. 'And it will be so much nicer when this is all over and you can be comfortable again.'

She stood up and went over to the long French windows. Rupert was outside, looking sad and forlorn, for he had been forbidden to come in during these last days, lest his boisterous behaviour be too rough for his mistress.

'Oh, poor thing,' Angela said. 'He looks so miserable out there.'

'Let him in,' Corinna said and stood up. 'I miss him and he cannot understand why he has been shut out.' She began to take a turn about the room, a hand to the small of her back as the ache became more of a pain. Behind her, she heard the panting and excited yelping that told her the dog had been let in and she turned just as he came bounding towards her, jumping up with the full force of his natural enthusiasm, his paws landing with a thud on her stomach. She gave a cry and staggered back, half falling and sitting on the sofa with a bump. 'Oh, the pain! It has started to hurt, Angela. Very badly . . .'

'I should never have let that brute in!'

'It wasn't his fault,' Corinna said. 'Besides, I told you to.' She clutched at her stomach as the pain ripped through her. 'Will you help me up the stairs, Angela – and then have the doctor summoned, please. I do not think Fitz's son is prepared to wait for another two weeks.'

Corinna screamed as the pain ripped through her again and again. Would the child never be born? She had sought her bed seven hours earlier and still the struggle went on. She had hoped the child would be born before Fitz's return so that he would not suffer, but now she longed for him. She wanted the comfort of his hand holding hers, the knowledge that he was with her. If she should die . . .

'Push, my lady,' a voice said close to her ear. 'I believe it is coming at last. One more push and we shall be there.'

'Reed . . .' She looked up, seeing his face through the mist of pain that seared her vision. 'I thought you were in town with Fitz.'

'I was, my lady, but he asked me to return yesterday – said he was uneasy in his mind and wanted me to be here should the child come early. He is on his way here even now, though he could not travel with me.'

'Fitz . . .' Her eyes filled with tears as the need for her husband swept over her. 'I am so tired, Reed . . . so tired.'

'You must not give up now,' Reed said. 'The battle is almost won and my lord will never forgive me if I let you leave him.'

'The doctor came but said it was in the Lord's hands and that I had some hours to go. He promised to return but has not,' Corinna said, her cheeks wet with tears. 'I believe he thought I would die and pleaded another pressing case.'

'We have no need of doctors,' Reed said as he looked down and saw the head emerging, its hair as dark as its father's. 'There, I can help you now, lass, it is all over, bar the last little push.'

Corinna felt the tears stream down her cheeks as she saw the child come out of her in a whoosh of blood and mess, to be scooped up by Reed in a linen wrap and placed in her arms so that she could feel him close to her.

'Oh, Reed . . .' she whispered. 'Tell me, is it the son we wanted?'

'Yes, you have a son, my lady; a beautiful lad, just like his father – and as much trouble to you, I daresay.'

Corinna laughed, kissing her child on the head, and closing her eyes for a moment. She was aware that Reed had moved away from the bed, and that someone else was there. Opening her eyes, she saw it was Fitz, and he looked as if he was crying.

'You should not weep, Fitz,' she told him. 'We have our son.'

'And you are alive,' he said and she saw the anguish he had suffered these past months in his face. 'You are alive, Corinna.'

'Of course I am,' she replied. 'For goodness sake, Fitz. Anyone would think I had been seriously ill. I have merely had a baby. It was quick and easy and no trouble at all. Ask Reed if you will; he will tell you. I shall be up and back to normal in days.'

'I know that Reed would declare black was blue to please you,' Fitz said, but he smiled as he took the child from her arms and looked down at him. 'He is lovely, Corinna.'

'He looks like you,' she said. 'Give him to my maid, Fitz, and come back to me later, when I am fit.'

'You need to sleep,' he said. 'And I, if truth be told, am hardly fit to be in your bedchamber. I have ridden through the day to get here and the dust of the journey is on me. I sent Reed yesterday for I was summoned to the Lords and could not leave before morning, and I was afraid for you.'

'As you see, there was no need,' she told him. 'Go away now, dearest, and when you come back bring Rupert to see me. He has been miserable being shut away from me, and he should be introduced to our son as soon as possible.'

'I have been told that it was Rupert who brought on your labour early.' Fitz looked stern. 'I am not sure I was right to give you such a clumsy animal. A lapdog would be better . . .'

'If that be true, sir,' Reed said, approaching the bed with a towel in his hands, 'then you should thank the dog for its good agency. Had your lady not given birth now, I fear the child might have grown too big for her to manage at all.'

Fitz looked from one to the other, and then he was laughing. 'I see that I can never hope to win when you have such friends,' he said. 'Very well, I shall bring the wretched thing with me – but if he thinks he is going to sleep on your bed, he is much mistaken . . .'

Corinna smiled, knowing that all was well. She need not have worried. Fitz would never harm her or those she loved, and the future stretched bright and full of promise before them.